More

An unexpected encounter in a bar promises Isabel Fields a chance to change her life. Sexual dominant Sebastian York, leads her on a passionate journey of sexual awakening that satisfies everything she's craved.

Their casual arrangement soon grows too confining as Sebastian ignites Isabel's long-buried desires and touches her heart. However, Sebastian may not prove to be the love of Izzy's life and just might leave her wanting more…

www.trollriverpub.com
More
The Evermore Series (Book 1)
Copyright © 2015 Rachel De Lune
ISBN: 978-1-939564-67-2
Cover Design: Rachel De Lune
Editor: P.A.K.

No part of this book may be reproduced or transmitted, with the exception of a reviewer who may quote passages in a review, without written prior permission from the publisher.

This is a work of fiction. All characters, names, events, incidents and places are of the author's imagination and not to be confused with fact. Any resemblance to living persons or events is merely coincidence.

WARNING: The author and publisher would solemnly advise you not to attempt any of the sexual or non-sexual actions of any of the characters in this book. Any damage physical, mental or emotional is the sole responsibility of the person/persons attempting such actions. Please be aware that this is a work of fiction and you are responsible for yourself and the consequences caused thereof.

Dear Reader,

Rachel has worked very hard on this particular piece of entertainment. This book was brought to you by hard labor and love. Please respect an artist's work for the enrichment we try to bring you. I humbly ask that you don't outright steal this child born on paper and brought to you by love. If you come by this book by nefarious means, and you are simply unable to give the purchase price, then take it with my blessing. But if you can purchase it and would like Rachel to continue to bring you great books, please purchase a copy to support her.

Thank you,

Troll River Publications

To U.S. Readers

I'd like to take this moment to let you know that Rachel is a writer living in the UK and while most terminology is the same, you may find some words or phrases odd. Knickers are underwear, "realise" is actually the correct spelling for "realize" in the UK and "flaking" is not ditching someone at a party.

Suffice it to say, if you find a word that blares out at you as "misspelled" blame the Atlantic Ocean for this diversity, not Rachel. This book has been properly edited and remains true to UK spelling and grammar. Thank you for your time!

Acknowledgement

The book you are about to read wouldn't have been possible without a few special people.

Firstly, to Elizabeth. Your initial faith in my little story was overwhelming. To think that a published author liked my work was huge for me. You gave me the initial belief that maybe, just maybe, I could do this. You have been a fabulous critique partner and I'm grateful to also call you a friend. Kris and M, you both endured early versions of my manuscript but still gave me the encouragement to keep going. Thank you. Thank you. Thank you. I've so enjoyed getting to know you and reading your stories and can't wait to see what's next. Hugs to you both.

To my American Mum, T. You have taught me so much since we first met. You have pushed me, supported me and even looked after me. You've helped to improve my writing and I am forever grateful. Your patience, kindness and talent know no bounds. If I am ever a successful writer, it will be because of you.

To Stephy, my wonderful publisher who saw something in my jumble of words and gave me the final encouragement needed to bring More to more than five people. I hope I can make you proud.

Lastly, to anyone who has purchased my words. I have my fingers crossed that you enjoy it. I know I loved writing it.

This has been an incredible journey and I know it's only just beginning.

A ship in harbor is safe, but that is not what ships are built for.
~ John A. Shedd

I'm invisible. My husband hasn't come on to me in months. Hell, Phil and I have barely talked in the last few weeks, let alone broached any type of physical contact. We exist within our own bubbles of life. He works, takes extra shifts at the show room—someone is always ready to buy a new car—or spends the evening out with his mates. When he is home it's, "Izzy, I've just sat down to watch *Top Gear*. Just give me half an hour." But it's never just half an hour.

I didn't notice to start with. My job at White Cube, a young marketing company in Bath, absorbs me. I plug in and I'm whisked away from reality and plunged into the world of digital marketing. I spend the whole day, every day, writing social media strategies for companies that want to leverage the best value they can out of the online world. I do lectures for business men and women in stuffy suits on how to "do social media."

Our lack of contact was a fact of our marriage and something I thought I'd grown accustomed to. I'd given up asking Phil to satisfy my sexual needs—any of my needs, for that matter—long ago. The last time I was physically turned on, I was reading some racy novel where the man couldn't keep his hands off the woman. They couldn't reach the bed quick enough and bodies and lips collided in a passion-induced frenzy. The man masterfully brought his woman to a state of orgasmic bliss, where she eagerly agreed to whatever he wanted. *Well, if I wish hard enough, it may happen.*

Even a little bit of that sounds fantastic. I long to feel desired and needed by Phil, and that couldn't be further from the way he makes me feel. It's hard to get excited over a pretty pink vibrator. I know that I need to communicate, to ask him more directly, but it's hard after getting ignored and side-lined for nearly ten years. He is my husband. I want him consumed by need for me. I want my satisfaction, my needs, to be his priority, but at this point, I would settle for an orgasm I didn't give myself.

I've been quiet for long enough. I can't continue to be idle in this relationship. I need to try harder. The realisation that Phil and I haven't been working for a long time—a very long time—frustrates and angers me. That I've ignored how bad things are makes me sad. *Maybe I can fix this. Maybe I can make him see me again, want me again.*

As I creep my Fiat 500 through the Bath city traffic, I play out what I want in my mind. For a long time, I've wanted to lose myself at the hands of someone else. To look into his eyes and feel utterly wanted. Like all he will ever see is me. The blatant heat in that look, telling me that I can put my trust in him. A look that tells me he knows every inch of my body and how to bring me to the height of pleasure. Because he knows me as a person. As a woman. Not just a wife to use when he feels horny or wants to get off. To have someone put me and my pleasure first melts me inside—hell, it makes me wet just thinking about it. To be listened to, considered. Attention on me that lasted past what was for dinner or the time it took him to get off. Phil wasn't being that someone, but I couldn't stay quiet. *No more.*

I will initiate things tonight. I will make him see me as more than the convenient woman in his bed. Screw "the way to a man's heart is through his stomach." I want to test the theory "the way to a man's heart is through offering him mind-blowing sex." I don't want to settle. I want Phil to be active in our relationship and show me why I should fight to hold onto our marriage.

For the first time in forever, I'm excited about seeing Phil. I pull up outside the house and hurry out of the car. I burst through the door, but my excitement turns to disappointment. I dump my bags as I walk into the hall. The silence of the house is deafening to me. He's not home. *Stupid girl.* My plan stumbles at the first hurdle. I resign myself to another evening spent alone in the house with only my phone and computer for company.

My mind doesn't switch off after climbing into bed. The sexual images I've explored circulate through my brain. My Tumblr blog is always my first port of call as I search for exactly what I want—erotic and sensual images of naked and bound women, waiting to receive their pleasure and pain, submitting to their Sir. The beautiful and peaceful poses of content women placing their sexual needs in the control of another resonate to my core and I slip my fingers between my legs. I cannot escape my deep craving to explore this form of connection with another.

The minutes slip past, and as each one rolls over, my anticipation and nerves grow. I have built the entire future of our relationship on the simple act of seducing my husband, and it has to be tonight. I won't have the courage tomorrow.

Phil's shadow creeps past me and into the bathroom. A shard of light splits the darkness and shines on the clock, illuminating the hands touching at twelve. *Where was Phil until midnight on a work night? The car dealership closes at eight o'clock.* I force the concern from my mind and wait for him to join me in our bed.

I have to phrase my requests the *right* way. Phil has a short fuse and he often reacts with no provocation. Once upon a time, he'd keep his temper in check, try to be less volatile. He's quit trying. One more sign our marriage is failing. I'm tired of being on guard all the time.

I take a deep breath. Okay then. *Just do it, Izzy.* When Phil joins me in bed, I roll over to face him.

"Oh, you're still awake." Phil freezes as if caught, clearly surprised that I've waited up.

"I thought we could spend some time… together."

His eyes penetrate through the gloom of the room before he rolls to the side and switches on the bedside lamp. A warm glow floods the room. A smirk twitches his face as he catches my chain of thought.

"Will you play with me tonight?" I try to sound sexy and confident.

He pauses to study me. "What do you mean by play with you?"

"I want you to play with my body. And, um, perhaps you could try tying my hands?" Another pause. I hold my breath. I was tired of being rejected so I stopped asking for him to satisfy me. He'd make the first move to have sex, but beyond that, he never took control. I can't take it anymore. My husband isn't interested enough to make a move on me. My discomfort grows at Phil's lingering silence. He's never shown interest in what I want. I got tired of having to ask for him to play with my body, touch my clit and my breasts. To kiss me like he actually wanted to kiss me. It made me feel so small having to ask the person I loved to do something for me. So I began to let it go. My needs weren't worth the hurt at being ignored and pushed to the side. *But I can't any longer. I want to be one of those bound women whose images inflame my imagination. I need him to take the lead. To dominate.*

As I play out the possibility in my mind, Phil retrieves the bathrobe off the door and pulls the sash from it. *Yes!* He is getting on board with this.

Once the sash is in his hands, he wastes no time in pulling my arms above my head and tying them to the headboard. My entire body heats and my arms relax. I want to spread my legs, and my sex starts to ache. I wish he would touch my skin. Slip my t-shirt up to reveal me inch by inch before teasing my nipples into hard peaks. Instead, he shoves my t-shirt up and mauls my breasts—his hands grabbing roughly before pinching my nipples. It hurts. He moves down to my thighs and jerks my legs apart. The tender kisses across my skin that I long for turn into hurried scrapes of his stubble on my belly in his rush to get to his prize. My vision of this evening is fast evaporating with each hurtful grope from Phil. I need some attentive care that indicates I'm important to him. I need him to think of me and my needs and bring me to the edge of a body-shattering orgasm. I want this. I can't keep quiet. Phil continues to kiss my thighs and pinches at my nipples.

"Please. Touch me, please. Push your finger in me and feel me," I beg. He doesn't answer. He grabs my hips and pulls me farther down the bed, stretching me out from where my hands are bound. He shoves my legs wider, spreading me completely for him. He stops to look at me for a moment and I suddenly feel a sliver of fear. *What will he do?* I push the fear aside and try to relax into the moment.

Leaning down, he nestles his lips next to my now-exposed sex before he flicks my clit with the tip of his tongue. Tremors ignite in my core and travel up my spine. I arch into the feeling. Months and months of unspoken words and empty nights are finally shattered. This might work.

"Do it again, yes... that feels good." My clit is so sensitive that I can already feel the distant build of climax, but he lifts his lips away from me, killing my budding orgasm. Frustration replaces my bliss and I huff out the air from my lungs.

"How do you want me?" Phil's voice focuses my attention back on him and away from my needy clit and aching sex. *No, I don't want to make any decisions in this. This is why I want to be bound and restrained.*

"I don't mind, but please, touch me first. I want this to be special." I breathe, coming down from my high.

"Okay then, baby." He lifts my legs, wrapping them around his hips, and strokes his cock. He wastes no time before he shoves into me.

"Argh!" I'm not ready, and it hurts.

He drives farther inside me. The stretching burns and it takes a minute for me to adjust. He doesn't stop or slow but buries as far into me as he can. He falls into a more relaxed rhythm that begins to rub against me in the right way.

"Don't change... keep doing that." *Mmm, yes, just there. Yes, yes.* He rubs against my clit just enough to give me that weightlessness, that wave, as it rolls up through my body to my chest. But it doesn't last for long. His grip tightens on my hips as he pulls in and out of me in quick, hard thrusts.

"Oh yeah, oh yes," Phil grinds out with clenched teeth as he hammers into me for the final time. He immediately lets me go and slumps forward against my chest. *No, no, no! This is for me as well, and you've... I'm not... I want to come!* I scream inside my mind, trapped under his body, unfulfilled and desperate for more.

"Phil, I want to come," I plead, his chest pinning me down into the bed. He takes a deep breath, ignoring my request as if I hadn't spoken.

"Mmm, thank you." He pushes off me and untangles my legs. He leans forward to untie my arms, sore from being pulled so far down. This isn't what I want. I want more than to be his fantasy screw. *How did my fantasy turn into his? No.* This was my plan and my idea.

"I haven't come. Will you still play with me?" I kneel up in front of him. I raise his hand to my breast and slowly press it against my raised nipple. I close his fingers around it and gently squeeze, showing how I want his touch. He seems to take notice and looks at me with a grin on his face. Turning over, I bend down so my elbows and chest rest on the bed, my bottom clearly on display for him. Phil used to like my bottom, and I hope it will get his attention. I stay down and wait for his interest. His hand slides up my naked thigh and glides over the arch of my bottom, continues up my back, and yanks my t-shirt up around my neck.

I want to come. I open my mouth before I can think any further than how badly I want to get off.

"I want you to make me come. Spank me while you tease my clit. Will you spank me, baby?"

His hand immediately stills on my skin.

"What!" His bark shakes me out of my needy, frustrated mind. I push up and sit, knees pulled to my chest. I shrink at his disparaging tone.

"What do you mean spank you? What the fuck? I'm not hitting my wife!"

"It's not hitting. I want to feel you do this to me."

"I'm not doing it."

"But this is something that I'm asking for, something I want us to try together. I want you to look after my needs, too."

"You want me to hit you? We just had sex, Izzy, surely that's enough. I tied you up."

"Yes, and you came, but I didn't. I need this from you, Phil. I need you to care enough about me to try something different. Please, Phil?" I kneel and grab for his arm, trying to disregard his anger.

"I'm not playing out your dirty little fantasy. What's gotten into you—asking to be slapped around? Asking for rough sex now, are we?"

"Please, I just thought…" I kneel up towards him.

"No, Izzy. Get your hands off me…"

"It's… It's not dirty."

"I said no." He knocks me back against the bed and raw anger flashes in his eyes.

I curl in on myself and wrap my arms tightly around my legs. Phil storms out of the bedroom. The violent slam of the door reverberates in the silence. I'm alone.

I feel as if I've been fucked over, which is ironic, as I have been. In my mind this scene went a different way. Humiliation extinguishes my last hope for resurrecting our marriage. Anger replaces humiliation as I consider the countless times I've gotten him off, but never once did he return the favour. It wasn't just the sex. His selfish indifference extended to all areas of our marriage.

Just once, I wanted him to come through for me and fulfil my innocent fantasy, to consider my wants and my needs. He took. He always just took.

I hear the front door close and assume he is gone. *Great. Just fucking great.* Tears gather in my eyes and my chest feels hollow. *Now what.*

* * *

A few weeks later

I walk into the bar, tentative and more nervous than I expected to be. It is perfectly acceptable for a girl to walk into a bar alone. The background conversation and companionable interaction of others sure as hell beats the silence and awkward avoidance between Phil and me at home. Tonight I've decided enough is enough. Phil didn't come back until Monday morning and barely spoke to me the following week. He wouldn't talk to me, wouldn't show any interest in me or in working this through. We simply went along with our own lives, going to work, cooking, cleaning, going to bed. I refuse to believe this is all my fault. We didn't reach this point simply from me asking to be spanked. The responsibility for the mess we are in isn't all mine.

The bar is friendly, yet intimate and fairly quiet, hardly surprising considering it is only Tuesday. I walk steadily towards the counter, careful not to look around and risk eye contact with anyone. I hop up onto one of the stools as gracefully as I can manage, which, in my case, means I barely manage to sit without falling off the damn thing. I'm not one of those elegant women who glide across the floor. I do wear the heels that would match such a move, but I rarely pull it off. I look down at my shoes. Black and grey suede straps wrap around my feet, a two-inch platform cushions the four-inch heel. My sexy shoes give me the lift I need and are the one indulgence I'll never give up. Thank heaven I can walk in heels.

I order a bottle of beer before I rest my elbows on the bar and hold my head in my hands. I need a moment. If I close my eyes and hold my breath for a second, everything will be okay, and my bleak despair at the future of my marriage will disappear. *Won't it?*

The barman places the beer in front of me before he returns to cleaning glasses. I take a long draw of the cool liquid to settle my nerves and my mind. I continue to drink, hoping the beer will actually wash away my problems. My marital issues are much bigger than a quick drink in a bar can fix. How have I not seen this coming? Phil always takes extra shifts. He seems to do anything apart from spend time with me, and that includes sex. The worst part is that I'm not bothered about it. I'm not bothered by my husband's lack of sexual desire for me. *After all the time we have been married, how can this have happened?* I drain the last of the beer and tip it towards the barman. "Another, please."

"Same for me." A velvety deep voice sounds from right behind my ear. Every nerve ending in my body awakens. The flesh on my neck tingles in response. The man slides effortlessly onto the stool next to mine, a hair's breadth away. I steal a quick look in his direction.

Dark hair frames a handsome face. One that could belong to my fantasy screen hero, complete with five o'clock shadow. A sexy smile across his lips gives his eyes a crystal quality that I could lose myself in. Instead, I whip my eyes back to my fingers, now clasped around my bottle for dear life. I think he chuckles, and I concentrate on not fidgeting. The barman returns with two bottles and places them in front of us.

"Cheers." That same velvet voice reverberates through my body. I slowly raise my eyes and look straight into two pools of blue liquid that stare right back at me. My entire body ignites with recognition and arousal floods me. He holds his bottle towards me. I have to concentrate to lift my bottle to his.

"Cheers," I croak. My cheeks flame as he smiles and his eyes light up with pleasure and amusement. I pull my gaze from his and focus on the beer. *Yes, the beer is my friend.* I sit as still as I possibly can and concentrate on drinking my beer without dribbling it down my chin or doing anything else horrifyingly embarrassing.

My reaction to the man startles me. My right side hums at the mere presence of him. I shift away from him on my stool and try to break the connection. I shouldn't feel this way. Despite my failing marriage, I am still married. I finish my drink with my heart beating out of my chest. I set the bottle down and swivel on the stool, ready to jump down. As I do, that gorgeous, deep voice strikes me again.

"I'm Seb. And you are?"

My eyes widen at his introduction. That sexy smile never leaves his lips.

"Izzy," I whisper. I don't think my lungs can take in oxygen anymore.

"A pleasure to meet you, Izzy."

I continue to look at him, unable to stop even if I wanted to. Something compels me to keep my eyes fixed on him. An alien feeling stirs my desires. The heat from my cheeks is ridiculous. I must be a bright shade of scarlet. That thought finally shakes my concentration. I stumble off my stool and pick up my bag.

"Leaving so soon?" He straightens his bespoke charcoal-grey suit. The cut accentuates his broad chest and I know he wouldn't achieve that with an off-the-peg Marks and Spencer.

"Um… yes. I, uh, need to get going," I stutter.

"Well, I'm sorry to hear that."

Does he really care if I leave? I look down and shift from foot to foot, as if I'm a love-struck sixteen-year-old. *What do I say now?* I risk another look, and my eyes wander up his body to his lips. A smile itches to spread across my face. As my eyes try to look anywhere but at his, he actually laughs. My stomach quivers and my thighs tingle in that oh-so-good way. *Good Lord, Izzy! Say something.* I take a breath to steady myself. "Okay, well, I, ah… need to go." I spin on my heels and walk as smoothly as possible to the door.

My sexual response to a complete stranger troubles my mind all the way home.

* * *

I pull the duvet cover higher over my body and snuggle down into bed. Did tonight really happen? I go out for the first time in months to escape the cold loneliness of my home life and get some perspective on my failing marriage, and I meet a man who sets my body on fire.

My stomach hasn't stopped turning, and that old, yet familiar, ache of desperate attraction does strange things to my breathing.

The door shuts and I hear the turn of the lock. Phil. He hasn't responded to my earlier text about what he was doing tonight. I don't care. Sadness comes with that realisation. It's late, but that's nothing new for Phil. Although, after meeting Seb tonight, I'm beginning to wonder a little more about what he's been doing so late. He can't be working. My mind flits back to the reaction I had to Seb. Instant and overwhelming. *Would it be such a leap to think that Phil's disinterest is due to another woman?*

I curl myself into a ball, lie as still as I can, and pretend to be asleep. The bathroom light streams through the crack in the door as he changes. A few minutes later, he comes into the bedroom and climbs into bed. The distance between us tonight seems cavernous, not the actual three inches between our bodies. *How could I not have seen this coming?* I squeeze my eyes closed and see Seb's clear blue eyes looking deep into mine and imagine, for a moment, what he would do if he climbed into bed with me.

* * *

I wake up early. My eyes take a moment to adjust. It's still dark in the bedroom and Phil's still asleep next to me. I've a big training session at work and need to be in early to set up. I hop out of bed, grab the items I left hanging on the back of the bathroom door and head for my shower. I make it downstairs without having to see Phil. I sigh. Guilt churns in my stomach at my physical reaction to Seb. Oh, those eyes. Those eyes will haunt my dreams for weeks to come. Coffee. I pour my morning cup and hope that my day will be enough of a distraction to keep my mind from Seb.

Driving to work, I go over my presentation. I hate presenting to a group and I'm always nervous. I know my subject thoroughly and I'm good at what I do, but I still give myself the mental pep talk as I park the car. It's a crisp morning. The last signs of summer are fading and there is an autumnal chill in the air. I cling to my files, fighting off the cool air as I walk across the car park. I enter the building and head to my desk. I toss my files on my desk and go in search of coffee.

The conference room isn't ready—no surprise—so I spend the next twenty minutes setting up for my session. Laptops, monitors, and cables—I'm surrounded by cables and nothing is working correctly. I scramble on the floor to connect everything to the power, check the laptops and then attempt, once again, to link the main monitor to my computer. *Why today? Why does it not work today?*

"Uh, hum." I hear a man behind me while I'm still on hands and knees sorting the cables. "Is this the right place for the social media introduction?"

That voice. I recognise that voice and my stomach lurches as liquid blue eyes flash through my mind. *This can't be happening. Not him. Not here, today, in my training session.*

"Excuse me," he says, a little more sternly and sounding somewhat annoyed.

I've not responded to his question and I'm still on my knees, my head hidden under a work table.

"Yes. Yes, it is," I reply in my most confident, self-assured voice. As carefully and gracefully as I can manage, I stand up and look towards him. Recognition registers across his face, drawing that sexy smile slowly across his lips and lightening his expression.

"Well, hello, Izzy." He offers his hand to shake, a polite and professional move given the circumstances. I take his proffered hand in mine and feel warmth and strength radiate through our touch.

"Hello. Ah... Seb. You're here for the training session?"

"Yes. I wasn't looking forward to it, but I think I just changed my mind."

There go my cheeks again. Red. I stand motionless and slightly dumbstruck. *What do I do? What can I say?*

"Okay, I'll... uh, be with you in a minute. Have you got a coffee or tea? They are laid up outside." I cast my eyes down to his hands. He cocks his head to the side and raises his coffee cup in salute.

I giggle nervously and turn towards my computer on the desk to hide my embarrassment. I open the programmes and presentations I will be using today and take a breath. *I can do this.* I mentally check myself, straighten my back, and face Seb. He has taken a seat at the conference table, set his drink down and is casually sitting with his legs crossed at the ankle and his arm resting on his knee. He's watching me.

His posture is relaxed and he looks totally at ease, the exact opposite of how I am feeling. As I summon the courage to speak to him again, another suited gentleman enters the room.

"Take a seat." I motion to the table, avoiding Seb's eyes, and return to my computer.

I focus on the screen in front of me as more people file into the room. I greet them pleasantly, all while keeping Seb in the corner of my view. He doesn't move, nor does he take his eyes from mine. *Please stop looking at me. You're making me—*

"Will you be starting anytime soon?"

His question throws me, and I'm momentarily flustered. "I think we're expecting one more. We'll start in a few minutes." I don't address him directly, but I can't help but steal a glance. He's grinning at me. This is going to be a long morning. I curse under my breath.

* * *

"If you have any further questions once you start your social profile, I can be found at any of these sites, or by email." I flick up the final slide with my social contact details and inwardly sigh. *I've gotten through it.* I sit down in relief. I keep my eyes on my screen to avoid the possibility of catching Seb's. I wait until I can't hear any more movement in the room before I raise my head, and look straight up into liquid blue. *Oh shit.*

"Not going to say goodbye?" he purrs. His velvet tones sing in my ears.

"I'm... ah... sorry. I hope you enjoyed the session?"

"Some elements of it, yes." His smile stretches slowly upwards.

My stomach turns and my lips part in response. *What is he doing to me?* I ask myself, frustrated that this relative stranger has such an effect on me. I stand and admire him for a moment. He's still sporting a five o'clock shadow. His hair is short and neat and a smoky black. His suit is a dark charcoal, matched with a white shirt and a lighter grey tie. He looks strong and in control, confident. My pulse quickens as I drink him in.

"I wanted to leave this with you last night, but you ran off before I had a chance." He places a card on the table and pushes it towards me. I pick it up and finger the thick white card, elegantly embossed with his name and a mobile number. "And it only seems fair as you've just given me all your contact details."

My brow furrows and I try to decipher what he means. He turns and gestures to the screen where there are several ways of contacting me still on display. "Oh, I see. Thanks." I absentmindedly rub my thumb across his name on the card, feeling the individual dips and rises of the letters.

"I expect you to call me, Izzy." With that, he turns and walks out of the room.

I sit back down, slightly dizzy and somewhat at a loss. I stare at the screen, which still has my Twitter, Facebook, and email details on it. All are my professional business accounts—I do this for my job, which I love, but I'm not going to post my personal details. *Nor my favourite sites.*

The rest of my day is quiet, so I take my time to sort out the room and return to my desk. I'm careful to keep Seb's business card in my pocket, out of sight of prying eyes. *Will I call him? Do I want to? What will it mean if I do?* Troubling questions plague me, and for the rest of the afternoon, I focus only on Seb, or rather, Mr. Sebastian York.

I write a few generic posts for the people in the training session today and wrap up some emails before I leave for home.

Home. At least today's relative excitement has kept my thoughts off Phil. It's unlikely I'll see him tonight. He's been avoiding home as much as possible. Or maybe he's seeing how absent he can be before I say or do anything in response. *Should I do anything? Should I say anything to him? Is it all my fault? Isn't marriage supposed to be a partnership? I seem to be the only one trying.* I shake my head as tears pool in my eyes. I'm thankful for the privacy of my car.

This is stupid. I try to convince myself that being a good wife means more to me than any desire I may harbour about exploring my sexuality—my desire for submission in the bedroom. I know this yearning will never leave. It is something that deep down I both crave and fear. *Something more.* I breathe in deeply and resign myself to the fact I will never experience my fantasy. I should not frustrate myself further. I should try to mend bridges with Phil.

The day has shaken off its cool start. I'm not looking forward to winter. The sun has a magical effect that brightens all situations, and with what I'm currently facing, I need the sunshine. I walk up to the front door and open it to a dark and empty house. Nothing new. The depressing thought breaks my last grip on my emotions and I sob in the hallway, mourning the marriage I once held such hope in. I stumble into the bathroom and turn on the water, seeking solace in the warm water, a substitute for the physical embrace I long for.

The bath is soothing and hot, and I am surprised at how good it feels. Bubbles and the scent of citrus envelope me. My body relaxes and my mind follows, seemingly content after my emotional break earlier. Sometimes I can cry my sorrows away and feel better, my own form of self-preservation. After the bath grows cold, I climb out, wrap myself in comfy pyjamas and grab my iPad, ready to sit in my chair and spend some time with my other "self."

I quickly get lost in the images showing exactly what I'm craving—submission, bondage, trust in another. I notice a new like and follow on my blog and I'm curious as to who is taking an interest in me on here. I don't do a lot of interacting. It's more for me to watch and imagine. I'm not interested in followers. Before I get a chance, my email alert rings. I tap the envelope icon and see Seb's name in my inbox.

> Izzy,
> You haven't called. I'm waiting. I had a very enlightening day and would very much like you to call me.
> S

Shit, shit, shit. I can't call him. *Can I?* My heart is suddenly in my mouth. I may not be able to get him out of my mind, but I never thought he'd actually contact me. I could email him—no harm in emailing. If I have a phone conversation with Seb, I'll be all over the place.

> Seb,
> I'm hoping enlightenment has come from the training session today. What would you like me to call you about? Are you having trouble with a new social platform?
> Izzy

This is so much easier than when I'm standing next to him. His presence—his very being—intimidates me. What would happen if I were ever alone with him?

> Izzy,
> I could say it was your training session, but that isn't the complete truth. I would like to talk about going for a drink. Maybe you could actually talk to me this time?
> S

That would be a problem. My mouth is bone dry.

> Seb,
> What do you mean by the complete truth?
> Izzy

Maybe he won't realise I'm frantically avoiding his other question. *Could I go out with him for a drink? There wouldn't really be any harm in a drink, would there?* But as I think that, I'm not being honest. I don't think I could have a conversation with him on the phone, let alone face to face.

> Izzy,
> Well, the training was, as I said, enlightening, but I was rather more interested in what I found out as a result of the training session. Don't avoid my question, Izzy. Drink. With me.
> S

> Seb,
> I'm not sure a drink is such a good idea. I'm married and wouldn't want to give you the wrong impression. I'm glad you learned something from me today.
> Izzy

> Izzy,
> Oh, I definitely learned something today. Is there any rule that says we couldn't go for a drink? Men and women drink together all the time and it doesn't mean anything. Drink. With me.
> S

Really? Does he mean that? A wave of hope floods through me as I remember my reaction to Seb at the bar and then again earlier today. I would like to see him again.

Seb,
If you're sure you want to go for just a drink then no, there shouldn't be anything to stop us. Should we meet again at the same bar?
Izzy

Izzy,
Good girl. I'll see you at the bar on Thursday night. 7pm.
S

More

What was it you told us today, Isabel? Choose one or two social platforms to start with. Well, Facebook is obvious, but I'd like to see what you do. You did say you can build your interactions by finding people that you're interested in? Well, I'm certainly interested in you.

I don't often believe in coincidence, but meeting you twice, seeing your instant reaction to me—how could I not be intrigued? Your lost look at the bar, your nervousness in my presence, both scream your vulnerability. It stirs all my base instincts to possess and comfort.

I grab my tablet and bring up my browser, starting at the social media sites Izzy talked about today. Facebook and Twitter hold nothing but marketing links. I want to find out more about Isabel Fields, and she gave me my starting point. I have a basic understanding of these platforms. I have yet to understand the fascination that people have with them. But the course saved me from being sent into another company this week. I have a great job, but it would be nice to do something that didn't involve going into a company and breaking it apart to maximize profit. Or worse, just not being able to turn it around and leaving it to the administrators.

I scroll through the mundane posts until I see a source from Tumblr. I click it and arrive at what appears to be a photography blog. I continue to scroll until I see a photo that raises my pulse. Clicking the black-and-white photo of a shadowed woman, I'm taken to another blog, this time filled with similar shots. But much more alluring. Bound and tethered, these photographs depict a woman's desires. The initials IF snap my attention. Why, oh why, didn't you give us all of your social profiles, Isabel?

I sit back in my chair, put my wine glass on the side and stare at my tablet. I click through the blog that now holds all of my attention. The IF appearing more and more. I click one more image and I follow the breadcrumb and arrive at a most unexpected website.

Well, well, well. I've stumbled on a profile that could only be for you, Izzy. Yes, after meeting you, I know this profile and content is definitely not for clients. It's certainly piqued my interest, though. Sweet, awkward Izzy Fields has a hidden profile on "Journey To Domination." Perhaps I'm mistaken and her shyness and innocence is not mere social awkwardness but signs of an aspect to her character that is closer to my heart. But she was almost shocked at speaking to a strange man—certainly too uncomfortable to show the usual flirty behaviour that I grew tired of years ago. Perhaps I shouldn't judge Izzy by her rather appealing cover. Perhaps there is more to Ms. Fields than a pretty woman who lacks social confidence.

God, her kneeling before me is something that's going to linger in my mind for a while. Fuck, I could barely concentrate after seeing her this morning, kneeling and bent over on the floor, attempting… well, whatever. It certainly sent my mind into action, picturing her in that same position, but in a totally different room. That thought will have to stay in check, though. She's already declared her attached status. But is she what she appears to be?

Hell, Natasha is going to have a field day when she finds out that I'm pursuing Izzy. She still thinks that I should defer to her—my mentor and first guide into the realm of BDSM—after all of these years. She doesn't understand the reasoning behind my relationship choices and possibly never will. I'm way past the occasional hook up with a sub.

Perhaps I'll get to see the real Isabel Fields on Thursday. Hopefully, she'll be less timid. Although that could just be a disguise. Women can often play the vulnerable card to their own selfish advantage. But she's fascinating. Although she's off-limits physically, I'm looking forward to Thursday. Yes, Isabel Fields, you definitely interest me.

Two

I can't believe I'm doing this, I tell myself for the hundredth time as I walk the short distance to the bar. I drove on purpose, so I couldn't have more than one drink. Less potential for disgraceful behaviour that way. The bar is the same as the night I met Seb: soft lighting, music playing, and a nice atmosphere. Not intimidating like some bars. Men crowded in small packs, watching for the next piece of meat to walk in.

I'm on time, but Seb isn't at the bar yet, so I steady my nerves with a few deep breaths. *This is just drinks, Izzy. Don't be so silly.* But as I say the words, I question my own integrity.

Phil and I have hardly spoken this week. I still can't talk about what happened a few weeks ago, and he certainly isn't in a hurry to bring it up. His work schedule seems crazy and he's in the house less than ever before. My seemingly brilliant plan has backfired beyond all imagination. I have a constant dull ache in my stomach when I think about where we could be heading. In my mind, it sounds ridiculous that one failed attempt at spicing things up could have me questioning my marriage, but it's more than that. Phil could never change and put my needs above his. His selfish and dubious behaviour isn't going to change. I've been accepting it for years. I can't keep doing it.

"Good evening, Isabel." His velvet voice tickles the back of my neck. I close my eyes at the sensation that his simple greeting draws from me.

"Good evening, Sebastian," I respond without turning or moving on my seat, but he doesn't join me.

"Shall we find a table? I've been looking forward to talking to you." His voice has me flustered already. I turn, and he holds out a hand. I feel this as a moment of truth. An offering. Of what, I'm not sure, but I take his hand. He leads me to one of the small tables around the edge of the bar, pulls out my chair for me to sit, and returns to the bar. I'm confused until I realise he's ordering drinks. He never asked what I'd like.

I sit and fidget anxiously until he returns with two glasses of clear liquid with plenty of ice and lime. *Gin and tonic, my favourite.*

"Thank you." I take the first sip and let the alcohol settle me, admonishing myself to not act like a silly teenager. I'm a grown and married woman, and I'm sure my status shouldn't require I stay at home and be miserable. I'm allowed to enjoy myself, and hopefully make a new friend.

"So..." I offer with a smile.

"So indeed. I'm pleased you've agreed to this. Cheers." Seb raises his glass and we clink softly. I hope that he'll take the lead in this. I can't remember the last time I spoke to a man who wasn't a work acquaintance. My silent prayer is answered.

"I'm going to guess that your visit to the bar the other night wasn't something you do too often?"

"Um, no. I can't remember the last time that I came to a bar on my own. I nearly didn't come in I was so nervous. Stupid, really." I try to hide my half snicker in my glass of gin and tonic.

"So that explains your 'rabbit in the headlights' reaction." His eyes hold mine and I do feel like that rabbit. "I'm sorry." He smiles. "I promise not to tease you anymore. Well, not very much, anyway." Seb's easy confidence lightens the weight of my nerves and I smile back at him—something that I find myself wanting to do. "Well, can I ask then, what made you come to the bar in the first place?"

"Oh, well... I suppose you could call it a bad day."

"Annoying men in suits causing you trouble in your training sessions?" His radiant smile eases my nerves.

"Oh no, nothing like that. I just... I needed a few minutes to myself and it had been so long since I'd been out for a drink."

"So not work... It must be personal reasons then. Care to share?" His question holds an air of genuine sincerity. He doesn't sound cocky or presumptuous. A look of concern replaces his sexy smile, and I want to unload my worries. But then I remember. I don't know him.

"Perhaps another time. What about you? What made you stop for a drink?"

"I was meeting someone, but they were running late." His eyes held my gaze. "Seeing you alone at the bar, I thought we could share a drink. And here we are."

"Yes, here we are. Do you live around here?"

"Nearby. You?"

"A little out of the city. I work in the centre, as you know. I've been here before for coffee during the day but rarely for a drink."

"Have you lived in Bath long?"

"Over ten years. When Phil and I got married, we moved down here."

"Phil's your husband?"

"Yes." I start turning my glass in nervous circles.

"What about family?"

"Both of our parents live on the other side of the country, so we rarely see them. It didn't used to matter because Phil and I were each other's family."

"Were?"

"I suppose somewhere along the line, Phil and I thought we only needed each other, and of course the jobs that we both found in Bath. But now, I'm not so sure. I'm not very close to my parents now." My fingers stop playing with the glass I've been turning round and round in my hands and I look up at Seb. It's clear he's been watching me, and I flush, suddenly embarrassed by the thoughts I happily shared with him—the same thoughts I was sure I didn't want to share with him. *Izzy, you know nothing of this man!* "I'm sorry. I didn't mean to say all of that."

"Please, don't be sorry. I'm glad you feel comfortable sharing that with me." His smile is warm and reassuring and my worries vanish. The unease that I first felt about meeting with Seb has abated and I'm suddenly very glad that I came. For a few moments, we simply sit. I steal glances at him, a little longer each time, whereas Seb seems content to watch me. I don't seem to be able to settle around this man. One minute, I'm nervous; the next, I empty my heart to him. I giggle to myself.

"What's so funny?"

"I told myself to stop acting like a teenager on a date before you met me here. And now that's exactly how I'm feeling, complete with the giggles."

"Are you always this nervous, Izzy?" He's almost laughing now, too.

"Sometimes. I guess it depends on the situation. I suppose I'm not used to going for a drink with someone who isn't already a friend."

"Well, can I suggest we change that tonight? I'd like for you to think of me as a friend."

"I might need to know a little more about you, then," I quip back. Seb's good humour is infectious.

"What would you like to know? I'll give you three questions. You can ask me anything."

Oh God, what do I ask?!?

"Um, well. Are you married?" *Stupid question, Izzy!*

"No, Izzy. I'm not married. Next?" Mischief dances in his eyes. He's clearly having fun with me.

"I thought you weren't going to tease me anymore?"

"I'm sorry. You do make it easy. I'll try to behave. Now, what else would you like to know in order to call us friends?"

"Well, what do you do? And... what's your favourite food?"

"I work for a change management firm, Phoenix Consulting. They have a branch here in Bath, and my favourite food is Italian. Friends now?" The sexy smile is back, and I laugh. Yes, friends would be nice. I smile back, and for the first time that evening, I relax.

* * *

The easy rhythm of banter flows after those first few anxious minutes. Time is eaten away. His favourite book is *Treasure Island.* He loves classical music and he's not a devout Christian. *Thank God.* I can't remember the last time I had an evening of pleasant conversation. I didn't realise how much I missed being with someone I like. With a man I like.

"Last call!" the bartender shouts.

"Oh my..." I look at my watch. It's 11.50. "The bar's closing. We'd better go." I stand before we're ushered out.

"So what's the verdict, Izzy?" Seb whispers as he guides me to the exit.

"Umm, about what?"

"About our drink. Was it innocent enough for you?"

I stop for a moment, mentally going over his question. If I concentrate hard, then yes—yes, this could be an innocent drink. "Yes, I think it was. Thank you for the drink."

"It was my pleasure, and I enjoy your company. I'm pleased I can now call myself your friend. I hope to see you again."

I can't help my answering smile at the compliment. "Okay, that would be nice."

"Coffee on Sunday?" he offers straightaway.

"Umm…" The weekend is supposed to be time for Phil and I, but we haven't done anything together in a long time. "Why not?" I smile up at Seb and can't help but look into his eyes. Eyes that I want to look into for longer than I should, eyes that I want to study whenever I choose. I swallow and take a step back. "So, will you text me the details?" I ask in a rush, trying to focus on anything but his eyes.

"Yes, Izzy."

I'm reminded of our first conversation by email and some of his cryptic answers.

"What did you mean when you said that you were more interested in what you found out as a result of the training session?" My question draws him in closer and I hold my breath for his answer.

"Take a guess."

"I don't know. That's why I asked." He smiles and I feel as if I'm falling under his spell.

"Well, shall we say we share some common inspirations? Your more secretive social media profile is very interesting, Izzy."

No! He couldn't possibly! My shock is plastered across my face and my cheeks go up in flame. I'm mortified. I thought I was so careful.

"Please don't do that." His expression knits in concern. "Don't cower in on yourself."

But what do I do? He knows. *God, can the ground swallow me up now, please.* Shit, he's technically a client.

"There is nothing to worry about," he whispers. He places his hand at the small of my back and we walk in silence to my car.

My keys jingle as I take them in my hand. I'm shaking from nerves. If he had suspicions about me before, my reaction certainly settles things. He takes my hand and helps me insert the key and opens my door

"Time to go." He leans over me as I sit in the driver's side seat. "Drive safely, and I'll see you Sunday. Goodnight."

"Goodnight."

As soon as he's out of sight, I slump in my seat and try to forget the last five minutes of the evening.

It is after midnight by the time I am home, and as I expected, the house is dark and Phil still isn't home. I put the kettle on and open the fridge for milk, glancing at Phil's schedule stuck on the door.

Today was supposed to be his day off, although he seems to take so many extra shifts that it doesn't really mean much. What shocks me is how little I notice or enquire after Phil and vice-versa. He didn't know I was going out tonight, nor have I asked when his next day off is or why he feels the need to work every hour under the sun. Going for a drink with Seb was easy. Phil's often been out and used a lame excuse. Has Phil found some other woman? Would that account for his disinterest? My mind springs to clichés of finding lipstick on his collar or a blonde hair on his shirt, and my heart pounds against my ribs at the thought of finding proof he'd been unfaithful.

Do I need to find evidence of Phil's cheating? Would proof that he had strayed justify my sexual response to Seb?

* * *

I don't want to challenge Phil about where he is spending his time and who with. I'm afraid to hear his answer.

I take my tea to bed and let the melancholy seep in. I'm alone. Alone and sad that the most connected I have felt to anyone in so long is with Seb. He is a stark contrast to the sadness that has been slowly consuming me. I felt alive and hopeful when I was with him less than an hour ago. I slip between the cold sheets, something that, although I hate it, I'm very used to now. My phone vibrates with an incoming text and I lean across to retrieve it.

> Goodnight, Isabel. See you Sunday. S

> Until Sunday, Sebastian. Izzy

And not for the first time, I go to sleep thinking of a tall and handsome not quite stranger with wonderful eyes—who isn't my husband.

* * *

"Come on, Izzy. Stay for another drink."

"Seb, I have spent more time with you than my husband the last few weeks. I need to go home." I didn't mean that to sound as accusatory as it did, and I see Seb's spine stiffen in response.

"Will he be home when you get back?" he retorts, knowing full well Phil won't be. I've confided in Seb these last few weeks. It started the first time we went for a drink. It wasn't intended, but he was ridiculously easy to talk to. He listened to me, and I found I wanted to share more and more with him.

"Don't you have better things to do on a Saturday night than to drink and talk with me?" I really hope that he doesn't. I love the time we spend together. I feel as if we are connecting and I want that with Seb. Very much so.

"And why wouldn't I want to spend my time with you, Izzy?"

He gives me his trademark smile and I'm a lost cause. He's been cautiously flirty with me in texts and emails, giving me hints that he might be attracted to me. But I'm not sure. Certainly not sure enough to tell him to stop. *You don't want him to stop!*

"One more drink, then," I concede, feeling slightly flirty myself.

One more drink turns into two, and I get tipsy. Alcohol is not always my friend. Seb is still in total command, his usual charming and polite self, guiding the conversation, putting me at ease and making me feel valued. *Wanted, perhaps?* I have been trying to ignore the butterflies and the ache low in my stomach that Seb controls. Each time we meet, I try to see him only as a friend, but at night as I drift to sleep, alone in my bed, thoughts of his eyes raking my body, his hands holding my face or my wrists, enter my mind unrestrained. It is my own personal heaven and hell.

Even as I think I shouldn't be feeling this way, my body heats. *Don't ruin this, Izzy. Don't lose him because you find him too attractive.*

As my mind thinks the words, Seb narrows his eyes and leans in closer.

"What were you just thinking? Because your cheeks are a beautiful pink and your eyes..." He pauses to look straight at me. "Look like you're turned on." My lips part as I draw in my gasp and I am left speechless. "Oh, Isabel, you're going to have to share. From the look on your face, I'm extremely interested in your thoughts."

I grab my drink and use it as a shield from his sudden closeness. *This is a bad idea. I should not drink with this man!* I finish my gin and tonic.

"I should go."

"Izzy, relax. You don't have to tell me if you don't want to, but I already have a good idea." He sits back and gazes at me. Confidence drifts from his smile, his relaxed state and the strong gaze levelled at me. He wears his usual suit, but he's taken the jacket off, no tie, and all I can think about is unbuttoning his shirt to see what he's like in the flesh. I'm cross at my own traitorous mind.

"Well, why don't you inform me, Seb? Since you seem so sure you already know," I snap back, embarrassed. I don't register my tone until I see his amused smile. *No more drink. Go now. Now.*

I start to rise, but he stands to meet me and grasps my shoulders so I can't leave. "I know that you're attracted to me, Isabel." His breath tickles my neck as he whispers the words in my ear. My heart pounds in my chest. "Relax. I won't do anything to make you uncomfortable. I know you're married and you believe in the vows that you made. But you'd be stupid to think that I didn't find every side of you attractive, too."

Every side? What does he mean by that?

I look up at him from behind my lashes. His outward confidence and the alcohol intoxicate me. "Why haven't you told me about your private profile? The one that shows the woman hiding inside?"

I'm locked in his spell and don't understand him. "What do you mean?"

"The profile on the BDSM site you've tried so hard to hide, but go home and indulge in most evenings." His comment immediately reminds me of our first "date" and him alluding to having found it. I, of course, completely ignored him and hoped he wouldn't bring it up again.

"You... You aren't supposed to know about that."

He takes my hand in his and rubs his thumb across my knuckles. "Don't hide it from me. I can help."

I gape at him. This time I'm not embarrassed that he's discovered the secret part to me that I've locked away inside. Heat and lust swamp my rational mind.

Seb pulls back a fraction to gently sweep a lock of hair off my face and tuck it behind my ear. His eyes are locked with mine and I am weak at the knees with thoughts of what he'll do next. *Kiss me.* He must be thinking about it. His eyes are on my mouth and I can't help but slowly lick my bottom lip with the tip of my tongue.

"He's a blind idiot, you know?"

I raise my eyebrows.

"Who?" The word comes out breathy, my body too hot and in need of water.

"Your husband." His tone is firm and harsh, not the gentle purr he used for me a moment ago. "Home now."

Before I realise it, he's taken my hand in his and is leading me out of the bar. We walk in silence the few minutes into the city, his hand still wrapped around mine. We stop at a taxi rank and he seats me inside the first available car.

"I'll see you soon, Izzy." With that, he closes the door and strides away.

I sit in silence all the way home. *What am I doing?* The past few weeks have been so… fun. I have connected to someone and I desperately want to keep that, but I am jeopardising my marriage. Worse, my time with Seb uncovers just how much my relationship with Phil lacks. My phone buzzes and I have an awful thought that it might be Phil wondering where I am.

Courage, Izzy. S

Courage? Courage for what? Seb is edging me towards an unknown something. But what do I need courage for? To talk to Phil about wanting more from our marriage, more from sex? Courage to admit to myself that I am undeniably attracted to Seb and can't go a single day without thinking of him, thinking of him giving me what Phil won't?

My mind battles with the thoughts I've been trying to lock away. But the key has been turned, and my eyes see visions of Seb's body against mine, lips crushed together, hands grabbing and urging each other forward, his palm on my backside before he reaches between my legs to find my clit. Desire, thick and heavy, flushes my body and my sex pulses in anticipation. "What are you doing to me, Seb? I can't do this." But even as I mutter the words to myself, I inwardly question my resolve.

* * *

"Iz? Do you want coffee?"

The muffled voice penetrates my cocoon of warmth and I realise I need to wake up. *Ohhh. But not that quickly.* My head throbs and I slump back down into bed.

"Iz, coffee?"

"Uh, yes, please." I attempt a type of shout, as Phil is downstairs. Downstairs—but at home and offering me coffee?

The next thing I'm aware of is Phil sitting on the bed next to me, a cup in his hand. It smells wonderful. I sit and attempt to pull myself up once again.

"Heavy night, Iz? That's not like you."

"Not a heavy night. I didn't keep track of how many drinks I had." I am automatically defensive and snappy, and my head pounds as I speak.

"Well, here's a coffee."

"Thanks. I didn't mean to snap." I offer a quick apology, as I don't really want to fight, especially the way I'm feeling now. "What about you? Where were you last night?" I take a sip of coffee and try to disguise the fact that I'm almost holding my breath for his response.

"Just at Jackson's. We watched a game and had a few beers. I crashed on the sofa." He provides the usual answer for when he's been out all night. "When shall we talk about it, Iz?"

As he utters the words, I mentally collapse on myself. *Not now, not feeling like this with Seb ingrained into my brain from last night.*

"What... uh, did you want to talk about?" I roll my eyes at how pathetic I sound.

"Why you asked me to spank you and tie you up. Why now, Iz? What's changed?"

The question hangs in the air. I close my eyes and pretend that this isn't happening. I knew this was coming. I've been trying to avoid it for as long as possible, even though it's put an even greater hole in the heart of our marriage.

I don't know how to explain any of my feelings to Phil, and I am even less sure of how he might react. He already freaked at what I asked. "Do you really want to know?"

"Yes. I think we should clear the air."

I let the breath I am holding in my lungs out and try not to fidget. "Okay, but try and listen." I pick a spot on the mug and think of Seb's message from last night. *Courage, Izzy.* "I want to explore a side of me that I've been denying for some time. I want us to connect, for you to listen to me and make sex about us instead of just you. I want to be able to put my satisfaction in your hands and know that you'll think of me, about what I might like." I peek up and see his stony face. "I want you to take control, to tell me what to do but also to take care of me. I want you to know how every touch affects my body. I want you so focused on me that you know how to satisfy me. I don't want to ask. And I don't want you to ignore what I tell you. Just show me, for once, what else there could be between us. And I want it to be a little naughtier." I pause and let that sink in before I go any further.

"So all these years I've not satisfied you? Gee, thanks, Izzy."

"No, that's not all of it. I feel like something's missing—"

He cuts me off before I can explain any further. "Too right, if you think I'm hitting my wife to get her off for a cheap thrill."

Phil stands and paces around the room. I can see he is torn and doesn't know what to do. "God, Iz. I thought it might have been a one-time thing. But you want this?" His voice is hard and accusatory, degrading me with his words.

Yes, I want to try. I long to give my submission. Why don't you know that or see it?

"Yes, I do." I'm not going to let him think I'm afraid of this. He asked to talk, but he can't handle the answer I gave him.

"Well, we might have a problem then, Izzy, because I won't hit you."

"I'm not saying hit me. I don't want violence. I mean… discipline. Sensation."

"Forget it."

"You won't even try this for me?" I plead, a little shocked by his words, and also at how weak my voice suddenly sounds. My heart races and I'm scared of where this conversation is heading. I've always thought deep down that Phil and I would work through everything—including this—each giving in or compromising.

"I don't do that type of stuff. It's not me."

No. I suddenly feel a rush of anger at how he is dismissing me. Again.

"Well, I hardly know what *is* you anymore, Phil. You're never here. You spend at least two nights a week 'out with Jackson'. Neither you or I knew where the other was last night. What does that say?"

He doesn't answer but he stops pacing. He narrows his eyes at me and I shiver at the malice I see there. He's trying to blame everything on me when he's just as much a part of this non-marriage as I am. The bedroom stuff was a chance to finally assert a side of me that I thought might help.

"Don't try and turn this on me."

"Phil, you must see it. You can't think that this is normal for a marriage. We don't talk. We don't communicate on any level. We don't have a relationship. We are simply roommates." I'm pleading for him to see what I see.

"So I like my space. You've never had a problem before."

"I think it's more than that." Since meeting Seb, I've started to think about Phil's actions. I'm sure he's hiding something. "I think you're seeing someone."

"Whatever." He storms out of the bedroom and clatters down the stairs. A few minutes later, the front door slams. *Clearly not, then.*

I slump back down into bed, my heart hammering in my chest and echoing in my head. *Did that really happen?* Phil and I have never communicated openly about serious subjects, but things were always more simple than this. We were drifting, and I didn't notice or care enough to question anything. Looking back over the last six months with fresh eyes, it's hard not to see the blindingly obvious. I was just another one of those wives who didn't consider the possibility that her husband was cheating on her.

I text my best friend, Jess, for a pick-me-up and wish we could flake in front of a film together. Knowing she'll always have my back is a huge relief as I contemplate my marriage.

Sorry, I'm out at the moment. Rain check? Jess x

I try to stop my thoughts from wandering to Seb, but struggle. Seb definitely isn't helping, but I'm confident that he isn't the catalyst for my troubled marriage. The night I met him I wasn't looking for anything other than relief from a cold, dark house. These past weeks with him have given me a glimpse of what a real relationship could be like. I'm afraid to let my defences down. I'm not strong enough to fight that sort of attraction.

Now I have the added questions about Phil to answer as well.

As I go about my routine, albeit slowly as I nurse my hangover, I can't help pondering all of Seb's traits—his self-assured, confident, and controlling nature balanced with his flirty side and his ability to listen and read me like a book, all wrapped up with a strong frame and the most arresting eyes I've ever seen. How would Seb react if I asked him to tie me up and spank me? The question is in my mind before I even realise it, and I nearly collapse on the bathroom floor. *No, I can't!* I can't think this way.

I need to talk about all of this, to explain to someone, that's all. I spend the rest of the day cleaning and filing, putting things away. I do anything I can think of to distract myself. Since I asked myself how Seb would react, I've tried to do everything I can to stop myself going there again. But no matter how clean the kitchen surfaces or the bathroom are, I can't stop the lust and desire, the images of carnal possibilities, from bubbling and festering under my skin. *No. I'm stronger than this.* I'm married. I made vows. No one said marriage would be easy. This is just a test. A fucking great big one, but still just a test. *Just a test, just a test.*

That becomes my mantra for the next few days. *Just a test, just a test.* I haven't heard from Seb, even though he is always on my mind. I have only *heard* Phil in the house, rather than actually speaking to him.

I'm miserable. I can't bring myself to talk to Phil and that damn thought—the question of how Seb would respond to my plea to be tied and spanked—has taken root and won't let go. I stare into my empty coffee mug and realise that I could have an answer to that question. I've been desperate to talk to someone and, although I have Jess who I can confide in, it feels almost humiliating to admit what I want and what is really happening to my marriage.

I know who I want to tell, and somehow I know he won't judge me. *You hope he won't judge you.* I've been circling this for the last few days and it's eating me up inside. I want to tell Seb about what happened, to see what he will say in return. This is a very dangerous path, one that is self-destructive and has little hope of ending happily, but I can't take the lonely emptiness I'm feeling anymore.

    I pack up my things from work and leave the office a little early to head straight to the bar. My mind is made up. Although this is the last thing I should be doing, part of me calmed the moment I made the decision to tell Seb. That scares me.

Three

Can you meet me? Please? Izzy

I press *send. That's it. I can't turn back now.* I order a gin and tonic and knock it back far too quickly, hoping that it will help me find the courage to actually tell Seb what I want.

I pick the bar where we first met, the bar where we've met each time since. It somehow seems fitting that it could be the first and last place I see him. And doesn't that send my heart pounding and my stomach churning? That's another little message from my body, reminding me of how crazy this all is. I've only known the guy for a few weeks and know next to nothing about him.

My phone buzzes across the bar top and I grab it quickly. *Maybe Seb's out of town and can't come? Maybe he's busy? With someone else?* If I don't do this today, I'm never going to have the courage to ask him. It's a gut reaction and one I have to see through.

Sure, Izzy, I'll be there in a few minutes. S

I close my eyes and remember Phil's face after I asked him to spank me. The anger when he realised that this is what I really want was plastered across his face. How he shut me out completely and dismissed me. He didn't want to understand. We've been together for eleven years, more if you count the two we dated, but does he really know me? *Hell, do I really know me?* I'm not even sure of that. I check my watch and silently curse Seb for taking his time.

I order a coffee to sober up. There's a knot in my stomach and I feel physically sick. It is that mixture of dread and excitement—the good kind of nerves that make your heart beat faster and your palms sweat.

I've gone over this too many times in my head. What will Seb think? Will he understand? How will I tell him? *Just say it. Come out and say it. Tell Seb that you need something more, that you want more.* The what-if's are ruining me.

There have been enough email and text messages with suggestive content, skirting around the topic of sex with flirting and innuendo. He's seen my profile on the BDSM site and I can guess he's also seen the images I like on Tumblr. There is clearly more to Seb than he openly portrays. Whether his controlled and sophisticated flirtation is simply a façade, I don't know, but I am going to find out.

Hands grip my shoulders and trail down my arms. Seb circles around me and takes the seat opposite, and I relax a little at seeing his face. He rewards me with his sexy smile. *Breathe. Just breathe.*

"Seb, I need to... well... want to tell you something important." I stumble over my words in my haste, but I have to get my thoughts out this minute or lose the small amount of Dutch courage I've built up. There's no room for "hi" or "hello."

"Okay, Izzy, what's so important?"

"It's just that... well..."

He reaches out for my hands. "I'm all yours. Take a breath and tell me."

"This is really hard to say." *Am I really going to tell him? This could ruin everything.*

"Come on, Izzy. Tell me."

His deep tones wrap around my chest and make my heart speed up. *I can do this. I want to do this.*

I focus on his chest and open my mouth to step over the line I desperately hope Seb doesn't want to keep in place. "Phil and I haven't really been 'together' for a while, not in the physical sense." I look up at him but he doesn't say anything. His thumb gently strokes my knuckles, giving me courage to say more. "He doesn't understand what I've told him I need. We've been growing apart for a long time and I'm not happy. I've changed, and I... I... Well, I need something different from our relationship. At least... I think I need it. But Phil can't... I've tried to explain, but he won't try to be the man I need him to be for me." I pause, hoping to re-gather my rambling thoughts. I risk another quick look into his face. His eyes are hard and he's sitting as still as a statue. Even his thumb on my hand has stopped moving. "He thinks I'm asking him to rough me up, and that's not it at all. I don't want violence. I want to submit." I look down for a moment. "I'm tired of being responsible for my own sexual pleasure. I want the freedom I'm hoping to find in submission. I want a partner who takes the time to arouse my mind and my body, and I want to abandon myself to him."

I study his face to see any emotion or reaction to what I'm trying to say. *Did I convey myself right? Does he get what I mean?*

The only thing I notice is the vein in his neck. It throbs hard and fast. My lips part as I imagine my tongue running up his neck to below his ear. I shake the thought away and focus again on his chest. "I asked him to tie my hands, and he did, but when I asked for something else, he got angry—well, a bit more than angry, actually."

"Did he hurt you, Izzy?"

"No, not physically." I relax my shoulders and let go of all the air inside me, physically slumping now that it is out. *Will he understand what I am trying to say?* I hope so. I want to be open with him. For some unknown reason, I feel I can trust him.

"It's just I told him it wasn't a one-off thing I wanted to try, and he... doesn't want that." Seb sits motionless. My eyes drop down, unwilling to see what I think must be rejection in Seb's face. I try to pull my hands away from his grip.

Seb grabs hold of my retreating hands and pulls them closer to him. "Izzy, are you asking me what I hope you are?"

I look up into his beautiful eyes. My world is lost in his hopeful gaze. Our eyes lock together and heat erupts from within me, warming my skin at this simple connection.

"Izzy, you need to be very clear with me on this." I nod, my courage already used up. "You are telling me that you want to experience submission at my hands, to cross a line, in order for you to understand if this is what you truly desire. You want to know the reality of submission... not the fantasy in your head or the online world you get lost in. Understand what it really is like to put yourself in another's hands—and you want it with me. Is this correct?"

I take in a breath, my mind racing in a million different directions. *Did he just offer me more? Is this really happening?* A smile spreads across my lips and I'm unable to stop the warmth that creeps across my cheeks. Our eyes still focus on each other. With my cheeks on fire, I nod. The hard grip he had on my hands gentles and his gaze softens. It is the only change in his expression. "But I'll need..." I pause, trying to give my brain time to process. "I need you to hold my hand, to guide me. I don't even know where to begin in this, and..."

"Shhh."

I break eye contact, suddenly shy about what I've admitted. *Shit, shit, shit.*

"I understand." He squeezes my fingers and chuckles.

I did it! My heart stampedes in my chest. If I don't get my breathing in check, I'm going to pass out. I can't look at him. My chest heaves with every breath. Adrenaline courses around my body. *This is it.* This is what has consumed my mind 24/7, and now I can't look at him.

My stomach takes a nosedive as his finger lightly runs down my jaw and tips my head up until my eyes follow and meet his. "This is the address of my flat." He hands me a beautiful, simple card with a few solitary lines of text. It's the same thick card as the one he first gave me, but this one also has an address in the city.

"7:30, Tuesday evening. Take a deep breath, knock on my door and I'll hold your hand. And, Isabel, don't be late."

Hearing my full name sends goose bumps across my skin. I'm struck by the intensity of the desire I feel for Seb as I look into his eyes. Aquamarine. They aren't blue, but a brilliant aquamarine. Blues and greens mix into a bright and clear shade that I hope conceals a darker promise. He still shows little emotion. *Smile. Please smile. Or something, anything.* I silently plead with him to give me his trademark smile. *Why did he call me Isabel? Is he cross with me?* But I want to hear him call me Isabel again. Over and over.

"Sebastian," I breathe. I finally see a response as his lips part to draw in a deep breath. "Okay." I put a voice to my acceptance and follow it up with a shy smile. But before I have a chance to fully register everything, he stands and walks out. I feel shocked and vulnerable but aroused as hell.

* * *

The next few days are the longest I've ever had to endure.

I play our conversation over and over in my head, trying to analyse and understand every word he said. I'm in a constant battle with my body and my mind. My body screams to follow through with my "confession" and go to Seb. My mind won't let me forget that Phil and I are still married. I am married. Unfortunately, Phil has done nothing to displace my suspicions over this week. He hasn't answered any of my texts, and he was out on both nights at the start of the week. He seems to only come home for a change of clothes. *What am I supposed to think?* I caught myself going through his pockets and checking his jacket the other night, but I found nothing incriminating. Yet.

Every time I close my eyes, I see Seb's beautifully dangerous, aquamarine eyes. Those eyes that make my core sizzle. They bring out a need in me that grows every day. I want to surrender and give my body to Seb. To put my needs in Sebastian's hands. I am becoming obsessed.

My secret retreat, my favourite social platform, is my only distraction. I open my iPad and click on the Tumblr app and wait for the images to load. Women, bound and restrained in submissive poses; men, caressing and pinching at breasts, spanking flesh and leaving their mark. All add fuel to the fire of my imagination. I skip out of the application and pull up my web history, scrolling through to 'Journey to Domination'. I open the blog and review the latest few posts. Words of submission, trust and freedom all play to my desire and the longing to feel what it's like to be the woman giving all of her control to her partner, to put her sexual needs in his hands, grows stronger. I want to submit. I need to know what being tied, blindfolded and flogged would do to my heart rate, my breathing and my pussy. I close the window and toss the iPad to the end of the sofa.

My days creep past, undistinguished, one after the other. Nothing changes in my life. I haven't grown horns overnight. No one is trying to hang me. My colleagues act normally around me despite what I am contemplating. That's the problem. I'm not contemplating anymore. I'm imagining what will happen when I put myself in Seb's hands.

* * *

Tuesday arrives and the clock stops ticking altogether. Everything at work drags. My concentration is shot. The hours creep by at a torturous pace. Five o'clock will never come.

I arrive home from work to an empty house. Phil is working. Again. It makes it easy, I suppose. I won't have to lie about where I'm going or where I have been. I run up the stairs and dash into the bathroom. Stripping, I turn the shower on and scrub my body. *Oh, shit. What am I supposed to wear? What have I got to wear?*

My obsessing only took me as far as the door to Seb's. How have I not considered the sorry state of my underwear before now? Of course, my mind automatically thinks he's going to want to have sex with me the minute he shuts the door. Seb agreed to help me experience submission. I assumed since Seb agreed, he had a certain amount of experience as a dominant, but we hadn't discussed the specifics. He left too soon.

I lather the shampoo into my hair, trying to relax my mind by rubbing my fingers into my scalp. *Black lace knickers, plain and simple.* I rinse the suds out of my long, chestnut hair and let the water wash over my body. Rubbing my shoulders, I try to relieve the tension and anxiety knotting my muscles. I hadn't realised how tense waiting can be.

I pull on my black underwear and my favourite chic but simple grey dress that hugs the small curves that I have. I leave my hair natural and down, roughly dried by the hairdryer and head out of the door a little before seven o'clock.

Four

As I slide out of the back of the taxi, I look up at the building in front of me. It's smart, well designed, and complements the surrounding older-style buildings. It fits Seb. I check my watch with his warning not to be late in mind. *Breathe, Izzy. Breathe. You want this.* Inhaling one last breath, I place one foot in front of the other. My heart is in my mouth and I can taste the excitement. I want this experience with Seb. To be able to feel what submission means in a sexual sense.

I shake my head free of all doubt, walk up to the intercom, press the button for apartment 62 and wait. The air is crisp and biting around me. The shivers of cold rival those of my anticipation. The enormity of what I am opening myself up to hits me. I take huge gulps of air and turn back to look at the street. The sound of his voice over the intercom recaptures my focus.

"Good evening, Isabel. Please open the glass door to your left. Go into the lobby and take the lift to the sixth floor. I'll meet you when you arrive."

With that, the door buzzes open, and I step over the threshold to meet him. No going back. I'll finally experience what I crave.

By the time the lift arrives, nerves and fears bubble into excitement. I am anxious to see Seb, to look at him, knowing he will be my guide, holding my hand and giving me an experience in submission. His reassurance that he will shepherd me through this experience gives me the courage I need.

The doors slide open and he is waiting for me. My entire body ignites as his eyes roam over me. My cheeks warm as I lower my gaze. I step out of the lift and take a few tentative steps towards him. He remains still and quiet, but I can feel a tension between us that isn't usually there.

He runs his finger down my jaw and gently lifts my head, exactly how he did only a few days ago. "Good evening."

Seb takes my hand and raises it to his lips, planting a sure and firm kiss there as if he's a noble knight. He lowers my hand but keeps it in his comforting grip.

"I'm glad you're here. Come in, Izzy."

I take another step, physically and figuratively, towards a new threshold with Seb. Exactly what I need. Something to look towards with hope.

Once inside, he closes the door and walks me into an open-plan room. His place is gorgeous—spacious as well as being filled with light. I take in the sleek, modern furniture. The subtle lighting contrasts well with the oak floor and aluminium appliances, hard, clean, and masculine. He leads me across the living area to a breakfast bar, and I sit in a tall chair. He looks into my eyes, and I see a hard edge to the blue shining at me. My stomach rolls so hard that I have to focus on not gasping for air. His eyes are filled with desire and I want to get lost in them. *Please, please, please, kiss me.*

He cups my face and strokes his thumbs over my cheeks, giving me permission to lean into him. Blood rushes through my veins and the staccato beat of my heart rings in my ears.

"You look even more divine than you did when I first met you."

His words make me long for him, and I can't believe this is actually happening. My cheeks warm, but I manage a timid 'thanks' in reply. *Divine—he thinks I'm divine.*

Soft lips press against mine, gently at first, but he's restrained, holding back. He pulls away too quickly, and I'm left wanting. I want everything from this man and he's only just kissed me. *Is that even possible?*

"So, would you like the tour?" He flashes the signature smile I want to call mine and I nod in agreement. He takes my hand in his and gently pulls me from my seat. Silently, Seb lets me soak in his surroundings. His flat is masculine, yet inviting and elegant with plenty of space. My eyes are drawn to the large dining room table at the other end of the kitchen area. His study is small and intimate. His desk dominates the room, set curiously in the centre, allowing us to walk around it entirely.

Black-and-white photographs of women's bodies are displayed in metallic frames throughout the rooms. *Why does he have women on his walls?* A horrible taste of envy coats my tongue. *I want him to want to look at me and not artistically posed, half-naked women in frames.*

I mentally chastise myself.

"This is my bedroom." He doesn't make any move to step over this threshold, so I simply take my fill as he stands to the side. A large bed with four tall posts dominates the space. The rest of the furniture is sparse, consisting of two double wardrobes, a full-length mirror and a single chair in the corner. There is another door, which I assume leads to his bathroom. I take in all the details before he pulls me away.

"One more room, Izzy," he says.

I follow him to the last room. He opens the door and pulls me inside. Cool, neutral tones relax my senses as Seb's hand gently drops mine. This room is smaller than his. The bed is made up with white linen, and the only colour in the room is two vibrant splashes of crimson silk in the form of cushions sitting atop a mountain of cream cushions. I look over at Seb and see his smile.

"This is your room to use as your personal space, whenever you are here." His eyes dance with pleasure and the calm the room had given me evaporates. "You can come in here whenever you want—if you need time or space, to freshen up or to prepare." His voice is soft and smooth, teasing me about what is to come.

The meaning in his words strikes me. He's taking the time to make sure I'm comfortable and at ease given the reason I'm here. He knows that I want to submit—experience the freedom that comes from handing over control—and submit to him. There will be a certain level of intimacy, and my earlier concern over underwear seems appropriate, now. I blush as nerves stir my stomach.

Power rolls from Seb's confident stance and all I feel is desired. Seb walks over to the dressing table, closing the distance between us. With each step toward me, the tension crackles. "I have some items for you. And I have some rules to explain. If you really want to experience 'more'—with me—these rules must come first." The air is saturated with tension, and chemistry bounces between us, eager to be allowed out to play. "Isabel, I see in you something very special. I believe you've been hiding, even from yourself, and my offer is to help you discover that hidden part of you. The process of this discovery comes with consequences to both of us, and you'll need to trust me."

Doubts flash through my mind. Is my desire to find the truth behind my sexual fantasies greater than the worth of my marriage? Or simply a reaction to the hopeless situation I feel I'm in?

"Izzy, don't shut down. Communication will be key. Talk to me."

Oh boy! "Phil never gave me what I wanted, what I need from our relationship. I tolerated his refusal and lack of interest in what I asked for. As the years ebbed away, so did the part of me that still wanted to fight for what I needed. I denied myself, thinking it was easier than fighting. But it's always been there—my longing to put myself in another's hands and experience pleasure. Phil still won't hear me, choosing to believe what I want is violent and dirty."

"I know, sweetheart, and that's why I'm offering this experience to you. This way you can make your own decision, safely."

My gut tells me I should follow through with the actions that brought me here.

"Yes."

"Good. This is the code to the lobby door downstairs and the key fob to my apartment." He hands me a slip of paper and a black plastic box the size of a matchbox. "For all of our subsequent meetings, I expect you to arrive beforehand and let yourself in."

The change in his speech brings me to attention. He is serious about this. "You should use this room as you would at home. Make any final preparations you wish. There will be a bottle of wine in the fridge and two glasses left out on the side. Pour two glasses and sit on a stool at the breakfast bar to wait for me. I will enter the apartment at our agreed time. You are to greet me, hand me my wine and kiss me as a welcome. We'll start our evening from there. Is this acceptable to you?"

Acceptable? My mind struggles to keep up, but I like the sound of it. Wine, the trust, the fact that he wants me in his apartment and intends to have me here again. Yes, yes to it all.

"Yes. Yes, it is," I reply, and I manage to make myself sound calm for once.

"Good. It's important to me that from now on you cross the threshold of your own free will, without suggestion or enticement from me. If, after I show you more, you don't like what you feel, you will have time to turn back without me persuading you otherwise. Understand?" I nod.

"I need to hear the words, Izzy." His voice drops, and I shiver. "Do you understand?"

"Yes." I long for his touch, his seductive whispering in my ear, helping me cross over to the unknown.

"Right. Now, are you wearing tights or stockings?"

"Umm... tights."

"I detest tights." His tone makes me want to fall to my knees and beg forgiveness. "Tights are unflattering, impossible to remove in a sensual way and do not provide me with the access I need. Never wear them again in my presence. If you must cover your legs, wear stockings or thigh highs."

"Okay. I'm sorry."

"There are consequences for breaking the rules. Not everything between us will be of a sexual nature. The submission you have been looking for comes from a multitude of things. I'm going to work on those as well, and following the rules is part of it." The edge to his voice promises delights yet to come, the delights I've only imagined until now. "If I find you wearing tights again, I will rip them off, tie you up with the remains and spank you."

Oh God, that sounds good. Is that what you're going to do to me now? The tips of my nipples tingle, my breath catches and my heart pounds in my ears. His fierce expression makes me want him all the more. My thoughts linger on his consequences and my sex pulses deliciously.

"Yes... I, um... understand," I finally choke out, desperately turned on.

"I wish to offer you a small gift."

Gift? A physical gift? Seb pulls out a beautiful black velvet box from the dressing table and opens the top. Nestled inside is a delicate anklet adorned with tiny pearls and clear crystals.

"I would like you to wear this anklet whenever you are happy to be totally mine, willing to obey me completely and allowing me total responsibility for your pleasures. If I see you wearing it when you are waiting for me in the kitchen, then I'll know that you will submit to me. Completely."

It's my turn to offer a smile for once. "Our language is jewellery?"

"Exactly." He closes the box and places it back on the dressing room table. I want to put it on now. *I'll submit to you now.* That's why I'm here, Seb.

He cups my face again. This time, he holds my gaze. Completely helpless in his hands, I am eager to please him. He leans in and explores my lips, scorching them with his passion. He pushes at my bottom lip. His tongue gently sweeps across my top lip, opening my mouth to his. I moan involuntarily as pressure consumes me and my mouth takes over. My lips move, devouring his as all of my hope and expectations surface. He releases my face. His hands run down my shoulders to my wrists and he traps them behind my back in a strong, controlling grip. The kiss burns wildly as our tongues seek each other out, exploring and teasing. It's filled with the anticipation of what's to come, and I'm wet with desire for him.

My body is awash with new feelings. Nerves and excitement mix with a raw sense of lust, and my head swims.

He pulls away and I instantly miss his lips. He rests his forehead against mine and breathes out slowly.

Please kiss me. Kiss me again. Now!

I feel more cherished and cared for in that moment than I have in as long as I can remember. That kiss unlocked all the emotions raging inside me, all the pain and disappointment, the sadness and frustration that I didn't even realise I'd held onto. It's all I can do not to break down in Seb's arms.

"Isabel, you taste so good."

How am I going to survive Seb? He kisses as if he wants to consume me. I'm going to pass out from pleasure. I don't say anything, but continue to breathe in through my mouth, my eyes closed, and concentrate on not passing out. My mind reels with thoughts stemming from the intensity of that kiss.

"What time do you have to leave?" he whispers.

"Midnight. Phil, when he does come home, gets in around 2 a.m."

"He doesn't always come home?"

"No. You know we're not close."

"In which case, Cinderella, I'll book your carriage now."

The mention of Phil's name saddens me. Technically, I'm being unfaithful. But I see no way to repair our marriage. Seb is resurrecting the part of me that Phil has slowly killed, and he makes it so easy. I feel alive with him. I get swept up in the physical sensations and can abandon myself to the pleasure. It is different from the emotionless service of Phil's needs I've grown accustomed to. I don't want to talk about leaving tonight. I've only just arrived.

Seb heads towards the kitchen. My thoughts and emotions swarm chaotically. *Deep breaths, Izzy.* Streams of chestnut hair fall across my back as I rock my head from side to side. I press my fingertips to my temples; my pulse is strong and steady. I force any negativity out of my mind. *No thoughts about Phil or our marriage—not tonight.*

With a new determination, I find Seb in the kitchen, pouring himself a drink.

"Would you care for a gin and tonic?" He crunches ice cubes out of the tray.

"Yes, please." The bottle of Hendrick's on the counter calls my name.

He mixes my drink. "Please take a seat. I'd like you to relax as well."

"Thank you." I perch on the stool and nervously play with my fingers as I wait for him. Relaxing isn't going to come easy.

"Do you think you'll be able to get rid of your nerves by the end of the night?"

My eyes flash to his. Is he serious? "I'll take that look as a no, then." He beams an alluring smile my way. Gone is the edgy, controlled man. Now the warmer, softer side of Seb rears his head.

"I love the red cushions in my room."

"I thought the room needed some colour, to reflect a bit of you, perhaps, Izzy." As he says the words, my cheeks blush and I look down at my drink.

"And right on cue!" He laughs and finishes his drink, then puts his glass down on the table. "Time is a wonderful thing. Time helps build excitement and elicits anticipation. Let's not leave that moment of first enlightenment for too much longer. When you are ready, go to your room, prepare yourself and come back to me here."

His words captivate me. They sink right to my core.

Time to take the plunge...

Sipping my Hendrick's and savouring the taste on my tongue, I slide off the stool. I try to find a confidence within me to ensure that I don't wobble and manage to lean in and kiss him on the cheek. In my most sassy voice, I say, "I'll just be a couple of minutes."

Shutting the door, I lean back against it and try to steady myself. My stomach feels as if it's housing butterflies. I'm relaxed at being in his presence, though. He manages to set every nerve ending and pulse point in my body buzzing with expectation while simultaneously putting me at ease.

I walk over to the bed and perch on the edge, not wanting to mess it up. *I want this. I want to see this through.* I pull my tights down and leave them on the bed. *Must buy complete new underwear collection, especially stockings and garters!* I stand, eager to get back to him, when the black velvet box holding the anklet catches my eye. *Am I ready to wear this tonight?* Do I really know what obeying and submitting is going to entail? It feels right when I'm with him. Hell, my body is dying to see where this could go. I want to give in and submit. I just need a little confidence. Seb said he'd help me. He'll give me the confidence. He won't be too hard on me straightaway. *Will he?*

"This is ridiculous." Cursing under my breath, I snatch the box and open it. I take out the delicate piece and raise my leg to fasten it around my ankle, taking my time as I symbolically step across another threshold.

I walk out and into the kitchen. The significance of this moment fills me with trepidation. *I can't do this without you, Seb.*

As if I spoke my thoughts aloud, Seb holds out his hand. Beckoning me towards him, he pulls me in and crushes me to his chest. His kiss envelops my mouth, claiming me, banishing my fear and doubt. He releases me and holds me at arm's length. Crystal blue eyes drown me with their desire. Heat spreads from my pussy and goose bumps erupt across my neck and arms.

"Stunning," he whispers. "Simply and beautifully stunning."

I'm in awe at his words and overwhelmed by the admiration in his eyes. This is exactly what I need. His eyes travel down my legs, now *sans* tights, and rest on my ankle.

Seb sucks in a breath. "Are you sure?"

"Yes, I want to. I still… I still want you to show me, make me feel what submission is really like. I'm nervous, though. " His commanding eyes pin me where I stand. "I want this, Sebastian. I need to see…" I trail off.

"And your marriage vows? Where is the line for you?"

A lump has formed in my throat. *Sex.* He's talking about sex, or at least variations of it. *Could I do that? With another man?*

"I… I'm not sure."

"You will need to be sure if you're wearing that anklet. I need to know how far I can take you. This can be all about the power exchange between us, you submitting to my control and getting the freedom you've been craving. Sex doesn't have to be part of it."

Freedom. The word sings in my ears. Shivers tremble through my limbs. This is what I want. With Seb, that attraction, the undercurrent, isn't going away, and the thought of not having his hands on me, not touching me—I'm not strong enough to resist his allure.

"Sex isn't where I want to draw the line between us." Whispering my confession, I try to adjust to my decision.

"On your knees."

Those three simple words in that velvet voice send my body flurrying to obey. My confession now forgotten, I kneel. My pulse quickens. A familiar ache in my stomach forces my breathing to labour.

"When I ask you to kneel, lower your gaze. This is another rule that I will enforce with a punishment I deem fit. Like the tights."

I cast my eyes towards the floor, breaking the contact that I've been seeking out. I hear him walk around behind me.

"You are truly beautiful like this, Isabel." From this position, I hear him rather than see him. "Stay like that for me. I want you to feel comfortable kneeling in front of me, at my command."

His words of praise send another wave of want through me and my pussy clenches. I try to breathe deeply and adjust to this new position. My weight presses my knees into the oak floor. My arms are restless by my sides, but I resist fidgeting. A deep breath stops my shoulders from tensing further but doesn't slow the rise and fall of my chest. I've only been kneeling for a few minutes, yet my knees are already protesting.

I wait.

The waiting seems to drift on for such a long time. With each passing moment, my anxiety rises. I try to relax. My mind concentrates on all the reasons I'm here. To find that something that's been missing from my life, the missing key that will unlock my inner self. I was never sure where to find it before now.

"You have beautiful hair, Isabel." His words bring me back to the now. He holds all of my attention. There is nothing else. Only Seb. Fingers rake my scalp as his hand makes a fist and pulls my head back. "But I don't want you to wear it down when you are with me. Put it up, or plait it simply."

That feels so good. Oh please, touch my skin, kiss my neck.

He pulls my hair into his hand again. This time he twists it around his wrist and tugs—not hard, but enough for me to gasp. My core contracts and my muscles tense, pulling my body upwards. Heat rushes through me; my pussy clenches tighter and sends a pulse of need to my stomach. I can feel how wet I am. The physical reaction I have to Seb is scintillating.

"Very good, Isabel." He maintains his hold of my hair as he lowers to his knees behind me. His warmth radiates against my back. "Well done on removing your tights. I see you're a quick learner. But you'll make a mistake soon, and you'll know what it feels like to be punished."

Punished? My body reacts immediately. Liquid want seeps from me, drenching my knickers. The gentle hum of desperation kicks up a gear. *How has he done this to me? Do I want to be punished? What if it hurts?*

"Yes," I pant out. "But please…"

"Don't worry. I'll always be beside you tonight." He lets my hair tumble down.

Always? Shit, where did that come from? And why did it sound so damn good?

"Now stand up and remove your knickers."

My body wants to respond to him, and my knickers will betray how much. They are soaking. *My knickers off—then there won't be anything in the way of him touching me, and God, I need him to touch me.*

My wobbly legs finally allow me to stand. In my shyness, I slide my hands underneath my dress , desperate to look sexy. Hooking my knickers to pull them down, I step out of them and look to Seb for my next instruction.

"Stand at the end of the bar and hold onto the edge. Hands close together. Feet wide apart."

Being commanded does good things to my pulse. My heart beats so quickly he must be able to hear it. Fear should be registering somewhere, nerves over what he could do to me. I barely know him, after all, but this feels natural. Soft rustling gives away Seb's position behind me, and my arms tremble in expectation. Seb places his left hand gently and directly over mine. He interlaces his fingers with mine, joining us. His right hand travels down the side of my body, following the contours of my hip. He doesn't stop. His hand runs to the hem of my dress, pulled taut as my legs are spread. Teasing between the fabric and my skin, he runs his fingers back and forth across the line of the two. "Don't move," he says.

Every hair on the back of my neck stands up.

Mentally, I'm begging for him to touch me, to feel how wet I am for him. If he were a mind reader, he'd hear me scream, *I'm yours to touch and to take. NOW!* I wonder whether he can hear my silent pleas.

Fingers skim up to the top of my thigh, between my legs, to find my dripping pussy.

"Ahh," I moan. A finger glides between my lips and eases inside me very slowly. As he moves, I arch my back. My head falls backwards and rests on his shoulder.

"You've clearly been denied what you so desperately need for too long. You're new at this, but you will learn to obey my orders. I'm going to help you."

The sensation of his finger toying with my most sensitive flesh clouds my mind. Then I remember his command to stay still. *Is he serious?* He's turning me on beyond all my hopes and he wants me to keep still? His finger continues to glide slowly between my swollen lips. *How... I can't... Oh, God, don't stop touching me... Please... I'm so close... I need to...*

"Take a small step backwards, then lean forward so you are resting on the bar, Isabel."

No... don't stop. Not now. Just a little bit more. I need release... You need to make me come...

I still for a second. The warning rasp in his voice rings clear in my mind. I obey. My bottom is positioned and ready for anything he wishes. My longing for this experience surpasses a quick orgasm. I want to feel everything Seb wants to give me. That includes more than the amazing pressure growing between my legs. I crave the total release that will only come from surrendering myself. Completely.

"Divine," he murmurs. I wait, something I'm quickly coming to realise I'll have to deal with.

Goose bumps follow the touch of his fingers as they run down the length of my back and follow the curve of my hips. He tugs at my dress, raising the hem so it bunches at my waist and completely exposes me. Warmth from the pressure of his palm spreads over my bottom cheek as he gently massages me in a circular motion. Then nothing. The absence of his touch sends a jolt of fear through me.

A loud slap of his hand on my left cheek followed by a warm glow pushes all the air out of my lungs. He follows with another spank in quick succession.

"Yes!"

The sharp sting radiates between my legs. He returns to rubbing and squeezing my bum, with both hands this time, before he delivers another series of smacks on alternating cheeks.

"Mmm," is my only answer this time as I relax into the force and feel of his hand on my skin. He gently rubs and kneads my skin, and follows with a quick spank or two until my whole bottom is alight with fire. My pussy is so wet I dribble down the inside of my thighs. My entire body feels alive and hums with excitement. I'm flushed everywhere and in a calm state of acceptance. He brings his hand down on me and leans forward.

His words whisper in my ear. "Now, shall I see if you enjoyed that little tease?" I hear the sexy smile in his voice as he runs his hand down over my bum, careful to avoid my crack, and heads straight for my throbbing and wet pussy.

"Oh God, Isabel. You're so wet," he growls into my ear. I nearly come on the spot hearing the warm appreciation in his voice. "Turn around and strip. Everything off. Now."

I immediately move. He takes hold of my hand to steady me as I turn, feeling light-headed.

He's going to see me completely naked. Shit, he's going to see me! I register my doubts, but my desire to obey his command is stronger. I stand tall, more than a little shaky. My legs are like jelly and my whole sex throbs with unsatisfied pleasure. I reach for the zip on my dress, keeping my eyes downcast, and slowly pull it down. I slide the straps off my shoulders. The fabric ripples down my body and pools at my feet. I gingerly step from the discarded garment and I'm left dressed only in my bra. Insecurities bombard my thoughts. I'll have to show him my breasts—my too-small breasts that never look desirable or flattering and can always do with an extra lift. Men always like bigger breasts, don't they? *Come on, Izzy. Have some faith. One last step. Say something, Seb... anything. Don't leave me hanging like this.*

"All of your clothes, Isabel. If I give you a command, I expect you to follow my instructions to the letter. Obedience is one of my rules and there will be consequences for not obeying."

With a quick gulp of air, my head falls slightly as his velvet tones echo in my ears, strong and sure. I reach around to unfasten my bra. It slides off and joins my dress on the floor. Now fully exposed to him, I place my hands behind me to stop from covering myself.

Please like me. Like what you see. I want you to want me.

A chill blankets my naked body as the cool air floats around my skin. I shiver but try to remain as still as I can. I look up at him, too nervous and insecure to wait, and I lock onto his eyes. I can see heat in them as he surveys my naked body, a controlled smile lifting the corners of his mouth.

"Gorgeous. I didn't think you could be any more exquisite, but you naked is the most breath taking thing I have ever seen." His words pull a smile from my lips and I have to fight the tingling of tears forming in my eyes. His approval and affection bathes me in a warmth I'd forgotten.

Seb holds out his hands and I eagerly walk forward a few small steps to take them. My sex is hot and desperately on edge. I want to come, and come soon. Once his hands touch mine, he walks slowly around behind me. I'm right here for him to see, to touch. *Will he?* In my head I start to beg. *Please, Sebastian, don't make me wait any more. Put your hands on my bare skin.*

My breathing hitches as he finally touches my skin. A meaningful touch gently sweeps over my shoulders and down my arms. His hands are firm and confident and his touch feels wonderful. I surrender without restraint. His lips tickle my shoulder as his hand wraps my waist. The kisses grow firmer, wetter. His lips cover my neck and shoulders as his other hand captures my breast. I'm lost in the feeling of being utterly devoured.

My breaths come in heaving gasps. I will his hand to move lower and finish what he started at the breakfast bar. I need him to touch me where heat is pooling so fast and furious. I want to spread my legs and beg for him to fuck me. I want to melt, and at the same time demand more.

"Sebastian, please," I beg. Finally his finger slips down directly onto my clit. I'm hit by a blissful wave of gratification that teases up and down my body. I'm so very close. My pussy and clit pulse as my whole body shakes with desire. He continues for a few more strokes before he pushes two fingers deep into me. He drops the other hand from my breast to press on my clit.

"Come for me now, Isabel," he commands.

I release a gasp as my eyes squeeze closed and I bite down on my lip. The force of my climax threatens to rip my body apart. Spasms force my hips to flex into this hand, prolonging the sensation. My legs turn to jelly as I relish the pulses still pumping through my limbs.

I'm spent.

I feel light-headed as he presses still deeper into me. He holds my clit and pussy tight as I continue to pulsate around his fingers, waiting until the intensity subsides. He removes his finger from my clit and wraps his strong arm around my chest beneath my breasts. With two fingers still inside me, he hugs me deep and close to him.

As I come around from the orgasm that has shattered me into millions of tiny pieces, I become aware of his hard cock pressing into the small of my back. He finally slides his fingers gently out of me. Maybe it's the endorphins making me brave, but coming all over his hand makes me want to feel Seb in my hand.

I turn around in his arms and kiss him. I want him to feel what he did to me. As my lips work against his, I press my body flush against his. He trembles as my stomach rubs against his hard length. He pulls back with a low groan. "Christ, Isabel." I kiss my way down his chin, his throat and chest, nipping and licking as I go, until I'm kneeling before him. I want to kneel in front of him, to please him. *I want to be here, kneeling before you.* I slowly raise my eyes to his and hold his gaze. My fingers fumble as I move them to release the button on his jeans. He grasps my wrists in his and moves them away, taking over and removing his jeans himself. He reaches inside his boxers, frees his stiff shaft from its confines and holds it before me, tempting me. I want to taste him, to flick my tongue over the tip of his cock. My thoughts startle me, but being with Seb brings out a part of me that I wasn't aware of. I feel sexy and wanton, and I love it. His eyes, now hooded and dark, stay locked with mine as a smile creeps across my lips. I want him, and I want to show him how much.

"Sebastian, I want to. Please let me show you how much."

"Wait. Not until I say." His words encase my body with desire. Not being able to express my want for this man is a new form of torture. I suck my bottom lip and bite down to distract myself from fidgeting.

"Stop sucking your lip and suck my dick, sweetheart."

In this post-orgasmic haze, my whole body still floats in bliss. I start at the base and lightly lick with the tip of my tongue. I tease up his shaft and across his inflamed head until I can taste the salty pre-come. He emits a deep moan as I suck him to the back of my throat. I snake my tongue over the length of his cock and lave its bulging head and then repeat, sliding my wet lips down.

He tastes good and he's so hard I feel the pulse of his heart through the veins in his shaft. The thought that desire for me has made him this way thrills me. I take him deeper into my mouth and suck harder. I'm as hot for him now as when he was teasing me. His cock swells in my mouth, stretching my lips wider. My free hand wraps his thigh to steady myself. The hard muscles of his upper leg bunch and electric tension zings through my palm. I want to push him over. I bring my other hand up and hold the base of his cock. I wrap my fingers around him and squeeze. He's holding back, showing me his restraint, but I want him to let go. *Go on, Izzy. Make him come!*

"Isabel, I am so close."

I pull off him but continue to gently pump him with my hand. "I know. I want you to come. Let go."

I lean my head forward to take him in my mouth, but he moves me back gently. I take the hint, but I don't want to stop. I run my hand quickly up and back along his shaft—back and forth, back and forth—until he comes. I pump all of his come into my hand until only a drop is left on his head. I flick the tip before gently kissing his cock clean.

"Thank you," he says in a deep sigh.

I take a breath and stand up in front of him. A storm of feelings thunder inside my chest. Pride and triumph reign against the guilt that I am experiencing this with another man. I'm being unfaithful.

"Can I... Are you okay if I go and take a shower?" He doesn't answer, but simply nods, and I take that as my cue. I'm suddenly very self-conscious. I head to the bathroom and wash my hands.

I look into the mirror, into the reflection of me—well, the new me who apparently likes being spanked. I reach in and turn the shower on. The steam fogs up the mirror, shielding my reflection. Stepping under the spray, my mind lets loose.

Did he really spank me and then make me come? Did I then fall to my knees and take him in my mouth? Of course I did, and I'd do it again. Hell, I think I'd do a lot more. *Would he have fucked me? Why didn't he? Oh, I want him even now, want his cock buried deep inside me.*

I try to make sense of all the questions in my mind as I let the water from the shower wash over me. I finish my quick rinse-off, and I suddenly feel naughty at the actions that played out in the kitchen.

I hear a knock at the door. "Come in." He opens the door but doesn't come inside.

"How do you feel, Isabel?" Seb asks quietly.

"Wonderful." I walk back over to the bed and sit on the edge, wrapping the bath towel around me. Seb stands motionless at the door. He seems to be deep in thought, which I can understand. I want to be able to relax, but I'm not sure if that's right. We crossed a line this evening, and it's going to change the dynamic between us.

Finally, he speaks. "I'm very pleased to hear that. I have your clothes. It's getting close to midnight."

"Oh... um, okay. I guess that means I need to go." Unease turns to awkwardness, and a little shard of disappointment hits me as I sit up on the bed. *Great! Way to bring a girl back to reality.*

"I'll leave you to get ready, Izzy."

Back to Izzy. Is this how it works?

"Thanks," is all I can squeeze out. He leaves me alone, and I take the opportunity to shake myself out of this silly mood. *You asked him to show you more. He did. He held your hand and your body, each step, and gave you what you wanted. What did you expect?*

My telling-off brings me to my senses and I get dressed. Remembering how good it was, I allow myself to smile. It feels good to smile. That too, has been missing from my relationship for too long. As I reach for my tights, I wonder whether he'll allow me to wear them home. I roll up the first leg and pull my foot up. The jewellery still twinkles at me from around my ankle. My smile is instinctive as I reach for the clasp and return it to the box on the dresser. *Please let there be more.*

I finish getting dressed and walk out of the room, sure that I'm never going to be the same again. Seb is waiting for me in the lounge.

"It's too late tonight, but there is a lot that we should talk about during the week. Okay, Izzy?"

"Okay."

"I need to check how you're feeling. Are you sore at all?"

"A little, but in a very good way. Thank you."

Seb crosses his arms and considers me for a moment. "Tonight was a test." I look up, startled. Seb laughs, "Don't panic. You passed. I needed to be sure that what I thought I saw in you—your submissive nature—really was there. Did you like what we did? Tonight was as much a taster for you as well." I study my feet and try to swallow the lump in my throat.

"Yes. It was a... good... experience."

Laughter lurks in his voice. "I hope I guided you safely through your first experience. I hope I 'held your hand'."

I glance up and catch his amused expression. I can't help but grin and nod. He grins back at me from across the room and I walk over to him. He pulls me into a gentle embrace and kisses my head as I wrap my arms around his waist.

We're both still for a moment before he releases me and reaches for my hand. He holds it and pulls me towards the door. I can't measure what happened between us tonight in just the time I've spent here. This is a pivotal point for me. My first real understanding of what I've only been able to hope for.

"When you come back, don't forget the rules." He delivers his final command in front of the lift.

"No, I won't." I don't even have to think before I answer. I stare into those beautiful clear eyes. His face is relaxed and calm, but I know now what lies beneath the surface. My earlier awkwardness is forgotten. I immediately want him again. To be here again and put myself in his control. I've had a small taste, and now I have a thirst that I'm not sure I'll be able to quench.

Five

On the street, Seb pauses before handing me into the waiting taxi. "Remember, what I said earlier," he murmurs. "You come here of your own free will. It is your choice to submit. I will push you a little more, but I promise to hold your hand through it. I'll see you at 7:30 p.m. on Friday."

I nod and the car door thunks closed and stark reality hits hard. The realisation of what I've just done, what I've allowed Seb to do to me, engulfs me. *I'm a horrible person. Who breaks their marriage vows so easily?* I slump back against the seat and close my eyes, the weight of my tears building.

My body—the body that Sebastian controlled brilliantly—feels utterly sated. The sensation is unfamiliar. It's been a long time since such physical satisfaction has been mine. I revel in the stunning physical pleasure Sebastian pulled from me with such effortless mastery. Having Sebastian take such care, put himself in this position, for me, heightens the emotions fighting to escape.

I cry silently to myself all the way home. I flee from the taxi and up to the front door, fumbling with the keys. The pitch black and my watery eyes make it hard to see. I finally get the keys in the lock and open the door. The privacy releases the dam holding back the flood. I sob hard and loud as I stumble up to my bedroom and fall onto the bed.

Everything that I wanted, everything that I desired, Seb gave to me. The attention and focus to know my body. But he isn't my husband. He's a man I barely know, yet who makes me feel like he's known my body for years.

My emotions overwhelm me.

The 'more', the experience of submitting that Phil would never give me, has led me to break my marriage vows. Vows that once upon a time meant everything to me. *Am I being selfish? I am a horrible, selfish person who puts my own needs above everyone else.*

Another roll of sobs breaks through and I bury my head into the pillows as the wonderful feelings of physical contentment collide with the emotional consequences of my actions tonight. I'll never be satisfied with the status quo again. Seb has ruined me for Phil. I take a few deep breaths to steady myself and hear the front door close downstairs. *Phil's back. Sleep—sleep—sleep. I need to be asleep.*

I turn off the waterworks, suddenly scared of what Phil would say if he found me awake and crying at two in the morning. *Game face on, or fall asleep.*

I cuddle myself up into the familiar position and I breathe slowly, focussing on the in and out of my breaths. Sure enough, Phil goes straight to the bathroom for a few minutes before he climbs into bed. The pungent smell of cigarettes doesn't mask a sickly sweet perfume that clings to him. That's new. He doesn't say a word, doesn't kiss me hello or goodnight, or even question why I'm in bed fully clothed. He does what he always does when he comes home. Goes straight to sleep as if I'm not there. I'm invisible.

Really? I am tearing myself apart for *this* man? The final thoughts that calm my mind before my body finally lets me sleep are of Seb, how he guided me from fantasy into reality and held my hand every step of the way. I finally have someone to share in my deepest desires.

Six

My phone vibrates across the side table. I attempt to open my eyes, but the swelling and soreness from last night's tears have welded them shut. I try again and grab my phone, determined to silence it for good. It clearly wants to ruin my morning. I'm still in my clothes from last night. *Clothes that Seb had me strip out of after he spanked me and gave me the best orgasm of my life!* Remembering the events of last night makes my body ache for the sated feeling again, the feeling of Seb and the freedom he awarded me.

"You'll be late, Iz!" Phil shouts up at me.

Phil! Guilt and pain comes back with a jolt. I was so caught up in lust and want for Seb that I forgot about Phil. I roll out of bed, not really wanting to do anything today. My body is weary and I want some space to digest everything in the light of day. I check my phone and see a text from Seb.

> Beautiful, amazing. I'm so proud of you. Thank you. Here's to Friday. S

The words fuzz as my eyes well up again, and I dive for the shower.

"Coffee's on the side. I need to run, too. I'll be late again, so don't wait up," Phil tosses at me as I come down to the kitchen. I barely see him as he rushes out, but I'm almost grateful. I sit and stare at the cup of coffee, just sitting there. I let the last few weeks' events run through my mind: my hopes of sticking my marriage back together with sex; wanting more from it and from Phil; meeting Seb and the light and hope he brought into my life even before last night. I continue to sit. I've drunk my coffee, but I don't attempt to move. My phone buzzing draws me back to the here and now, and I glance at it. My boss.

> Where are you? Mark

I hadn't realised how long I've sat here. I quickly fire back my response.

> Sorry – not well. Will be in tomorrow. Izzy

The next text I send is one I should have sent long before now.

> HELP! Are you free? X

I watch my phone, waiting for Jess to answer my plea and praying that she's not busy.

> What's up, hun? You don't sound good. I'll pop over. I'm off today. X

My tension releases as I read her few words. I put the kettle back on, and my mind runs over everything that has happened. Again. I decide I'll leave some of the Seb details out for now. The mess with Phil is enough for one day. Jess has always been my best friend, and although we don't talk or see each other every day, we're always there for each other. Like today.

* * *

"Phil and I are fighting."

"Really? I'm sorry, Iz, but that's not necessarily a bad thing." Jess states.

"I know you don't like him, and I'm sorry that I've taken so long to wake up to him…"

"Finally." She interrupts, clearly happier about this conversation than I thought she'd be.

"Jess, just let me talk to you, alright."

"Okay, hun. Sorry."

"I don't think I can cope with Phil ignoring me any longer. He's taken me for granted, starved me of any sort of affection and never considered my needs and wishes." I sip my tea, hoping she won't see me as giving up. "I asked him to do something for me… in the bedroom. To tie my hands and actually make me feel, give me an orgasm for once. He ignored everything I asked for, as usual, and I think it broke me. It hurts to say these things, even to my best friend. Phil's rejection hurt. An orgasm wasn't worth going through another knock-back from Phil, so I got used to being disregarded, accepted it and buried my feelings."

"Izzy, why haven't you told me any of this before? You clearly haven't just woken up and decided this is how you feel. You should have come to me sooner."

She's right, of course. Although she sounds harsh, more than anything else, she's upset because I've kept her in the dark.

"I don't really know… I'm… ashamed my marriage isn't working. Hasn't been working for a very long time. After trying to fix things and going from bad to worse, what am I supposed to do?" I hold the mug in my hand as if the lukewarm tea can offer me the answer.

Hurt, sadness and sympathy fill Jess's expression. She reaches for my hand. "It's not my decision, Izzy. This is something you need to work out. But you need someone who is good for you and to you, and even if you are married, leaving your husband isn't the end of your life. Plenty of people get divorced." She picks up her tea and drains the remaining liquid.

I sag at her implication. "Jess, I don't know. I've stuck with him for so long. Being married and a good wife used to mean everything to me. Can I really quit?" The words agitate me, and my fidgeting isn't enough. I stand and walk around the kitchen, filling the kettle back up as I do. I want to tell her the other part of my confession.

"I'm saying that now, rather than later, might be an easier option. You've been with Phil so long, you probably didn't even know who you were when you married him. And even I've seen him change over the years." Her voice hardens and she looks away.

I gape at Jess. She always has this scary ability to look at things in plain light and tell me the honest truth. This is what I would say if the situation were reversed. She doesn't even know the worst part yet. If I tell her I've been unfaithful, will she judge me? *She won't. She's your rock.*

"There's more, Jess. I met someone. It wasn't on purpose. I'd had a shitty day and stopped at a bar for a drink. There was this very handsome guy who came and talked to me, and I completely ran away. He was so intimidating, you know, in that sexy but scary good way, and I couldn't get him out of my head. I gave a presentation the next day and he was one of the attendees. He left me his card and I emailed 'Hi'. We hung out, talked, drank together and just clicked. There was a constant undercurrent of attraction, initially just a physical attraction. We both knew it was there but we didn't act on it." Jess has all of her attention on me now. "He's smart and patient and pays me attention. That sounds like such a cliché thing to say, but after so long with no interest from Phil, you can't imagine how good that made me feel. It was easy to talk to him, to fall into an easy friendship. He understands me. All of me." For once, Jess seems stunned at my admission. She won't like what I'm telling her about me having an affair. She's been on the receiving end herself, but her dislike of Phil might just outweigh her dislike of cheating in this instance.

"Stop looking at me like that, Izzy. I'm not the one about to break into tears. I'm glad you told me. You shouldn't have been worrying about all of this. God, Izzy, I'm so mad at you. You shouldn't go through this alone..." she holds me in a pointed stare... "and keep a better eye on Phil."

"What's that supposed to mean?" I frown and fidget in my seat. Her mouth compresses in a tight line.

"I'm just saying that he should be paying more attention to his wife." She stops her words mid-speech and shakes her head. "Look, I have to go, but I don't want to wait for the divorce papers to come through before I hear from you again. I'm proud of you. I know how much your marriage has meant to you, but I can't be upset that you're finally realising what a jerk Phil is." She stands and puts her cup on the side.

I suspect I know what she started to say and I want to press her to finish, but Jess is discretion personified. I've never been able to pry information out of her she wasn't ready to give. "I know, Jess. About Phil. He's been having an affair. I'm not ready to face him with it just yet. Or the divorce question. I..." I can't finish the sentence because I'm not even sure what I want.

"Look." Jess's tone softens. She knows I'm a moment away from breaking into tears. "You've been through a lot, but think about your future. Do you want to be like this in another five years, ten years or when you have children? You've never really shared all the details of your relationship, but there is something clearly not right between you and Phil. Now that you've admitted it to yourself, and you seem to have met someone that has sparked an interest, perhaps it will help you make a decision you should have made years ago. " She smiles and walks over to hug me tight.

"Thank you," is all I say. I can't think of anything more.

After Jess leaves, the house is quiet again. I remember a time, soon after Phil and I were married, when I never would have imagined being unfaithful and was proud to be his wife. That version of Izzy is a far stretch from the girl who has just spent a night of fantasy with a man she isn't married to. I've changed somewhere along the way. I've grown up, discovered more about myself and perhaps lost part of me as well. Jess's comment about not really knowing myself keeps coming back to me, and I think I agree. *Is the growing gap between Phil and I justification for what I am doing? Of course not. But does being married to Phil mean I have to be unhappy for the rest of my life? Do I not deserve to have happiness?*

I'm at a loss and decide to submerge myself for a few hours in my now second-favourite pastime and log on to my BDSM profile. I play for a while and add some content before I feel restless. The imagery I'm seeing isn't just fantasy anymore. I understand the heat that flashes across your skin after it's spanked. Seeing it on-screen only heightens my want for more experiences with Seb.

Spilling my worries to Jess has helped, but she's given me more to think about. One thing, though—nothing she said made me think any differently about Seb.

I will still go to see him on Friday, and I'll enjoy every second of it. My mind flashes with images of his face, his eyes, and how it felt last night with his skin against mine. I'm utterly certain that I'll do it again.

For the rest of the day, I clean the house and play on a few social sites. I shake off my emotional funk and try to think positively. Jess is right. I try to make two mental boxes in my head: one for Phil and my marriage, and the other for Seb.

Separating them doesn't stop me thinking about Seb, and almost as soon as he pops into my head, my mind conjures vivid details. His kisses and his touch, the room, the anklet, and the sheer vulnerability I felt when he undressed me. Shit… What will I wear? I remember my previous thought about lingerie and decide to go shopping after work tomorrow. For the first time today, a small smile creeps across my face as I go back to cleaning the bathroom.

Seven

I walk into Oh La La and immediately feel intimidated. I haven't bought sexy lingerie in years. I've gotten by perfectly well with my simple but feminine bras and knickers. *What would Seb like? What would he like me in? What do I want to wear for him?* The first couple of items are easy. Black, lacy, balcony bras with matching knickers. The bras emphasise what little bust I have without going for the obviously padded extra, and they are very pretty. *Stockings and thigh highs.* Seb's words are still in my mind as I walk over to the hosiery section. The memory of his strong and commanding voice washes over my body and sends shivers to my pussy. I choose a modest black and nude pair of thigh highs before I opt for a decidedly sexier option—black lace tops with a tiny ribbon woven through.

I choose stockings as well, so I can feel Seb snap the clasps with his hands. Black again, more sheer this time, but of course lace is a must. I ponder what I need to accompany them. A simple garter belt? Or could I risk something a bit more… provocative? A corset or bustier with garters included? I'm beginning to enjoy all of the options. Better yet, I'm imagining all the ways Seb could remove them.

I grab a simple belt, but then an elegant black corset with a lace panel, wide ribbons laced at the front and ending with a bow at the bottom catches my eye. *Would Seb like to untie me as well as tie me up?* I've always loved the way corsets help to give that hourglass figure I've always coveted. I love how classy and elegant corsets seem, but with a naughty edge of being a hidden delight. Perfect for careful unwrapping. Slow and seductive. *Ummm, Seb unwrapping me slowly and sensually, kissing my skin as he loosens the ribbon at the front, dipping to suck my nipple in his mouth.*

The daydream seals the deal and I grab my size off the rack. When I look for the changing rooms, I'm distracted by a display of side-tie knickers. I finger through the plain black satin with thin ties to find my size and add them to my pile.

After stripping, sucking, tying, and swapping a few sizes around, I emerge from the changing room with arms full of lace and concede to pay for the lot. I don't even know whether I will get a chance to show Seb all of this, but I hope so. *He wanted me to come back, but how many times? How long is this going to last, to work?*

My thoughts put a decidedly sour note to my otherwise enjoyable evening spree. I head for home. *Shit, will Phil be home? Is he working?* He can't see any of this. Hell, I haven't worn anything for him in years and now I'm eagerly trying corsets and side-tie knickers for Seb. My stomach rolls as anguish grips me and my heart hammers in my chest. *What if Phil finds out? What will he think of me? Will he even care?*

That stray thought makes me think about when Phil and I last connected, on any level, about anything. I can't even pinpoint it. We are just two people living around each other. I want so much more out of a relationship. *Do I deserve more?*

The same argument that has gone through my mind the last couple of days flashes through it again. I'm married. It's the fundamental reason I shouldn't be doing this. This reality clashes against my need to surrender to a partner who will take charge of my desires and ensure my satisfaction. I yearn to yield to a man who will guide me into the world of submission and domination that figures so prominently in my sexual fantasies. And that man is not Phil. It's Seb—Sebastian. *And you're back to square one again, Izzy.*

Before I head back to my car, I stop in one of my favourite shoe shops. I've just spent a fortune on underwear, but shoes make me feel good. They are my indulgence that always makes me happier. There is a pair of black heels with a pretty gold ankle strap that I treat myself to. They would go really well with some of the lingerie.

I get back to my car and drive. Not even four-inch black heels can lift my mood. The lights of the city give way to quieter streets as I approach home. The lights are on when I get to the front of the house, so I plan my safest route—straight up the stairs to stash my naughty purchases under the bed. I push the door open and breathe a sigh of relief that the TV is on in the front room.

"Hi!" I call out as I nearly run up the stairs. I don't hear any response, and I dive for the bed, shoving the bags under and covering them quickly with an empty rucksack. I can't keep these here. *Could I leave them in the extra room with Seb?* He did say it was my room to use, and he wants me to come back. The black-and-white photos of women gracing his walls flash through my mind. It would be nice to have something of me there as a reminder. A sign, perhaps, that I'm in his life.

I go downstairs and make a cup of tea before I face Phil. My guilt is under control, for now. I put the teaspoon down on the side as my phone alerts me to a new message. As if on cue, Seb has texted to ask me about my day.

I thought you'd be finished for the day. I'm looking forward to tomorrow night. And remember, Isabel, no tights. S

I smile involuntarily and close my phone before Phil notices anything. I am very much looking forward to tomorrow, and now I have something sexy to wear—for Seb.

Eight

I check my watch as I walk across the lobby of Seb's apartment building to call the lift. 7:12 p.m. I still have enough time to get ready before he arrives. His apartment is a lovely space. It has elegant and masculine edges to the décor, with striking contrast in textures and colours. I want to explore, curious as to what lies behind his closed cupboards. *He trusts you with his apartment and you sneak around?*

That naughty feeling adds to the anticipation of what is coming later tonight. I make a mental note to arrive earlier next time so I can explore.

What does he keep in his bedside drawer? What if it scares me? What if I don't want to see? Can I invade his privacy like this? I could look at his books and music, though. There is surely no harm in that. First, I walk to the spare room, which I am trying to think of as mine, and drop my bag at the corner of the wardrobe. I sit on the bed and roll my tights down. I pause to imagine how good it would feel to have him rip them from me and tie me with them. Simply imagining the strength and power he'd have over me makes my insides turn and my stomach ache. Heat tingles in my veins. *How would he punish me if I did wear my tights?*

I ease into my nude thigh highs, sliding them to the top of my thighs, and pull my skirt back down. Automatically, I feel sexy, both from my choice in hosiery and my thoughts of Seb. I'm doing this at his command. I walk over to the dresser to retrieve the anklet out of its box. I take it without thinking and place it around my ankle. *What will he ask of me tonight? Will I obey and submit without hesitation? Of course I will. This is all that has been playing in my mind since Tuesday.*

My inexperience with BDSM makes me nervous, but I can trust Seb. There is still the question of sex. I told him last time that he can cross that line. As soon as I left last time, beyond all of the guilt and confusion assaulting me, I knew I wanted to push the experience we shared, and I am going to let Seb take me as far as he wants. I tie my hair in a plait to the side. He wants my hair like this, and I liked how it sent quivers of vulnerability and desire dancing down my back when he pulled on it. With that thought, I take out my sky-high heels from my bag and slip them on. They're a luxury of mine. Simple and elegant, you can't beat black heels. *I hope Seb likes them.*

Right... Quick check in the mirror before I walk out to wait in the kitchen for him to arrive.

A bottle of Sauvignon Blanc is chilling in the fridge and two glasses are waiting on the side, as promised. I open the wine and pour two glasses, then sit on one of the bar stools in preparation. The cool, crisp liquid calms the nervous fluttering in my stomach. *What is he going to do to me tonight? Challenge me to surrender further? Will he punish me if I disobey?*

Before that thought has time to linger, the door opens. I turn. Seb strides confidently across the living area, bags of food in his hands and a brown leather messenger bag over his shoulder.

Jeez, he looks good and I'm wet for him already. That thought sends my entire body into a hot flush. My cheeks pink at how easily this man turns me on.

"Good evening, Isabel." The formality in his voice portrays him as the perfect gentlemen. I know better.

"Good evening, Sebastian. Your wine." I hand him the glass and kiss him on those delightfully soft lips—a quick welcome only.

"Thank you. We will start with dinner this evening. There are things I would like to discuss with you." He looks me up and down, and it sends a pulse of heat between my legs. *Does he like my appearance?* I can't maintain eye contact and lower my eyes. I catch the slight twitch of his lips—a smile. "We'll start with a light selection of breads with dipping oil, followed by stir fry. Nothing too heavy. I don't wish you to feel too full later. Dessert will be a surprise. And you'll be blindfolded."

Blindfolded? I pause slightly, and my heart quickens.

"Now, if you would be so kind as to set the table in the dining area, I'll prepare the starter."

I watch him move into the kitchen and take that as my cue to fulfil my task. I set the table for two so we'll be opposite each other. I sit in one of the scroll-back dining chairs to watch Seb prepare the food. The last drops from my wine glass pass my lips as Seb walks to the table with the starters. My mouth waters at the smell of warm bread. I have the choice of a number of oils and balsamic vinegar, all neatly presented with basil and other embellishments.

"So, Izzy, have you had a good day?"

I'm Izzy now. Okay then, a little conversation to calm things down. I am beginning to understand that when Seb calls me Izzy, I am the 'friend at the bar'. When he addresses me more formally, as Isabel, I am the woman he dominates in the bedroom. "Yeah, it's not been bad. We've got a few new clients recently, which is good news, and people are happy about it. More work, but the office seems good. How about you?"

"Oh, I'm busy enough. At least I had the thought of you this evening to keep me focused. Talking of which, I haven't got any more dates in the diary beyond tonight. Do you wish to continue our arrangement?" His direct question startles me. Do I want to continue? *Hell yes!*

"Yes, yes, please... Haven't we just begun?"

"Yes, although I wanted to check in with you. It's especially important for us to have clear and honest communication. You need to be able to tell me what you are thinking, and trust that I'll deal with those feelings appropriately. So... how did you feel about what we did the other night?" He looks at me with his blue eyes and I almost fall under his spell as the words wrap me in a protective blanket. "Well?"

Oh crap, that's my cue!

"The other night... I felt desired, for the first time in years." I pick a spot on the table and muster the rest of the feelings that have been plaguing me. "Your command and control gave me the trust I needed... to be vulnerable and give in to my desire to submit. You, you took my trust and rewarded me." I raise my head and smile at Seb. "You guided me through my fantasy." I busy myself with the bread and tear a small morsel to dip into the oil. "I know we haven't gone very far. But I already doubt that I will be able to go back to the way things were before..." My voice trails off.

I don't say anything more, but continue to nibble at the delicious bread and oil. Seb clears the plates and returns to refill our now empty glasses.

"Isabel, I want to discuss you and your physical needs."

Back to Isabel. Okay.

"Alright. What... what do you mean by physical needs?"

"Before this week, when we first met here, how many times had you had an orgasm this year?"

Shit. I look down and cross my legs under the table. "I don't keep count." I hug myself as if to hold the pieces of my shattered composure together. My eyes find a photo on the wall and I concentrate on the image.

"A rough estimate, Isabel."

I shift in my chair and play with the end of my plait, stroking it between my fingers soothingly. His eyes watch me intently as he waits. I drop my gaze into my lap. The silence lengthens and I clear my throat. "Probably around a dozen."

"Probably more or probably less?"

"Probably less," I whisper.

"Isabel, it's October. That is, on average, one orgasm a month."

I straighten in my chair, place my hands in my lap and face him. I raise my chin with a jerk. "I know, Sebastian. I don't need you to remind me."

"I think you do need me to remind you. That is not enough for a woman with your needs. Do you ever take matters into your own hands?" His voice is harsh and stern, as if he's trying to open me up while telling me off. As hard as it is, though, I want to answer him. *Did he really ask if I play with myself to get off?*

"The dozen includes those times."

"Tell me about the times when you have come."

Details! I inwardly squirm as the heat in my cheeks burns and I think about it. *Isn't the shame of admitting that measly number enough?*

"Well, at the beginning of our relationship, Phil always made sure I came, but that faded away. He only makes sure he comes now. I've learned to live with it."

"The details of when you come, Isabel." His tone is sharp, and I realise I'm not following his commands and certainly not without hesitation. I take a deep breath and find the words.

"Most of the times I'm on top. I put on a show and play with my breasts, trying to encourage him before rubbing my clit while riding him. When he doesn't want me on top, I normally wait until he's asleep and then go to the bathroom to finish myself off." My eyes focus on anything other than Seb as I confess.

"Stand up, remove your knickers and sit back on the chair."

Wait... Hold on... What? Here? Now? I try not to let my hesitation show, but before I can rein it back, my mouth opens and words spill out.

"Sebastian, the blinds are open."

"No one can possibly see from the ground, and the window cleaner doesn't work at eight at night. Do it, now."

I stand. I wobble on my heels. The wine has gone to my head and the additional height isn't helping. My hands lift the hem of my skirt and slide the material up my legs so I can hook my thumbs into the waistband of my now slightly wet lacy knickers. Peeling them over my hips, I wiggle my legs and the wisp of material falls to the floor. I attempt to retrieve them in a moderately sexy way. Seb holds his hand out across the table and I place my damp panties in his palm. Obeying Seb's demand sends a bolt of lust straight to my core.

"Good girl. Now open your legs and place each one on the outside of the front of the chair legs. Slide your feet backwards and wrap each foot around the inside of the chair leg, then slide your skirt up so I can see you."

I do as I'm instructed, and in this position, my knees are forced open, wider than I would really like, and my skirt has ridden up to my waist. He's looking right at me... down there... and I sit with my legs splayed for him, doing what he asks of me.

"You have such a cute pussy. You are going to make yourself come in front of me. Now. I want you to follow my exact instructions. If he won't look after your needs, I'll teach you how to do it yourself."

Cute? I can't keep up with him. His unpredictable demands are keeping me off balance and tense. Before I can process anything more, Seb begins his instructions.

"Stroke your upper thighs slowly with the palm of your hand and the flat of your fingers, but don't touch your labia." I do as he commands. "Good girl. Slowly now, keep stroking those thighs."

Am I really doing this? Okay, so I'm enjoying this... a little bit, anyway. God, what if it were his hands?

"Now take the middle finger of your right hand and suck it into your mouth. Make it nice and wet and then slide it gently between the lips of your labia. Now, very slowly, rub your clit. Slow down. There's no rush. This can take the next four hours if it has to."

Four hours? No way. There is no way that I'm going to last much more than four minutes, let alone hours. I've not been this wet, this turned on in—

"Now stop rubbing and place your finger right on top of your clit. Good, now press down on it hard... and release. And again. Press hard then release. Good."

Oh, I didn't know that felt this good... Umm. I'm trying to do what I'm told, but I want to do more, move faster. My nerves are awakening.

"Now move your finger in tiny little circles around that tight bud. Slowly... Good. You can go back to rubbing again, but I want you to do it at half the speed you were."

I can't quite believe that I'm enjoying this, sitting here on a chair in the middle of his dining room, fully clothed except for my knickers. My legs are wantonly spread apart and he's perfectly relaxed opposite me as I touch myself, per his instruction. It's crazy.

"Isabel, are you wet?" he asks, as if it's the most natural thing to say. My body relaxes into the vulnerability of the situation and of being exposed to him in a new, more intimate way. I push any and all my insecurities aside and answer him.

"Yes, Sebastian. I'm... I'm soaking wet. Please..."

"Take your index finger and slide it down the side of your inner lips. Do not touch your clit. Now do the same on the other side with your ring finger. Now both fingers together, one each side. Good girl. Close your eyes and let your head fall back. Now, with those two fingers, start rubbing right in line with your clit and then stretch your lips wide apart." His words make me needy, yet I flush with embarrassment. "Wider than that, Isabel. Stretch them so your clit is tight." He purrs his instructions, a deep and soothing voice that automatically has me trusting yet hot as hell.

Don't think, Izzy. Just do it. Don't worry about him. Follow the sound of his voice and hope he keeps talking to you. God, my clit is burning and I can feel my pussy opening, wanting this.

"Now, with your free middle finger, gently tap your clit."

"Tap?"

"Yes, tap it, Isabel. Now do it harder. Slap it. Tell your clit off for being impatient."

A bolt of pleasure runs straight from my clit through my body as my finger makes contact. The sensation isn't pure pleasure, though. It is tinged with pain, just on the fringe, driving my desire, and I begin to pant. My orgasm builds and every fibre of my being begs to come.

"Now take your fingers, place them on the top of your lips and close them tight together. Rub your whole hand over the top of your mons. No sneaking a finger between your wet folds. Good girl. Now rub yourself again with one finger, but this time I want to see really long strokes. Go from the very top of your slit to the opening of your pretty little cunt. Very slowly slide your finger up inside you... That's too far. Slide back a little so you are just an inch inside. Now explore, feel yourself, what you like, what spots you like to press."

The frenzy of lust streaking through my body makes focussing on Seb's words difficult. I'm desperate to come. But I want to obey him. I've never touched myself like this before, never taken the time to, and I am struggling with how good I'm feeling. My whole body is alive with nerve endings ready to ignite. Small tremors beg to grow from within me, but I still want more.

"Sebastian," I breathe out. "I can't take much more of this."

"Oh, but you can take much more, Isabel. On another night, I will make this last ten times longer. Now I want you to use both hands. Put your finger back inside your pussy and use the middle finger from your other hand to stroke your clit, but at half the speed that your mind is telling you. Now tell me, does that make you feel naughty?"

"Yes. God, yes. Very."

"Now, open your eyes and look directly at me as you make yourself come with both hands."

I mentally battle to open my eyes and then to hold his gaze. My entire body heats as I look into the cool depths of his eyes. My clit throbs, my pussy contracts around my finger and I can feel that I'm going to come, right in front of him. I focus on my fingers and the feel of my wet pussy. I never imagined that I could touch myself in front of someone, let alone Seb. His words coax me deeper into my fantasy. My legs are wide, reflecting my vulnerability, but I also feel alive, every part of my body strung as taut as a piano wire, and it's Seb who is playing me.

I want to please him. I want to earn the smile on his face, his approval at my obedience. I hold my stare and move my fingers to tip me over. Pleasure explodes from my core, rushing through my body in a heated wave. My voice sounds a desperate cry, deep and throaty. "Argh. Mmm." I can't hide how good it feels as I let go. I come hard and hot with Seb watching me, instructing me, and I can't stop the appreciative noises that escape from my lips.

"Good girl. Press your finger in tight to your clit and leave the other inside to feel what you've done. Slide your finger out, and come over here and place it in my mouth. I want to taste you."

I'm still recovering from my orgasm so I'm a little slow in recognising all the words he's said. Place it in my mouth. I want to taste you. How can you turn me on by saying things like that after what you've just done to my body? So gorgeously crude.

I try and re-orientate myself as I stand and take the few steps around the table to Seb. I look directly at him as I raise my hot and sticky finger to his lips. I wait for him to open them and tentatively push my finger inside his mouth. Immediately he envelops my finger and caresses it with his tongue. Desire pulses to my already wet sex. His own desire is unmasked as I look into his eyes. The blue is clouded with promises of yet more to come.

"Hmm. Thank you, Isabel. Well done. Now, how do you feel?"

I slump back into the chair as I think about his question. *How do I feel?* As if he's mentally fucked me, and I'm desperate to feel him on my skin. I'm astonished I could make myself come for someone. But it's not just someone. This is Seb.

"It was a little awkward... I was embarrassed. But the look in your eyes and the tone of your voice..." A small smile creeps over Seb's lips.

"Go on."

I take a deep breath. "I've never felt so turned on. Your desire for me, your instruction... I wanted to please you and obey you." My eyes sink to my lap and I pull at my hem, covering myself back up. I run my palms over my thighs to alleviate my need to fidget. "Will we, um... could I do this more often?"

"You will. I'm going to give you homework, Isabel. You must make yourself come every day this week, finishing Friday. Do you think you can do that?"

Oh, shit. Seriously? There is no way I'm going to be able to do that.

"I'll try."

"Isabel, you will do more than try. Explore your body, feel yourself, what gets you hot and wet, what makes you want to touch more. You will bring yourself to orgasm regularly, but I want you to experiment. No more rubbing yourself off to an unsatisfactory climax. Touch yourself, play with your clit, your pussy, your perfect breasts. Hold yourself on the edge of climax before giving into your body that's screaming to come. You will make yourself come each day." He doesn't try to hide his sexy smile as he delivers his instruction. "You will then text me to advise me of your daily achievement, and bonus marks if you text me while your fingers are still wet with your desire." A stern look replaces his smile and straightens my spine. "There will be consequences if you fail. I will know if you lie to me."

I think I'm going to come again...

"Okay," I manage to say, my voice thick with need.

"Good girl. Now for the main course." Sebastian stands and crosses to the kitchen, clearly satisfied that a small part of him is going to be guiding me outside of the apartment, when we aren't together. I sit alone at the table, still buzzing with warmth from my orgasm. *Who have I become?* Me, little, quiet Izzy, performing with brazen abandon and enjoying it? This could be something I could easily get used to, and like a drug, become addicted.

I watch Seb prepare our dinner with exacting precision and mastery—as in command in his kitchen as he is everywhere else. I smile inwardly at this stolen glimpse of him, at ease in his home.

Where he has invited you and instructed you to make yourself come at the dining table.

My cheeks heat and I cast my eyes towards the table as Seb brings the plates of stir-fry across.

We enjoy easy conversation over dinner. I have relaxed and have a fixed grin on my face, but he has a knowing look in his eyes. As we finish off the last morsels, he dabs at the corner of his mouth with the starched white napkin and sets it down slowly on the table. His gaze holds mine and something dark flickers in his blue eyes.

"Now for dessert."

Nine

Seb clears the plates away and returns holding a black satin blindfold.

The air crackles and my head swims with a light-headed sensation as I watch him move towards me. With no hesitation, he walks behind me, places the blindfold securely but delicately over my eyes and ties a knot at the back of my head. The satin ties brush against my exposed neck as he releases them. With this single action, depriving me of sight, Seb establishes his control over me.

"Can you see anything?"

"Nothing." My heartbeat already thrums in my chest and I try to steady my breathing.

"Good." The light pad of his feet on the wood tells me he's moved away, and my anxiety peaks. I can't see Seb and can't look to him for guidance. Fear creeps into my mind. The cool air over my heated pussy reminds me of my vulnerability. I twist my feet, fidgeting, and feel the delicate symbol of my surrender still fastened around my ankle. I focus on that—the meaning behind the jewellery. I want this feeling of being open to his desires, his will, and at his command. The blindfold has offered me a thin shield of security and I'm grateful.

His warm breath on my neck signals his return.

"Open your mouth," he commands gently. I slowly part my lips, a little hesitant as to what to expect. As I do, my tongue tastes the cool metal of a spoon before an intense rush of chocolate floods my mouth. Rich, deep, and velvety smooth, the chocolate melts in my mouth as I clasp my lips and pull it from the spoon. The tip of something soft on my lips encourages me to open. The sensations of taste and touch are heightened by my lack of sight. I bite down into a ripe strawberry and juice bursts in my mouth and escapes past my lips. Before it can drip, material tickles my lips as Seb dabs with a cotton napkin.

He continues to feed me the chocolate torte and strawberries in turn, and I enjoy every bite.

Without saying a word, he takes both my hands. "Stand." His deep whisper matches the velvety chocolate taste that still lingers in my mouth. He leads me slowly across the room. From the brief knowledge I have of the flat, I must be standing somewhere in his bedroom. He releases my hands. A single finger glides down the side of my cheek.

"I'm going to strip you naked." It's a statement—no question or hesitation in his voice. He undresses me. Each of his movements is planned to ignite my senses even further—a wisp of contact followed by a well-placed hand. Each time his hands come into contact with my body, I heat. The cover of the blindfold helps me feel less self-conscious about his actions, and I succumb to the building tension in the pit of my stomach. As my skirt hits the floor, I step out of it. Seb returns to the buttons on my blouse, revealing the black lace that covers my breasts. He bends to whisper in my ear.

"New underwear, Isabel?"

Oh, shit. What do I say? That I wanted to buy new underwear to please you, to feel sexy in?

"Yes." I hope he can't see how my cheeks are warming.

"I like," he replies, and I think I almost feel a smile against my neck.

He continues to run his fingers over my skin, taking his time with me. I'm burning with anticipation. His hands play around my hips, toying with me. He undoes my bra and runs his hands over my shoulders to free my breasts.

"Although you look unbelievably sexy standing there in thigh highs and heels, that's not what I want tonight."

I draw a breath and feel my pussy pulse at those words. *What does he want?*

I don't know how long he's taken to undress me. Minutes—if that—but it's as if he's lavished attention on me all night. I'm desperate to feel what it's like to be under this man, feel his strength and maybe a glimpse of lost restraint as our bodies join.

"Step out of your shoes, Isabel."

I do and immediately feel his fingers slip around the tops of my thigh highs. He's literally stripping me in front of him, and I'm helpless. I feel… good. Free. The choices have been taken from me and I can just enjoy.

"You're wearing your anklet again. Are you sure? Have you thought about how far you want to cross your vows?" His fingers close round my ankle and I feel him remove the jewellery to allow my thigh high past.

"I want… I want to submit. To you. Completely." I'm panting, imagining Seb's cock as it pounds into my pussy. He secures the anklet back in place and continues to rub around my calves and slide up to the back of my thighs. With every inch his hands travel, I lose more of myself to his touch.

I can sense him standing next to me, his mere presence turning my body into a pliant plaything.

"You'll have sex with me, after you beg me for it." His words are a definitive statement. He turns me around, now without a scrap of material on, and gently lowers me back onto the bed.

"Are you feeling brave?"

Am I feeling brave? I seem to be stuck repeating his words over in my mind as if I can't grasp them. I'm feeling desperately needy. I want Sebastian. I'm going to do whatever he asks.

"Please… Yes… Yes, anything."

He pushes me back so I'm lying down and he pulls each wrist above my head. He wraps soft, silken material around each wrist before tugging on them. He secures the material to the headboard. My arms are now tensioned above me. I give another piece of myself over to Seb as he secures me, taking my trust and returning it with his control. Before I can fight it, he's taken each ankle and pulled them wide to the corners, spreading me out. Muffled movement is my only indication he's still with me, getting louder before the bed dips to the side of me. My heart is in my mouth and I'm ready to burst. His soft lips plant kisses down my neck, carefully between my small, pert breasts, avoiding my sensitive tips, and on down to my navel.

My body screams at me to move. I want to struggle, but I can't. This should be terrifying and scary. Intimidating. Instead, my heart beats harder. Faster.

After worshipping my body with kisses, he pauses, and it sounds as if he is taking a drink. Then I feel his presence over my left breast. His lips brush against my nipple and entice an instant reaction. He sucks it deep into his mouth. It's cold and I gasp as an ice cube presses against the tip of my nipple. I don't know whether it's the cold ice or the attention that makes my nipple go rock hard. He then repeats the process on the right and causes the same instant response. All I can hear is my deep and heavy breathing as I try to cope with what he's doing to my body. I can't speak. I'm not sure what I'd say if I could. I'm a mass of feeling.

Warm fingers tweak the very tips of my nipples and he pinches them softly. I moan and my body arches off the bed. Sensations awaken through my skin as I feel the spike straight to my clit. My pussy clenches and weeps in response. I press my breasts up into his hands, desperate for more contact, for him to do that again, to keep doing it.

Taking my cue, he pinches my nipples again and my body responds, arching up at his touch, desperate for him to keep going. And he does. He gently stretches them up and my moan turns into a small scream of pleasure. *What is he doing to me?* This is intense. I inwardly beg him to run his finger down to touch my pussy and my clit and feel what he's done to me—to feel how wet he's made me.

Seb caresses my legs, running his splayed hands over each and every contour. I urge him to go higher, flexing my hips, hoping with every sweep that he'll provide relief from this slow torture. I'm panting and willing his fingers to find their way to my aching core.

Finally, he runs a single finger down my slit and pushes straight inside me. The ease of his journey gives away how wet I am. It brings a new high to my pleasure, mixed with immediate relief. The muscles I didn't even realise I was holding tight relax. But before I can enjoy it, the feeling is gone. Seb removes his finger, and I strain to hear what he's doing.

I hear the sound of clothes hitting the floor and then his lips are on my ankles, moving quickly up my legs, heading straight for the inside of my thighs. *No, no, Seb. Wait... Please.* A sliver of fear melts into my blood. I can't stop him. I'm tied up and at his mercy and I have no power. The feeling swallows me. With my lack of sight, my senses are heightened and everything feels stronger, more potent. It's an addictive feeling.

Before I can engage my voice to tell him not to go down on me, his tongue is on my clit and I let loose a loud gasp. Seb nuzzles his head between my spread legs and gently runs his tongue up until he's flicking my clit, answering my unspoken words of need. *God, yes!*

I try to keep my body still, but I'm no longer in control. Its reactions are all Seb's. He can command me and use my body as he sees fit. He keeps the tip of his tongue lightly pressed to the bundle of nerves and I'm balancing on the edge of a body-shattering orgasm. My muscles are winding up, contracting within me. He keeps the pressure constant, teasing my body even now, and he pushes his hands underneath my bum to lift my hips to him further. His tongue then works faster and presses harder into me, running up and down and dipping inside me. He builds me to a crescendo and as he flicks the tip of his tongue onto my clit, he drives his thumb inside me just as I let go and tip over the edge.

"Ohhh… Yeeesss!" I scream out as the pulses rush through me. I can't contain the need to give voice to my release, my ecstasy.

Once I come down from my orgasm, Seb lowers me back onto the bed.

His teeth sink into the pulse point in my thigh and I groan, caught in a frenzy of lust. Hands and lips cover my neck, breasts and chest, but it's not what I want. "Yes, Seb. Please, please fuck me. I need you." I don't care how I sound. I feel empty and need him inside me—to feel him lose control with me.

"You've pleased me, Isabel. You haven't held back."

"Please… Please. I need you!" His heat retreats but he returns quickly, ripping a condom open. He positions the tip of his cock and gently presses inside, filling me up.

"Christ, Isabel!" His voice is deep and raspy, telling me he's as affected as I am. *Yes! How can you feel this good?* He moves, slowly at first, pulling out, making my stretched core flutter with pleasure. I smile as his pace quickens and I relax into the wanton and sexy creature he's created, free of decision and eager to enjoy.

And then he really moves, pulling out and slamming back into me, making my body quake at the intensity of his actions. How desperate I am for him to fuck me and do it hard. *More… Please.*

He pounds into me for several more thrusts before my body's climbing again. He's hitting me hard and in just the right spot. I've never been taken before—not in this primal way. His body tenses with mine. I want to tense my legs but I can't and it only adds to the pleasure. As he thrusts harder and harder, the friction builds and my body heats. Fire burns in my veins as I'm forced into another shattering orgasm. My pussy clenches around his cock, pulsing over him, and I feel him go rigid as he comes deep inside me.

He relaxes his body, his head coming to rest on mine, and we're quiet for a moment, surrounded by the sound of our breathing as we both struggle to regain our senses. My insides have turned to liquid and I may be physically unable to move.

The quiet stretches out and I'm overcome. My raw emotions bubble under the surface, a reaction to the intensity of the time we've shared this evening. I feel totally vulnerable to this man. Content and satisfied. But above all, I feel connected. The dream I'd given up on. I have to try to not break down. I need to break the spell—the magical spell that exists between us now, binding me to him. He's not mine.

"Thank you, Sebastian," I murmur breathlessly. Seb gently pulls himself out of me and I slump deep into the bed beneath me, completely spent from the experience that is Sebastian. I can't hear what he's doing, but I don't really care. I cling to the afterglow of truly satisfying sex, careful to keep my emotions in check.

He unties my wrists and ankles and places a brief kiss on my lips but leaves the blindfold on. I can easily untie it when I'm ready.

"Take your time. I'll be in the lounge with a drink for you when you're ready." He doesn't say anything else. He just leaves.

I do take my time. My body is limp and sated. I slowly rise and pull the blindfold from my eyes. Light swamps me, and I take a moment for my sight to adjust to the room. I'm sitting in the middle of the bed amidst crumpled sheets, feeling thoroughly fucked. My skin is warm and my soul feels light. I head to the bathroom to wash up before dressing in my clothes. When I'm ready, I walk out to find him in a large chair with a glass of wine in his hand. There is a tall glass of sparkling clear liquid on the table in front of him. As I walk over to him, he motions for me to drink. I bend and kneel on the floor at his side. My drink, happily not wine, is cool and quenching, and I drink down half straightaway. Seb's hand runs through my hair and it sets me at ease. We sit in silence until I can no longer ignore that I need to leave.

"What time is it?" I whisper, not really wanting to break the perfect contentment that surrounds us.

"A little after midnight." My heart pounds. I need to leave now. I need to be home before Phil gets in. *But I don't want to leave.*

"How are you feeling, Izzy?" His gentle tone is soothing.

"I'm good. I just… don't want to leave." I sigh. "But I suppose I must. It's after midnight."

"Come on then, Cinderella." He stands and gently helps me to my feet.

I realise all of my things are still in my room and that I'll need to take off my anklet, so I head to the bedroom. "I won't be a minute." Gathering my bags quickly, I replace the anklet in its black box and return. As I walk towards the door, I glance up to see the black-and-white photographs of beautiful women, and a wave of unease washes over me. *Do I measure up? In Seb's eyes, do I measure up to what he likes?*

I try to knock that thought straight out of my mind. I was feeling perfectly calm and happy before it invaded. My mood is calmer than the previous visit with Seb, and I want it to continue.

"Don't forget the homework, Isabel." Seb's comment shakes me from my thoughts, and I suddenly remember the beginning of our evening.

"No, I won't."

"Are you free next Friday?"

Friday? That's a whole week. Can't I see you before that?

"Um, yes. Yes, Friday is fine." I can't keep the edge of disappointment from my voice, and he clearly reads it.

"I've a busy week and I want to be able to give you my undivided attention when I see you, Isabel."

"Okay. Friday is fine."

"Besides, I want you to keep me posted with your progress. Every day, remember, and that includes Friday." He smiles warmly down at me, and I can't help but answer with my own.

"Thank you for tonight. It was… definitely more." I feel shy as I say the words, but he leans to kiss me, so softly and gently that I know he feels the connection we shared tonight.

"You are more than welcome. You pleased me immensely tonight. This week I want you to think about what limits and conditions you wish to place on what we do during your evenings with me. By having intercourse with you I broke a self-imposed restriction. It won't happen again until you ask me to."

"I more or less begged you. I wouldn't change anything we did."

A wry smile tugs at his mouth. "Yes, you did, and I'm glad you have no regrets, but I should not have lost my self-control. I consider myself a good Dom. A good Dom is a controlled Dom. I wasn't tonight."

The soft lilt in his voice envelops me in yet more satisfaction. He is as reluctant to let me go as I am to leave. I open the door slowly before I turn to smile. We head to the lobby in silence, the signal to the end of the evening. The taxi is waiting and it feels as if I'm in a dream state, weak limbed and light-headed. My body's on autopilot as I get in, sit back and relax. My mind returns to Seb's bed.

Sebastian

Much like the first evening when I watched her leave, I'm left feeling empty. Tonight surpassed all my expectations and destroyed my carefully made plans. I underestimated my attraction to her. I sit down to finish my wine, but my mind lingers on the evening, recalling all of her reactions, all of her beauty.

Fuck, those heels... and the anklet. She tested my control on many different levels and I bet she didn't even realise. Her natural submission fuelled my dominance. Watching her as she followed my instructions on how to get herself off—her finger running over her bare pussy lips—I thought I was going to come in my trousers like a teenager.

She might want to experience her own version of sexual submission and hand her body over to my command, but where are her boundaries? How much can I ask of her before she backs off in fear or disgust? I suppose the only way to find out is to continue on this path and explore her limits with her. She has a quick, intelligent and inquisitive mind. She wants to taste that freedom where obedience, desire, and submission mix. I'd like to take her to that place—if I don't send her fleeing in fear first.

She took it all so naturally. Her body's reactions were fucking beautiful, arching up into my mouth and hands as I played with her sweet pink nipples. I can still smell her musky scent on my fingers and taste her in my mouth. Fuck, she was so wet I could barely stop myself from eating her and seeing how quickly she could come.

I stop my mental tape recording, as I'm getting hard and I've got to wait all week before I can see her again.

I never meant to fuck her. That was a line I drew for myself, but I couldn't say no when she begged so delightfully. It was her choice.

Keeping this arrangement balanced was always going to be tricky. God, Izzy is keeping me on my toes. Finding new ways to test her boundaries stirs feelings in me that have been dormant a long time. My original plan to show her only a power exchange lasted as long as it took for her to tell me she wanted a more sexual experience. It was a relief. I wanted her as much as she wanted me. Worse, my feelings are engaged. I take the glasses to the kitchen, but I can't escape her presence.

I'm confident that I can show her more of my true nature, be harder with her. I won't sugar-coat it like I have done with others. In the future, I want to see her like she was earlier—a beautifully sexy woman spread out and willingly restrained. That's what I've been looking for. A woman who isn't afraid to submit to me. Who trusts my actions as a Dom, who craves the control I want to possess over her.

Maybe she'll turn out to be a tourist like all the others—simply playing along, pretending, then scurrying back after the novelty of a bit of kinky sex wears off. When they realised that what I needed from them was their total submission, not just role-play, they ran. I'm fed up with tempering my nature in the hopes that I'll find the right woman. Sure, Natasha could set me up with a submissive to play with, but I'm well beyond wanting a temporary relationship that only lasts as long as a scene.

Izzy is the temptation of everything I want. There is no way I will be able to sleep in my bed tonight, not with her smell and the results of two orgasms all over the covers. I make myself a coffee and walk down to my study. I'll sleep in the other guest room. I have to stop thinking about her, but all I can see is her kneeling before me, waiting for me, submitting to me. God, I want her submission and hope that it runs as deeply as I need in a woman. I crave the power exchange, and I've already built a good trust with her. With Izzy, it could be fucking amazing.

Jesus! I get up from my desk and grab a proper drink from the kitchen, knocking back the whisky and letting the burn settle me. I've offered to show Isabel what true submission feels like. How deep does her submissive nature truly run? Could she be my perfect complement? Is my search over?

There remains a huge hurdle. She's a married woman. What is she going to do about her marriage? Will her husband let her go? I must remember she's not mine, even if all my instincts are crying out to pursue her and make her mine.

The desire to discover if Izzy is the elusive 'one' teases my heart with tantalizing possibilities. The question that plagues me is can I keep from becoming too emotionally invested? I must. I'm the one with the control. I shudder, envisioning the damage she could do if I lose that control—if she becomes too important to me.

Ten

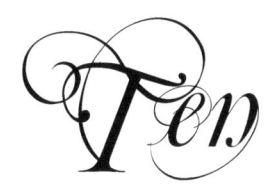

Saturday

I can barely peel my eyelids open when my alarm rings. It's Saturday, so I simply hit it and roll back over in bed, determined to stay in my satisfied doze, rested and content to do nothing else. Phil is at work—I presume. He has the morning shift. All the wonderful visions from last night dance through my brain, reminding me of how good Seb made me feel.

"You need to understand your body and its needs. You must make yourself come every day this week." Even remembering his words makes me squirm in my bed, tensing all my muscles and then stretching, feeling my body relax. *Can I really play with myself and make myself come for Seb?*

Even as I doubt I can do it, my hand slowly crawls down my stomach and passes under the waistband of my pyjama shorts. The loose cotton provides easy access for my now wandering hand, and my fingers glide on either side of my labia. My hesitant fingers only need a moment to build confidence before they slide between my lips to find my clit. I gently tease myself in tiny circles before I run my finger down and push inside a little.

My eyes close and I imagine Seb watches me—watches me as I push my finger in deeper. "Mmm." My pulse quickens as my appreciation grows. It's not as though I've never done this before, but this is the first time I picture another man's face in the process.

Thoughts of Seb send a wave of heat directly to my pussy, and I move my finger to focus on my clit. *My naughty little clit.* I'm going to come quickly, so I squeeze my eyes shut and propel myself over the edge. "Mmm" I release and my finger stills, my pussy still pulsing over my hand. My body slowly comes back down as I lie still for a few minutes, peacefully listening for my heart to quieten. It didn't compare to what Seb did to me. It was neither as intense nor as satisfying.

I ponder what to do with my day now that I'm actually awake. Surely there is something to keep my mind away from Seb, but that is impossible after what I've just done. Before I pull myself out of bed for the day, I reach for my phone.

> I've completed the homework you set for me for today. Izzy

> Good girl. Did you enjoy it? S

> Yes, although I preferred it when you watched, or when you touched me.

Can I say that to him? It's only a text.

> We'll get to that, Isabel. Don't worry. But I want you to continue with your homework. Remember, every day and bonus points for texting when your fingers are still wet. S

> Then I just earned some bonus points.

> And I earned a difficult day thinking about those naughty fingers. S

I blush as I read his text. It's easier to think about following this instruction knowing the effect it will have on Seb. I want to hear his praise more often.

After I throw some clothes on and brush my teeth, I head downstairs for coffee and reflect on what I've done with Seb. My mind is full of erotic visions of what has been and hopefully what I've still yet to experience. I want him to challenge me gently. I think I've known that ever since I first put on the anklet. The problem I have now is that I don't really know what else to expect. Giving up control of my sexual needs is natural with Seb. Something that I long ago gave up on with Phil. How far will Seb take me? Do I even know where my limits are? I have plenty of ideas of things he might try, all courtesy of my Tumblr and BDSM private profile pages. Seb called himself a controlled Dom. I witnessed the slight traits of a Dom—the subtle changes that made my nerves stand on end and my sex ache with anticipation. Will I get to see more of that side to him?

The rest of the day is uneventful and I'm left, once again, to my own devices at home. I do very little, aside from keeping up to date with the latest posts from Tumblr and exploring a little deeper into the BDSM sites I've always browsed but never interacted with.

It's late by the time Phil shows his face, too late to have just finished work. He heads straight to bed. We're talking even less than before, if that's even possible. The guilt that I'm feeling is hard to live with, even though our relationship was failing before I met Seb. I'm not making an effort, though. I don't want to make the effort, and what does that say about me?

* * *

Sunday

Saturday helped to ease my nerves concerning playing with myself without Seb's instruction. It's early morning and a Sunday. The perfect opportunity for a leisurely shower where I can experiment. Phil is downstairs and won't disturb me. I take off my dressing gown and step into the shower. I luxuriate in the water soaking me and turn the heat up to relax my muscles. Working my fingers into my scalp eases some of my latent worries, and the stress washes away with the bubbles. I pick up the shower gel and squirt a generous amount into my palm and lather it up. Instead of rushing with the wash and rinse, I take time to let my hands run over my arms and my chest, exploring my skin. I've never done this. Before long, the bathroom has filled with steam. I move my hand to the apex of my thighs and gently graze my middle finger between my labia. I try to remember all of Seb's instructions to tease myself and build myself up. However, I'm impatient and tease my clit almost straightaway.

My reaction is instant, and I can't understand why I've never tried this before. I can touch and tease and rub where I need to, bring myself right to the edge quickly. Seb can't instruct me to go slow here. I want to feel that wave of heat rush throughout my body.

I run my finger once or twice down my slit and push inside. I'm slick, not wet from the water, but from how my body reacts to my own touch. As I press my finger inside, my stomach tenses with desire and an ache or longing to have something thrust deep into me. I swirl my finger and return to my clit. The hot water streaming down my body heats me further and I want to reach that high. I rub quickly on the tip of my fleshy clit until my legs go weak. With my arm out to steady myself, I let go and succumb to the rush of bliss throughout my body.

I take a few breaths and try not to swallow too much water before I finish my regular shower routine. *Two days down, five to go!*

After the longest shower I've ever had, I finally step out and grab my towel to dry off. I pull on my dressing gown and walk into the bedroom. A text from Seb awaits me.

> As you seemed so eager to please yourself yesterday, I thought I'd see how you were feeling today? S

I grin at the thought I pleased him. The high from coming has loosened me up. I have no problem telling him exactly what I want to.

> Well, my body is still wet from the shower, and if I wasn't in the shower, my fingers would still be slick. Izzy

> Good girl. Remember to listen to your body. I'm looking forward to the rest of the week. S

* * *

Monday
After how good the shower was yesterday morning, I decide that I'm going to spend a little extra time in the shower every morning this week. It feels so good to get that release, that warm feeling throughout my body. Today, getting myself off was easier than yesterday, and I even have a slight glow to my cheeks as I rush to finish getting ready for work.

> I've completed my homework for today… and I think I found how I like to do my homework the best. Izzy

> Really? You've only been fingering yourself for a couple of days and you already think you know how you like it best? Isabel, you need to experiment a lot more. S

> No, I mean I know that I like it in the shower, where I'm not going to be disturbed. Izzy

> The shower. That sounds... Well, let's just say I'm going to have an interesting day thinking about it. S

His text puts another great smile on my face. I happily go to work, content in how my body feels and eagerly looking forward to my morning shower tomorrow.

* * *

Tuesday
Oh no, no, no! Shit! Phil has left early for his morning shift and although I usually lie in bed for a little bit longer, content to keep warm in the covers, I must have fallen back into a deep sleep. I seem to be sleeping especially well at the moment. Perhaps they should recommend a daily orgasm as a cure for insomnia.

But I'm late. Really late. Too late for a shower, with barely time to get ready, I literally fall into my clothes and bolt out of the door, grabbing my keys and bag as I dash to the car.

Damn, I had been looking forward to having my own little happy time again and now I can't. *Shit!*

As I arrive late for work, the sound of my phone has me scrambling to find it.

> Don't forget Jackson's tonight. I'll pick you up. Phil

No, no, no! I can't believe how this day is going already, and it's only 9:10 a.m. Phil's dinner plans for tonight had completely slipped my mind. Not surprising as we don't talk. I'm astonished that Phil still wants me to go with him. I shouldn't be. He does this. Having a wife is convenient for social gatherings with his work colleagues.

I'm not going to be able to complete the homework. A slight panic at displeasing Seb washes over me and I have butterflies in my tummy.

Perhaps if I text Seb and explain I'll be able to make up for it tomorrow. Asking Seb for permission to come seems an alien concept... but also rather naughty. How does he manage to keep his command over me and my desires even when he's not with me? It's 11:30 before I work up the courage to text him.

> Hi, Seb, I had a bit of a disaster this morning and didn't get a chance to take a shower. I've got to be out tonight and so won't be able to find time to finish my homework today. Can I make up for it tomorrow instead? Izzy

> Isabel, that would be breaking the rules. Have you had your lunch break yet? S

Why does he want to know when lunch is? *Perhaps he could meet me and help me out?*

> No. Taking lunch in 30 minutes. Izzy

He leaves me hanging until the half hour is up.

> Go straight to your office bathroom, find a quiet cubical and complete your homework there. S

Did he really just ask me to make myself come in the toilet at work?

I shake my head and pick up my bag. After a quick glance left and right, I stand up. The ridiculous feeling that people will know what I'm going to do dissipates as I enter the ladies. I open the end cubical and lock the door, mentally wrestling with myself.

How is he controlling me like this? I want to. I want to do as he says.

I sit and lower my knickers. I'm already turned on. In only a few days, my body has learned to expect this and has turned into some sex-hungry ball of neediness. The position doesn't feel normal—my knickers stretched around my ankles—so I pull them off and put them on top of my bag. I run my finger between my legs and find my damp clit. *What the hell am I doing? This is mad, but, but… I want to do it.*

I've never considered the naughty girl fantasy before, but I see the appeal. My phone buzzes with a new text and I know instantly it will be Seb.

> Are you doing as you're told? S

With one finger still rubbing my clit, I fumble and text back.

> Yes. I can't believe you've got me doing this. Guess where my other finger is right now.

> Well done. Don't forget to use some of those details I showed you at the table. Tap your clit, and let me know when you've come. S

The mention of the table and the feel of my finger tapping on my clit launch a surge of desire through my already turned-on body. Hearing Seb's voice in my head is enough to make me open my mouth to breathe in some much-needed air.

I'm already close, picturing Seb and his hand showing me what to do. I close my eyes and imagine that I'm back at his dining room table, sitting in the chair, and rub my clit a little harder, tapping. I'm spanking my own clit. The soft vibrations add to my building orgasm. I bite my lip and try not to make a sound as I force myself over the edge and feel the release tingle and shiver through my body. I don't want to open my eyes to focus on the absurd reality of my surroundings, but finally I do. I grab for my phone.

> Homework completed. I'm pleased you're impressed. Izzy

For the rest of the day, I can barely focus on what I have to accomplish. All of the want and desire that Seb brings out of me simmers under the surface, and I have a strange sort of satisfaction at actually impressing him with my naughty little act at lunchtime.

Phil picks me up straight from work and sours my mood.

"Hurry up, Iz, or we're going to be late," he snaps before I even have time to sit in the car.

"Alright, I'm coming."

My mind races while I stare out of the window. The lights pass by in a blur of yellow and white. I don't speak to Phil. I'm sulking because I don't want to be here. I let out a long sigh. What happened between us that stopped us enjoying each other's company? I've tolerated these evenings in the past, mainly in my attempt to show give and take in the relationship. Another area that Phil was content to take and never to give. I should have stood up to him before now about his behaviour.

My thoughts do nothing to snap me out of this quiet spell, and luckily we arrive soon after.

I've known Jackson for years. He works with Phil at the garage in the sales team, and his wife has always been pleasant. There are a couple of others I don't know at the house, together with the area boss that I've met at the Christmas parties I'm also forced to attend.

We are offered drinks and Phil abandons me, making a beeline for the other guests. I'm left holding my glass of wine, lingering at the door to the dining room.

He knows these people, but I don't. He hasn't even introduced me. Do I not even warrant that anymore? I'm his invisible wife. We don't go out together, don't socialize together. We lead completely separate lives.

A laugh brings my focus back to the room. The source of the laugh is a pretty blonde. Phil must know these other people well, or more accurately, the blonde. He sits on the arm of the sofa while she paws at his arm, clearly finding whatever they are talking about amusing.

That's my husband! The words pop into my head, but not with the venom or possession that should come from a wife. I don't care. I watch another woman throw herself at my husband and I don't care. *Is she the one?* I wonder if I were to get close to her would I smell the sickly scent that he couldn't mask the other night? The correct reaction would be defensive jealousy, fury even. A smile spreads across my face when I realise I don't care. *Sebastian.* I want to be with him, not stuck here tonight.

It's obvious that Phil isn't always working or staying with Jackson when he says he is. My suspicions are confirmed. Again, I'm struck by my lack of reaction. I watch for a few moments longer before I've had enough. If Phil is going to drag me here, he's going to have to deal with me.

"So, are you going to introduce me?" I smile my sweetest smile at Phil and see everything I need to know in his eyes. Resentment flashes in them before he covers it over. He doesn't want me near her. *Well, tough. I don't want to be here at all, so deal with it.*

"Um... yeah. This is Sophie. Sophie, this is Iz."

I aim my smile at her to see how she deals with me.

"Hi," is all she replies. She's unable to look me in the eye and I recognize the guilt in her posture. I can't understand why Phil would drag me here if he knew Sophie would be here. Why introduce his wife to the woman he must be sleeping with?

The rest of the evening is uneventful, but I'm now stewing in my own mixed-up thoughts and I am not pleasant company.

Phil clearly doesn't want me and is very obviously into someone else prettier than me, taller than me, and much more curvy. I've supported him for years and tried to do everything right, so how have I ended up here, not caring that he's rubbing his bit-on-the-side in my face? Why are we still together?

The ride home is silent. I go straight to bed. My mind churns and my guilt changes into some unnamed emotion, something different, which keeps me awake.

Phil climbs into bed with me and his hand creeps under my t-shirt. I remain still, shocked at his behaviour.

"What are you doing?" I'm certainly not in the mood for anything physical.

"Come on, Iz. I haven't had anything from you in months. You were asking for a lot more than a little sex a few weeks ago. Come here. It'll be good." He rolls towards me and kisses my neck. My body tenses and I don't know how to respond. I don't want this. *Not you... You don't know what I need or what I want. You don't even want me.* But how can I say no to my husband? He'll know something's wrong, and I'm not strong enough to lie to him. Not tonight. Not how I'm feeling. God, I don't even know how I feel.

"Phil, not tonight. I'm tired and you barely talked to me all evening. You were too busy flirting with that blonde woman. You can't turn me on like a light switch." I try to sound as gentle as I can, but he won't listen to the tone of my voice.

"Iz, come on." He tries once more and my anger boils through my veins.

"No. I said no. Not tonight. Just... let me be, Phil." I roll over and curl in on myself, hoping that's the end of it.

"You can be a real bitch, you know, Iz? One minute you want me to spank you while having sex and the next you don't want me to touch you? What's up with that? And before you throw me out, I'm sleeping in the spare room. Don't want you to feel uncomfortable with me in the same bed as you." He throws back the covers and storms out. The door slams. Possibly on whatever is left of our marriage.

That's not fair! I scream at him in my head. I don't know what to think at the moment. I don't want to be with Phil. I can't be with him while I'm with Seb. I'm cheating on Phil and I know that's not right. In principle it's not right, but I don't want to be unfaithful to Seb while I'm with him. How can I have such conflicting thoughts and feelings at the same time? How can I be thinking I should be faithful to someone other than my husband?

Tears seep from my eyes as I wrap my arms around myself, trying to calm and console my heart. All I really want is for Seb's strong arms to wrap me up and make everything go away. He can't, though. He's only showing me a physical need I have. He wants me happy, having a little fun and showing me something new. He'll walk away when he's had enough, and I'll be left to try to pick up the pieces.

Eleven

Wednesday

I wake before my alarm and listen to determine whether Phil is anywhere in the house. It's all quiet, so I creep out of bed. As I peek around the doorframe, I still hear nothing. He must have gone to work already, so I go back into the bedroom and start the day. After the fight with Phil, my enthusiasm to pleasure myself has been waning. Guilt has gnawed at my insides that I'm happy to let another man instruct me to come, but won't let my husband touch me. Still… I don't want to let Seb down. I can't. There isn't a future where I can see Phil and I still together. Phil has already moved on, and I think her name is Sophie. I should have finished things before I even met Seb—but hey. The hands on the clock won't give me a pass and turn back just for me.

I start the shower and resolutely try to change my feelings. I won't let last night ruin everything. Today is a new day and maybe Phil and I can be civilised and talk about last night—talk about our problems and our future. *There isn't a future that ends happily with Phil.*

The water is hot, and I drench myself under the stream before I reach for the body wash. As soon as my hands start to wash, I recognise the tingling throughout my body. I'm already twitching to get off, to release the tension, to forget about everything and get lost in sensation.

I move my hand down, now familiar with the actions that will get my heart beating and my body aching. My fingers slide down and dip into my waiting pussy. I close my eyes to the water and relax into the now familiar feeling.

"What the fuck, Iz?" Phil shouts through the shower door at me. My eyes snap back open. My hand retracts and covers my body, startled and embarrassed at being caught touching myself. Even through the fogged glass, it would be clear where my hand was.

"I'm just finishing in the shower, Phil. Give me a minute." I try to even out my voice and turn my back to the glass and away from Phil.

"I don't believe you. You won't let me touch you but you're rubbing yourself off like a cheap slut in the shower the next morning? What's gotten into you? You're a selfish bitch."

The humiliation I felt when I first asked Phil to spank me is suddenly all I feel.

"I'm not a selfish bitch. We can talk tonight. I'll be late for work. Please?" My fumbled words sound meagre and weak, and I hate myself for not being stronger. *Just for now. Let it be enough for now.* I can't face Phil now, not naked in the shower, trying to fulfil another man's wishes. *Wanting* to fulfil another man's wishes.

He doesn't respond, and after what seems like hours, I finally turn around. Phil's gone and the bathroom is empty. I turn the shower off and dry myself quickly. I pull on the first work outfit I come to and scurry down the stairs.

"Phil?" I call out, and hope that I can at least say something to him before I head to work. There's no response. The guilt rumbles in my stomach for everything I'm doing. The dread of having a conversation with Phil to explain my actions makes me feel sick. What can I possibly say to explain? Sorry, Seb, but I don't think that I'm going to get to finish my homework today.

The workday seems to pass at an excruciatingly slow pace. As usual, when I want or need the time to pass quickly, the clock conspires against me. I barely speak to anyone during the day and keep my head down, hoping I can get an early exit.

Will Phil even talk to me, hear me out? Hear me out about what? What am I going to say, exactly? That I don't want him to touch me or be with me, and that I want someone else? *Seb*. Seb knows what my body craves—what I need—and gives it to me willingly. Thoughts of my marriage are grey and hazy. I don't want to stay married, yet I can't quite bring myself to end things. *Why can't I?*

Tears well in my eyes as I suddenly realise the enormity of the conversation that is looming. Is Phil as unhappy as I am? I am deeply unhappy.

All of the raw and painful feelings constrict my chest and I struggle to hold the tears back. I've been unfaithful because I couldn't cope with the constant neglect and lack of affection. I needed something else, something more, and couldn't simply sit back any longer. I naively thought that none of last week's actions would have such a profound emotional effect on my relationship with Phil. Finally, I am waking up and feeling alive. I want to do everything that Seb instructed me to do. At the same time, Phil and I are growing further apart.

I decide that I can no longer sit and stew at my desk about all the mights and maybes that await me at home. I need to take responsibility for my actions and confront Phil. I gather my things from my desk, shove my laptop into my bag, and head for the door. As I'm leaving, my phone buzzes in my pocket and my stomach rolls in response, anticipating a tirade from Phil.

> Isabel, I haven't heard from you all day, and with your recent eagerness I wanted to check in on your homework. I hope you're enjoying yourself? S

Shit! No, not now... I can't deal with both men. My head is literally going to explode with everything crashing around in it.

> Sorry, today's not been a good one. I'll txt later. Izzy

> Izzy, are you okay? S

Izzy... He wants to make sure I'm okay. But I'm not. *I'm not okay, Seb, and I don't really know what to do right now. Can you guide me through this as well?* My wishful plea turns my stomach. How can I be thinking that? I'm being a spoiled little girl who needs to grow up.

> I'll txt u later, OK? Got to go.

The entire way home, I can't settle. My feet tap. My fingers drum. Shifting and fidgeting doesn't calm my racing heart. I park the car and walk up to the front door. As I push it open, I take a very deep breath on yet another threshold, this one somewhat unwelcome.

"I'm in here, Iz."

Please don't be mad. Please don't hate me. God, what am I going to say? I peek into the front room and see him in the chair, watching sports on the TV.

"Hi," I mumble, unsure of my own voice.

"So... You said we need to talk. Where do you want to start?"

"I don't know really. I couldn't do it this morning."

"Huh... because you were too busy fingering yourself in the shower, Iz. I saw, don't worry!" There's no gentle introduction to this conversation. He attacks me—straight for the jugular.

"Please, Phil. I didn't do it to hurt you."

"Then why did you do it? You didn't want any last night." His voice is filled with anger, his posture giving away his own agitated state.

"I just... I needed to. My body, I... I wanted to come, and I like doing it to myself." I cast my eyes down and hope the uncertainty in my voice masks my indiscretion. *You're not lying to him. You do want it. You wanted to make yourself come.*

"I could have done it. Or better yet, you could have had sex with me last night."

"I didn't want to have sex with you last night. I'm not a switch that you can flick on and off, and besides, I was angry with you last night." As the words escape my lips, I realise that I've opened this up to a much bigger fight.

"What do you mean, you were angry with me?"

I inwardly take a deep breath and steel myself for this. *How did he not know that I was angry?* It was as plain as day and I couldn't have made it any more obvious after the way he acted at Jackson's.

"You took me to a party where I knew no one. You promptly abandon me at the door. You didn't care to introduce me to people you were clearly 'friends' with, and you allow some girl to paw all over you. We drove home in utter silence and then you expected sex? Really? And you can't imagine why I was angry?" I can't keep the acidic tone from my voice. My nerves settle and anger builds when I remember how I felt watching Sophie with Phil.

"She wasn't pawing at me, Iz, and I did introduce you. You're so sensitive." He shrugs it off.

I'm not prepared to let this go. Not now. "I introduced *myself*, Phil and she *was* pawing you, and you clearly didn't have a problem with it!" I shout. I suddenly want to vent all my fear, my hurt, my need for more out of our marriage, out of my life, at him.

"Iz, come on... She's just a friend. I'm sorry I didn't introduce you earlier. That's all, Iz. I promise." He sounds nervous. I've hit a nerve.

"You know what's sad? I'm not particularly bothered about Sophie and you, Phil. Are you sleeping with her?"

"Don't do this, Iz. We're supposed to be talking about why you don't want me to touch you, but you're perfectly happy to do it yourself. I'm not discussing a simple friendship with another woman." Phil stands abruptly. "You really are a bitch, you know."

"Don't storm out again, Phil. We have to sort this out."

"I'm not listening to you anymore. You can keep your dirty little fantasies. Don't expect me back tonight." With that, he storms out of the room.

The slam of the door echoes around the house. My meagre attempt to stand up to him has failed, and I'm left reeling from my surge of frustration and anger. I know he's being unfaithful. It was clear from Sophie's reaction to me that my suspicions are valid.

He's not the only one, though. I have been unfaithful, too. I'm just as much to blame. I drag myself up from the sofa and head upstairs to the bedroom. It's too early to go to bed, but right now that's all I want to do—fall asleep to escape my thoughts and feelings. *Everything is supposed to look better in the morning, isn't it?*

My mood hampers my speed as I get undressed for bed, but I finally manage to pull the covers up to my chin after I climb in. I reach over for my phone and notice a couple of new text messages.

You're meant to be my wife, Izzy. Phil

As I read his words, a tear escapes and runs down my cheek. The word 'wife' rings in my heart and I'm sad that I don't feel it. I haven't felt like a wife for a long time.

> It takes two to make a marriage. You haven't been a husband to me in a long time. Izzy

I pull up the un-opened message on my screen.

> Izzy, I'm worried. You haven't texted back and it's late. What's happened? S

And what am I supposed to say to that?

> It's just been a bad day. I'm sorry.

As I put the phone down on the side table, it rings. It's Seb. *Can I do this? Can I talk to him now?* But I'm already answering his call, desperate to hear his deep voice. I hope it can soothe me and help to arrange my thoughts into some form of rational order.

"Hi."

"Hi yourself. Now what's wrong? You haven't been yourself all day and I can tell, so think before you try to lie to me, Izzy." His authoritative tone immediately makes my body relax, even though I don't think I can emotionally deal with an explanation. He's taken charge by simply stating what he expects, how I should react. The way I'm feeling now—caught between turmoil and confusion—it's amazingly seductive. *So why can't I just tell him what's on my mind?*

"Seb, I'm tired. I had a bad day. Couple of days, really, and…" *Shall I tell him I've failed? That I couldn't complete my homework? Will he be disappointed in me?* "And, um, I've not done my homework." I want to feel valued, part of something, and

Seb is offering to help me with that. I'm so tied up in knots. I should be sorting my life out without Seb needing to rescue me. But he is rescuing me. And I'm throwing it back in his face.

I wait for his response and hope that I don't have to deal with another argument.

"Why did you fail, Isabel? I thought you were enjoying your homework from your text message yesterday." His hard tone is not quite telling me off, but it's not too far from it.

"I've just... I had a fight with Phil, and it's sort of filled up my day. I can't just drop everything to fit it in. Sometimes life gets in the way." My answer is defensive, reactionary. Again, I wait for his response.

"Do you want to talk about it?" Those words from Seb are both the best and worst thing he could say. When I'm looking for support, he's the one offering it to me.

"Why would you offer me that? Surely you're not interested in hearing about it?"

"I am interested in everything that concerns you, Izzy, this especially so. You confided in me before we ventured down this path. I know you are struggling in your marriage. I want you to feel comfortable talking about these things with me, even if they are hard and painful. If anything, it's more important now. I told you about having clear and honest communication—clearly something we need to work on. Now, talk to me." Those last words are laced with authority, and I'm warming to him, wanting to share my feelings without the fear of rejection or humiliation.

"It's... I was... Phil caught me playing with myself in the shower. He wasn't really happy with it." I pause to see whether he will say anything or expect me to continue. He'll want more of an explanation. I breathe in a little to see whether he's going to interject, but nothing. His patience is frustrating, but forces me to continue. "And he didn't like it because I didn't want to have sex with him the previous night." I rush the last few words on my exhale.

"Why didn't you want to have sex with him, Izzy?" His calm tone confuses me more.

"That's what you want to know? I... I don't know, Seb. I couldn't. Look, it's been a really long day. I need to go to sleep."

"Don't do that, Isabel. Don't run away from me. I want to help. The type of relationship that we have... it's not just about what happens when we're together. I said that I would hold your hand every step of the way. That includes helping you come to terms with your feelings." His voice is strong and sure. The shivers that run up my spine tell me how affected I am by this man and how he seems to understand what I need before I do. Can I deal with Seb, *Sebastian*, knowing everything to do with Phil?

"I'm sorry I failed at the homework. Am I still going to see you on Friday?"

"Yes, Isabel. I still want to see you on Friday. Very much so. I have something in mind that might help you." He almost purrs the last words, and despite how awful I feel at how I don't seem to be able to express my feelings the way I want to, I'm desperate to see him.

"Okay, so I'll see you on Friday." I try to finish the conversation even though my body is already warming to his voice and his words.

"Okay then, Isabel. You clearly don't trust me enough yet to completely open up. But you will. Don't forget what I've said, especially about being honest. I expect that from our relationship, so I'm giving you a little more time. This is still all very new to you. But remember, this conversation isn't over, and you did fail on your homework. There will be consequences." Although his words are hard, his voice softens the blow. Perhaps there is even a hint of a smile in his voice at the mention of consequences.

"Goodnight, Seb."

"Goodnight, Izzy. Sweet dreams."

* * *

Thursday

After how utterly dreadful yesterday was, I wake and hope that today can be an improvement. *Yes, today is going to be better.* I pull myself out of bed after silencing my phone. Wandering into the bathroom, I put the shower on and wait for it to get hot before I climb in and let the water submerge me in my thoughts. I can always think clearly in the shower, and I attempt to order the chaos that is my mind and emotions.

That is, I used to be able to think clearly before I started making myself come in the shower. *Just imagine how it would feel if Seb was in here with you.* Rushing through the usual routine, I grab a towel and dry off.

My daydreaming doesn't stop, though, and Seb's words from last night drift back to me. He was concerned, genuinely interested in hearing what was wrong, and even offered to help me through it. I wanted more, and he's given it to me. I wanted him to be gentle and guide me into this darker side of my sexual desires, and he has. What else do I want from him? Can I give him something in return, or is he just having fun? No. *He wouldn't want to deal with my marital issues if that's all he wanted. He'd just fuck me and leave.*

My mind is still filled with confusion over Seb. He said he wasn't finished with the conversation, that he wanted to help with my feelings. A huge part of me wants to trust in that. So far, Seb has known what I needed before I have. *Will he be right again?* I trust Seb—it's almost an automatic response. But have I opened up to him on an emotional level? Fully? My actions say otherwise. Perhaps I'm not ready to let him behind every wall. It isn't easy, after training myself to be quiet and not speak my true feelings for so long. *Enough! Get dressed and get on with your day.*

I listen to myself and diligently finish getting ready for work.

I descend downstairs into the quiet of the house. It's always quiet. Phil usually leaves before me, but this morning, knowing why he isn't here, the silence seems worse.

Our marriage is not working. Should I give up so quickly? Will this be what it's like? Living in quiet with no one to share my life with? Should I admit defeat and end things?

The silence does nothing to ease my thoughts about the future, and I decide to get to work as quickly as I can.

Work is a busy and welcome distraction. My mind clearly hasn't been focussing on what it should have been lately, and my workload is piling up. I open up my inbox and try, hard, to keep my mind on the screen in front of me. My fingers drift across the keys and click the mouse, but a very small part of my mind is still with Seb and Phil. God, even thinking about them in the same sentence seems wrong. Before long, my phone buzzes with a new message.

> How are you feeling this morning, Izzy? I want to make sure you're better today. S

Before I can even stop them, my lips smile and my mood lifts.

> Better, thank you. How is your day going? Izzy

> Well, now that I know you're okay. I'm looking forward to tomorrow. S

> So am I ☺

I've pressed send before I consider what I've typed. I am pleased to be seeing him tomorrow. My body craves his, and being around him brings me a sense of ease. I'm able to put my desires in his hands without worry that they won't be fulfilled. It's freeing—a weight lifted from my chest. *That's what you need, Izzy, and don't beat yourself up about wanting it. You can have it. You've had it handed to you on a plate by an incredibly strong and handsome guy who does things to your body you've only dreamed about. How many girls get to say that?*

Remember your homework, Isabel. S

Shit, really? Still?

I don't think I can, Seb. I'm sorry.

Of course you can. You're at work now, aren't you? You need this, Isabel. Trust me. S

Trust you? Of course I trust you, and that's what's scaring me.

I don't reply. It's nearly lunchtime, and I grab my coat and bag, walk down the stairs to the lobby and into town, snug in my coat as the cold air swirls around me. Autumn is definitely here. I'm not looking forward to months of cold to come. The season seems to mirror my marriage—things are dying. A cold wind is replacing the sun's warmth. With my shoulders slumped, I lift my face and let the wind wash over me. *Izzy, snap out of this.*

All I seem to be doing lately is telling myself off in my own head. I know that even without Seb, I would be in the same situation with Phil. Before I met Seb, things weren't right between us. I want Seb. I want what he can show me. For once, can I do something for myself? No one else but me?

I am the one who always has to make the decisions, to take the lead, to say how it needs to be. I don't want the burden anymore. I want the freedom that comes from allowing someone else the responsibility of making the decisions in my life, or at least in the bedroom. I want to be able to trust that my emotional needs and my sexual wants will be met. I want to experience the satisfaction of being the focus of someone else's concern.

Seb does that for me. *And it's fantastic!* Without even meaning to, I build a vision of him in my mind—his voice, his words, his hands on my bum as he spanks me.

With the image of Seb spanking me over his breakfast bar rooted in my mind, I walk quickly back to the office. I nearly run up the stairs and head straight for the toilets. As I lock myself in the cubicle, I waste no time pulling my trousers and knickers down. My hand knows exactly what to do, and I dip my middle finger between my lips to touch my clit.

I bask in the physical sensation as it pulses through me. I feel naughty and aroused all at the same time. That I'm obeying Seb's commands adds to the high. I push my finger inside myself, teasing myself, working myself up before returning to my needy clit.

I didn't realise how much I wanted to come until I started. I'm desperate to feel that release, that point where every nerve ending in my body sings with pleasure and everything else disappears. I rub harder and tap my clit until my orgasm breaks free. My hand thrusts out, pressing against the cubical wall for balance. I sigh as my eyes close, and I submit to the wave of heat that floods through me. I take a breath in and open my eyes. Nothing has changed. I'm still in the toilets at work. If I'm going to experience everything that Seb is prepared to offer me, I need to trust him with my feelings as well as my body. With that realisation and my silent commitment to hold true to it, I pull out my phone.

> Homework complete. At work. Do bonus points make up for yesterday? Izzy

> No, Isabel, they don't, but well done. My place, tomorrow at 7 p.m. S

More

> Can't wait. Izzy.

As I text him, I realise that it's true. I can't wait. Something has shifted. Maybe the internal back and forth of conversation in my mind has finally paid off. I am going to go after what I want.

Twelve

I wake up, a giddy sensation radiating through me. It's Friday morning, and despite the last few days being an emotional rollercoaster, I feel as if I'm waking up on my birthday, unable to contain my excitement and joy at getting to unwrap my presents. I rush my homework, taking no time to bring myself to climax with thoughts of Seb, vivid in my mind. I continue getting ready for work and arrive in record time.

Seb said seven o'clock , and I want to be ready before I head over to his place. I plan to leave work early tonight to ensure enough time to make every inch of me as ready as possible.

The hands on the clock are my personal torture devices. I spend the day clock watching and flicking between checking my emails and text messages. I still haven't heard from Phil, and I feel that I need to make the first move.

I hope I've given you enough space to cool off. We can't let this carry on. Will I see you tomorrow? Izzy

I nearly end it with my customary 'I love you', but think better of it. *Do I still love Phil?* I don't know anymore. Perhaps it is more the memory of love, but that isn't enough, not now that I've experienced the depth of real feeling from Seb. God, only a taste and I can't wait for more. Submitting to Seb has been liberating.

Before I get drawn into my own internal debate over right and wrong, what I want and what I have, I take a deep breath and focus on how my body feels. Since stepping across that line with Seb, my body has come alive. Putting my faith in that surely won't lead me astray. I practically burst into the house—I'm that eager to go upstairs. Stripping as I enter the bathroom, I jump straight into the shower. I wash my hair and grab the body scrub to make sure I'm buffed as smooth as possible. I make a mental note to check when my next waxing appointment is, actually eager for once to make sure I am hair-free now that it isn't just for my benefit.

Finishing quickly, I dry off, wrap the towel around me and go to my underwear drawer. As I slip into the lace and silk, I peek at myself in the mirror.

Apart from the fact that my boobs are too small for my body, I don't look too bad. My pale skin looks like ivory contrasted against the black lingerie. My legs look long and shapely in the thigh highs. My wardrobe doesn't scream 'sex appeal' but I do have a few dresses that I think flatter and suit me. I choose a short, fitted dress—again, black—and pair it with some high heels. This is where I can have some fun. My shoe collection is my extravagance and I won't give it up.

My black patent heels are my go-to choice, but I opt for my dusky pink heels with a black lace pattern, a t-bar and ankle strap. They have a small platform so I can walk comfortably in them. Just.

My nerves make me fidget in the back seat of the taxi. Butterflies are awake in my stomach at the thought of seeing Seb once more, feeling him touch me, and hopefully going further. He asked me to think about where my limits were to our arrangement. I knew sex wasn't one of them, but I hadn't figured out the rest. My mind skips back to the images of women from my Tumblr, bound, flogged, laid out for the pleasing of someone else. My body hums with energy. My excitement makes me light-headed.

Calm down, Izzy! I'm not even with him yet and I'm already dizzy for him. I don't even know what he's going to do to me, but the unknown is a part of the buzz. The uncertainty and the danger all fuse together into a naughty mix of emotions which I relish.

I watch the road ahead of me. The lights contrast with the black night and I become lost in the darkness, thinking of my evening of pleasure.

I pay for the taxi and step out. For a moment, I am rooted in place. I need a few moments to compose myself and prepare for what may happen. Although I'm excited, there is still a small part of me that understands that this isn't right. My yo-yo mind relaxes, and I advance towards the lift and press the button to call it down. As the numbers descend, my heart hammers in my chest. The lift slows and the doors open. He said he wanted to finish our conversation, and that he wants to be there to support me through every step. I'm hoping that he will be a lot more physical with me than just offering his verbal support. I'm hoping for his hands over my body, making my pussy wet and my clit throb, and then commanding me to do whatever he wants.

I'm not quite ready for the deep and meaningful yet. After I exit on Seb's floor and let myself in, I walk through the apartment and head straight for my room. On the dressing table in its box is my anklet. The velvet box is soft in my hand and squeaks as I open it up. The anklet sits there, winking at me. All the excitement and pleasure that it can unlock twinkles and entices me. I quickly pull it from its velvet bed and bend down to fasten it around my ankle before heading into the kitchen. The wine glasses are waiting on the counter and the Sauvignon Blanc is chilling in the fridge. I open it, pour two glasses, and then seat myself on a bar stool.

I check my watch. 6:55 p.m. Five minutes to spare. The crisp and fruity liquid floods my mouth as I take a sip. I remember how I felt prior to hearing Seb's voice on the phone Wednesday evening—exhausted, deflated and shut down. He's already shown me how easily I respond to his words and his touch. But there is still part of me closed to him. I want to change that. I want to let him in, not just physically, but emotionally as well.

The sound of the door shutting startles me.

"Good evening, Isabel." Seb walks through the sitting area to join me in the kitchen. His hand captures my loosely plaited hair and smooths it over my shoulder with a gentle tug. Soft lips brush my cheek with such deliberate poise that my breath hitches.

"Good evening, Sebastian. Your wine." I offer him the glass I poured a few moments ago and place a sweet kiss on his lips.

"Thank you. Cheers." His glass clinks with mine. I smile and look up into his beautifully dangerous eyes. I watch him as his gaze runs down my body, taking in my legs and pausing at my feet.

"I hope you've got some time tonight. I have a lot planned for us. First things first, however. Dinner. It will take a few minutes to prepare."

"I have time."

"Excellent. Don't drink more than one glass of wine with dinner." His usual sexy smile's back, teasing me with those words. *What if I have too much to drink? What would waking up with Seb be like? Would he let me stay the night?*

"Okay, one glass, then." I smile in return, pleased to see things seem as normal as they have always been with us.

"Dinner will be simple and sweet tonight. I'm preparing spaghetti with tomato sauce and parmesan."

He's spoiling me with his care and it means everything. The novelty of a man making dinner for me touches a vulnerable place inside. It's a rarity that anyone ever cooks for me. I watch him prepare the food. It wouldn't matter what he prepared, I'd eat it because he'd made it for me.

"I love Italian and that sounds great. I've hardly eaten all day."

"Why is that, Isabel? You need to eat. Make sure you eat properly." His tone is clipped but I don't take offence.

"I had a busy day and I had somewhere I wanted to be fairly early tonight." I dip my head and look up at him through my lashes.

"Is that right?" He reaches for me, taking my face in his hands, and rewards me with a deep kiss. His lips press into mine and I open my mouth to him willingly. The strokes of his tongue across my bottom lip instantly heat my blood. Goose bumps cover my skin and my legs want to open to him. His tongue pushes into my mouth and I push back, showing him I'm willing and definitely wanting in this. But he pulls away and moves down my jaw to my neck, taking my pulse with each kiss. I moan, unable to stop myself. *Do that again. Keep kissing my neck, there... again.*

I melt as he trails kisses across my collarbone and up the other side of my neck. He takes his time. Lazy licks and wet kisses continue until he reaches my ear. As his teeth close around my lobe, my pussy pulses at the wild desire he stirs within me. He bites a fraction harder, kicking my lust up to knicker-wetting levels. *Jeez!*

"I could make this last all evening, Isabel. I think you would be happy for that." His whisper titillates as his hand runs up the inside of my leg. Passing the top of my thigh highs, he slides his hand to my pussy. His touch is barely there before he slides under the edge of my knickers and strokes down my slit.

"Oh, Isabel, wet already and I've barely touched you." His velvet words send shivers down my spine. I try to readjust my sitting position so he can touch me deeper. The ache from my sex screams for attention, for Seb to do more, push his finger inside me, here in the kitchen.

"No, Isabel. You've been a naughty girl this week and haven't completed your homework. As much as I would love to make you come with nothing other than my hand, I have much more planned."

Naughty. I like being called naughty. Shockingly, I want Sebastian to show me exactly what he does to a naughty girl. But I can't say anything. My cheeks heat and I have to close my eyes and breathe deeply to calm down. His lips barely touch my ear and I can hear his breathing. He's affected as much as I am.

"You need to know how ready you are, Isabel, how ready your body is. I've only just begun and you are already turned on to the point that I could slide my fingers inside you easily. You want this, don't you? I want you to tell me how much you want this." The drop in his voice oozes sex. It's hypnotic. He could read the label on a jar of marmite and I would find it sexy. My mind takes a moment to register that he's actually asked me a question and is waiting for a response.

"Uh-huh," is all I can manage. My pussy is desperate and achy, and I can feel my throat tighten. Nervous anticipation creeps through me as his words make me feel almost queasy.

"You can do better than that, Isabel. I want you to tell me how you are feeling, what you want."

I start to inwardly plead—again. *Please, no. Don't make me say it. I want you to do it to me, not tell you about it. Touch me, make me stand up and bend me over the bar, spank me again and tell me I've been naughty before fucking me.*

"I'm waiting, Isabel." His command sends me over the edge.

"I, uh, want…" My voice is breathy and I'm finding it very hard to concentrate on speaking. "I want you to… touch me. To undress me and bend me over the bar again… To, um, spank me and then… and then fuck me." My panting breaths don't deliver the oxygen I need to stop me from shaking. My mouth is dry and my heart is pounding. None of that can destroy my personal triumph at saying the words. *I did it!*

"Very good, Isabel. That sounds very good, and believe me, fucking you while you lean over this bar, feeling your pussy quiver in need while I thrust into you before forcing you to come, is something I will be doing to you." He cages me with his body, crowding my space, and all I can do is breathe him in. "But not tonight."

I hear the grin in his words and a small part of me likes that he's enjoying this. The rest of me is in open rebellion at being denied. Sebastian pulls away from me, his hands sliding down my arms to my hands. I open my eyes and am met with his beautiful eyes. They are a clear blue now, icy and cool in colour, hiding all the lust and danger that I saw earlier tonight.

"Isabel, let me be very clear about what you are asking for. You want your experience of submission to me to include intercourse."

"Yes." My mind is still locked in the fantasy I described to him.

"Okay. We need to finish our conversation from the other evening. I think over dinner would be a good start."

No, I don't want to talk! I nod. It's all I can do at the moment. He's done it again. I've told him what I want, even though I really didn't want to. *How does he do it?*

"Good. Stay here and finish your wine while I put the pasta together." All of a sudden, he is back to charming Seb. He releases my hands and walks around to the other side of the kitchen, giving me a very clear view of his bum. *His very, very fine bum.* He collects all the ingredients together and starts the water boiling.

"Isabel, you told me why you failed your homework on Wednesday, but completed it yesterday. Can you tell me why you did that?" He continues in his preparations as he asks the question, and I'm taken aback.

What do you mean, why did I do it yesterday? You said I had to do it, not to forget about it. Were you tricking me?

"I wanted to do it," I answer as simply as I can. "I wanted to please you."

"Good. That's very good. Do you like how it makes you feel?"

"Yes." My reply is laced with nerves and I drop my head to look at my feet. He can't even see me.

The rich, sweet aroma of tomato and basil fill the kitchen and my stomach rumbles. In an attempt to stall this conversation, I ask how much longer dinner will be.

"Only a minute or two. We'll eat at the bar tonight. Will you please grab some place settings and refill my wine."

Good, it's worked.

"Don't think I'm done with you, Isabel."

I do as he asked and then sit while he serves a delicious looking pile of spaghetti. I wait for him to sit next to me before I pick up my fork. As I take my first bite, he places his hand just above my knee. I pause. My heartbeat hitches before I allow myself to take the first mouthful. Again, as the fork touches my lips, he runs his hand under my dress to mid-thigh. His touch is distracting. I don't know what I should do. Do I continue eating? Yes, yes, of course. But the feel of his hand on my leg sends sparks all over my body. I don't know what to concentrate on, the food or his touch.

"Enjoying your food, Isabel?"

"It's delicious, Sebastian. Thank you." I look at the food and avoid his eyes, worried he'll see the want hidden inside them.

"You're very welcome," he purrs as he gently caresses my leg with one hand. He digs into his own dish with the other.

Every time I bring a fork to my mouth, he squeezes, rubs or strokes my thigh, going higher or lower, teasing me as I try to concentrate on eating.

Why is he doing this to me? He's driving me crazy. I want him. He knows that already. Why is he teasing me? What does he want from me?

It takes a lot longer than usual to finish a simple bowl of pasta, however delicious it is, but I finally clear my plate.

"Well done, Isabel. I trust you enjoyed your meal?"

"Yes, the spaghetti was delicious, thank you, although I was somewhat distracted."

"Well, I have some other distractions in store for you. That was simply the warm up. Now…" He moves off his stool and stands in front of me. He twists my seat so I am no longer facing the bar. His stance is harder and the air is filled with the crackle of tension. I'm inwardly hoping he'll re-consider turning down the bar sex. "I want you to follow every one of my instructions."

The authority he puts behind those words nearly brings me to my knees. All the air in my lungs leaves my body and my pulse races. Bar sex forgotten for now, all my mind focuses on is Sebastian and doing what he wants. *Dear Lord!*

Thirteen

"Slide off the stool, Isabel, and kiss me."

My body instantly obeys. I look up at him. I'm drawn to his crystal cool blue eyes that give nothing away—no sign of what runs through his mind.

I want to pour all my need and hurt into one small physical act. I place my hands on his hard chest and slowly run them up towards his neck as he bends to meet my lips. Leaning in, I press mine against his, slowly to start with, gently moving and opening my mouth. I slide my tongue against his lips. Sparks ignite at every place we touch. Greedily, I pull his head harder in to me and run my hands through his hair as I breathe out and open my mouth fully to him, showing him how much I want to obey. As my passion grows, so does the force of our tongues, duelling and tasting each other. His lips scorch mine with his lust, wiping away any shred of doubt in my mind of his desire for me. My lips press back, wanting to get as close to him as I can. My chest heaves against Seb's as I fight to balance my breaths. My heart beat drums through my ears, dulling everything else around me. He stops.

He pulls back and takes a step away. My body and my lips miss his contact and I have to hold myself in check before I reach out for him. "Thank you, Isabel. Now walk into the front room and strip for me. Slowly."

With my heart still pounding, I step towards the living area and stop. With my back to him, I look down at my shoes, hoping he'll let me keep them on. *You've done this for him before. Take your clothes off. Don't think. Act. You're only wearing underwear and a dress. It won't take long.*

I count to ten and then pull myself up to my full five-feet-three-inches. The zip is within my grasp. I draw it down the side of my dress and open it.

"Stop." I hear his voice and the thud of his shoes walking to me. He passes me and sits back in one of the armchairs to the side of me. "Now, stand in front of me and look at me as you take your clothes off."

Oh, shit!

I turn around and look him in the eyes. Still nothing other than those beautiful colours reflect back at me, this time more green—perhaps from the darker lighting.

Counting again, I slide the straps of my dress off my shoulders. I pause for a moment as it pools at my waist. I try, as seductively as my stiff and uncoordinated body can, to move my hips and wiggle the dress down to the floor. I step forward, closer to Sebastian and out of the dress, leaving my thigh highs, knickers, and bra in place.

I reach around, unfasten my bra, and let it drop to the ground. Remembering his instruction to strip slowly, I attempt my own tease, knowing the knickers will help. I take each of the ribbons keeping my knickers together at the side and play the thick black fabric between the tips of my fingers. Slowly I begin to pull, millimetre by millimetre, until they unravel. The material unknots and the two triangles of black satin fall from my body.

"Leave the rest on, Isabel."

I hear the edge in his voice. Those few words ignite my desire and send a sexy shiver through my body, giving me the reassurance that I'm desperately craving. *Thank you. I love my heels!* They give me some of the inner confidence of a sexy vixen. Without them, the plain girl I am takes centre stage.

I remain standing, unsure of what to do next. I focus on breathing. *In and out. In and out.* He's trying to get me comfortable with being naked in front of him, and I'm fighting the urge to cover myself every second. I am not going to break. I want to please him. His words guide my body into a place of comfort. Even if my mind isn't there with it.

"You are an amazingly alluring creature, Isabel. Exquisite. I could admire you for hours, but for now I would like you to put this on." He pulls a folded piece of black material out of his pocket. I reach out to meet his hand and recognise the silk blindfold he used on me the last time I was here. I unfold it and place it over my eyes, seeking comfort in the darkness. I tie it behind my head and drop my arms by my sides.

"Now, don't move unless I tell you to. Relax and listen to your body. If you're uncomfortable at any point—and I mean it—just tell me and I'll stop."

My body is already answering him. I have that ache in the pit of my stomach. My pussy has already been teased and wants more, but I stand still and wait for his instruction. The muffled sounds of him moving around me don't help my restlessness. Not knowing what he's doing adds to my apprehension. Suddenly I feel a hand around my ankle and fingers at my shoe strap.

"Lift your foot." I do as I'm told and he follows suit on the other leg, removing my shoes. His hands linger on my anklet.

"I need to take your anklet off, but I'll put it back on after I peel you out of your thigh highs." The sound of those words while Seb's hands are wrapped around my ankle sends my head reeling. He runs both hands up my right leg, to the top of the thigh high, and slides his thumbs underneath the lace trim. Keeping to his word, he peels it down the top of my thigh, skimming his fingers over my skin as he trails the material to my foot. I lift it again, unstable from the sensations he is creating in me. He repeats the leisurely seduction on my left leg. It is beyond erotic and I am ready to open my thighs to him. He seems to burn a trail on my skin with his touch, and I can feel myself growing wet.

Before his hands leave me, he refastens the anklet, confirming I will do anything he asks of me tonight.

"Now kneel."

The power he holds over me is incredible. I moan in my submission to his command. I can't help it. His lips are nearly on my neck and I want so much more of him. Gently lowering myself, I press into my knees and try to find a comfortable position. My mind churns with the possibilities ahead of me. *More pleasure, or perhaps a little pain? Both?* All I can do is wait. Then I feel it. A cool but soft piece of material—firm material—drags gently and slowly down my spine, and it feels amazing. There is enough pressure to keep it from tickling but it's gentle enough not to hurt. *What is that? Leather. It's leather. What's he going to use on me?* I try to silence my racing thoughts and succumb to the feelings Sebastian draws from me. My imagination is my worst enemy. Tension builds in my body and between my legs.

Seb continues to draw patterns over my skin with the leather, around my side, over my stomach and between my breasts. The leather leaves my skin for a second before it slaps down on my breast and catches my nipple.

"Ahhh!" I gasp in surprise at the sting and how it immediately connects to my pussy. A flood of desire seeps out of me.

"I asked you the other night why you didn't want to sleep with Phil, and you ran away from the question. You will answer me now, Isabel." His voice is hard and doesn't waver. He is in complete control of me. Kneeling for him, blindfolded, I want to answer. But do I even know the answer? As I try to gather my thoughts, the leather returns to my skin, giving me little nips and flicks all over my chest, back and thighs. *I can't concentrate on thinking when you're doing that to me. It feels too good.*

"I'm waiting, Isabel, and I don't like to be kept waiting." A strike flashes my skin with pain before it simmers. My bottom stings at a hard smack as residual heat licks up my spine.

"I... I didn't want to." I sigh, confused as to what my body is feeling and what my head is trying to pull together.

"I know that already, Isabel. Why didn't you want to? He's your husband."

"I know he's my husband, Sebastian. You don't need to remind me." I can't keep the hurt out of my voice. My body is willing me to stay still, but I'm desperate to turn and face him.

"So why, Isabel?"

"Because... he doesn't satisfy me."

"Why not, Isabel? Don't hold back from me. That's an order."

Why did you have to say that? You know I want to obey you, but I don't really know. Please!

"He doesn't give me more. I'm just a means to get off. That's not enough. I want to feel important, cared for..."

"I knew that before we even started this. That is why I offered to help introduce you to this lifestyle, safely." *Smack.* "Now tell me why, or I will spank you until you do."

Please, come on, Izzy. Just... get it out. Say whatever comes into your head. Focus on that and not your pussy, or his voice, his commands. You want this. You want him.

"With Phil, I feel nothing but resentment. He treats me as if I'm at his beck-and-call. Used and thrown aside until he wants to get off again. I can't accept that anymore. When I'm with you, you take care of me, you see me. You see all of me, including my sexual needs. You instinctively know how I'll react, and you guide me to a pleasure I've never know before." My thoughts finally break through, suddenly surfacing as coherent words. "I want to put my trust in you, experience where you can take me. I won't let Phil take what he wants from me anymore. My body, my feelings are mine to give, and I want to give them to you. I want to feel a connection—the connection that we have. I don't think I can go back to the life I lived before I met you." I exhale and hang my head, almost ashamed of my admission. I've just admitted that I don't want my husband.

"Good girl. Now, run your hand over your nipples. Feel how hard they are, how aroused you are." Seb's words are clinical, and it chills me. I'm still reeling from my admission and take a few moments to follow his instruction. He doesn't seem concerned at all, more as if he expected it. "Isabel."

"Yes," I squeak.

"You're not following my instruction. You have your anklet on."

"I'm sorry. I'm just…"

"Take a breath and stop thinking about what you just told me. We'll have time for that later. Right now…" He punctuates his words with a hard tug on my hair and pulls my head back. "I want you to do exactly as I tell you. Understand?" He whispers the last word into my ear and I shudder all over, my body completely attuned to his voice.

He repeats the first set of instructions, and this time I follow them. He's right. In response to the authority in his voice, I don't have to think. I respond and although it's my own hands on my body, they are there at Seb's instruction.

"Run your hands down your body and slide your finger past your clit to see how wet you are. You're turned on, Isabel. Your body wants this. You want this. You need this and you shouldn't feel ashamed of it. It's a beautiful thing to behold—a fragile yet strong woman kneeling before me. I can see the fight in you, your unsureness of what your body is telling you it needs. Feel yourself, Isabel." Strong fingers slip between mine and move my hand to my pussy, holding my hand to my skin. His body slides behind me and his arms encircle me. He moves my hands, positioning me—his own marionette. My hands move to his command, exploring every inch of my body.

"Your body is so responsive. Feel, Isabel, and don't let any preconceived ideas of how you 'should' behave get in the way of what you want." His words soothe and calm my fears as they sink into my soul, but I desperately want him to touch me rather than guide me.

"Sebastian?" His name is my plea, and I hope he'll understand what I'm asking. Seb has turned my world upside down, and after my confession I need his strength and guidance more than ever. I need to feel that the trust I am putting in him is founded.

"Spread your legs and put your hands on the floor."

Oh yes, thank you!

The rustle of clothes tells me he's undressing. It's followed by the rip of a packet, and a moment later he returns and runs a hand down my back. My scalp prickles deliciously as he pulls my hair. I open my mouth in response and tilt my head. The head of his hard cock nudges at the entrance to my sex and his arm wraps around me, his finger seeking my clit. I moan at the joint assault on my throbbing flesh. He slides his cock over my creamy lips before he pushes slowly inside me. From this position I'm completely open to him, and he slides in deep—both physically and mentally.

He keeps one hand around my waist, his talented finger holding my clit captive. He grips my hip and thrusts into me. He slowly pulls out, balancing right on the edge of me before he slams back in. The jolt through my body adds to the sensation of being thoroughly taken. I release the tension I've been holding through my limbs and relax under his pleasure. I submit all of myself to him. He pushes deeper and harder each time he enters me. My arms are tiring, but I can't drop to the floor. He's going to force my orgasm. My sex is already oversensitive. My muscles tighten at the slide of his cock in my juices.

With his next thrust, the walls of my pussy spasm. My body pulses as the awareness of my impending climax sweeps my entire body. My cheeks flush, my breath labours, and my fingers dig into the rug. I let out a deep, throaty cry as he finally tips me over that blissful edge.

"Yeeesss." Even after I'm spent, he continues his claim on my body, preventing me from relaxing completely after coming so hard. His body slaps against my behind with each jolt forward and nerves dance down my spine. I'm not sure I can keep still as he's bucking against me. His fingers grip my hips, ruthless in his hold of me.

"Yes. There... Fuck." His curse leaves his lips in a delicious growl, followed by a rumbling moan as he presses into me before he stills. My arms are dead weights, stiff and tired from being stretched out, and my knees are raw. After what feels like a lifetime, he pulls out of me and runs his hands up from my hips and back to my shoulders. His arms slide around me and he gently pulls me up and back into him until I'm sitting in his lap. He unties my blindfold and leans around to kiss the side of my face.

"Good?" he asks, his voice low and husky.

"Hmmm," is all I manage. He's literally drained the life out of me, and I am exhausted.

"Well, if it was as enjoyable for you as it was for me, I'll take the 'hmmm' as a yes. Come on. I want you in my bed."

My heart flutters at his words, but I don't think about the meaning they could hold.

Seb carries me to his room and lays me on the bed. I turn to curl up, content with closing my eyes and breathing in his smell, but he has other plans.

"Oh no you don't. I'm not done with you yet." His stern, masculine voice cuts through the sleep invading my mind. I crack open my eyes to be greeted with his glorious, naked body before me. I can only look and admire. I think it's the first time I've seen him completely naked, and I certainly enjoy the view. His thighs look hard, beautifully carved muscles covering his body. His shoulders are wide and he has a broad chest speckled with hair that leads down—in that lovely v shape—to his waist. He's distracting and I want to run my hands all over him. "You, young lady, have been naughty this week." His wicked grin stretches across his face and his eyes twinkle at me. "And naughty girls need to be punished."

I'm now fully awake and my sex is already throbbing at his words.

"Hands above your head, Isabel." He leans over me and captures my mouth with his. His hands force my arms straighter and run along every muscle in my arms. He quickly leans across the bed and fastens my hands together with a length of thin silk and then to the headboard. He leans back once his work is done and looks as if he's admiring the view. "Very nice. Now, as you couldn't make yourself come every day last week, I'm going to give you an extra lesson. But as I've tied your hands, you won't be able to move or help yourself. Understand?"

I look up into his face and nod.

"Good girl. And just so we're clear, you won't be making yourself come for the next week. That will be your punishment. And I expect you to follow it through this time, Isabel. It gives me great pleasure to see you obey my wishes."

Crap! This is going to be torture. I whimper in response as he lies down next to me and runs soft kisses over my jaw and down my neck. It's been less than ten minutes since he fucked a shattering orgasm out of me, yet I can feel myself getting hot. My body warms to his touch and desire washes over my skin, pooling between my legs. *How is he this good? Experience, lots of experience.* I frown at where my dark thoughts take me.

"Ow!" I gasp as Seb pinches one of my nipples between his teeth.

"Stay with me, Isabel. In this moment." His voice centres me, while his fingers and lips continue their assault across my skin.

"Now, this week, you're not allowed to do this, Isabel," he whispers in my ear as his fingers trail down over my pubic mound and stroke my soft lips. "And you can't do this." He presses one finger down onto my clit and circles it before he runs the very tip of his finger farther down to feel how wet my pussy is. "And you definitely can't do this."

I cry out as he thrusts two fingers into me and I pull on my restraints in response.

"Oh, baby, you're so wet for me, so ready. And you will deny yourself all week. Do. You. Under. Stand. Me?" He punctuates each syllable with a thrust of his fingers, deeper and harder every time. Then he stops and curls them around to rub my g-spot, sending me free falling into another orgasm.

"Fuck, Isabel, you're beautiful when you come for me." My eyes are closed and I struggle to bring my breathing back under control when he pushes my knees up towards my chest. "I'm going to take you hard and fast, Isabel. Don't come this time. I want you frustrated." He pauses to roll on a condom before pushing inside me. I was anticipating a violent thrust, but he takes his time until he's sheathed inside my drenched pussy. My respite is short-lived, though, as he pulls back and slams into me.

I moan each time he drives back into me, and my body takes over. It feels so deep like this, but with every stroke he brings me closer, teasing me and riding me higher to my climax. I can already feel the tensing of my stomach muscles and my sex, and I can't do anything to still the sensation.

"No you don't, Isabel. Look at me. Breathe. Do not come." He growls out his command.

I try hard to concentrate on his face, his eyes—now darker and brooding. I don't think about what he's doing. I want to give him this, to do as he wants. The tension is etched on his face and

I pray that he's close. I clench my jaw, biting back the release that I'm scared will explode in a matter of strokes. With my arms bound, I can't do anything but accept. Pumping hard, he crashes into me for a last time, finding his own release before he stills, leaving me perilously close to the edge.

I whimper and gasp as he quickly pulls out of me.

"Good girl," he murmurs against my lips as he consoles me with a kiss.

I ache. All over. I'm a ball of frustration. I'm desperate for him to touch me and give me my release. I try to squeeze my legs together in an attempt to find some relief.

"Oh no you don't, Isabel." Seb strides back into the bedroom. He pulls my hands free and tugs me towards him. He holds my face in his hands and looks deep into my eyes. I feel more vulnerable than I did when I was tied up. "No. You won't make yourself come this week. Understand?" His tone gives no room for negotiation, clearly commanding me to obey, and although I want to come—desperately—I also feel soothed that he is giving me this to do. Even though I'm not sure about it, I want to do as he says. I nod my head in acceptance. "Okay then. Come." He gently pulls me through his bedroom and out into the hall, unconcerned at my nakedness.

As we pass, my eyes automatically lock onto the photographs in the hall. *I hate them.* Are these photos of Seb's previous conquests? *Is this what I am? A conquest?* How can I ask that? Until I'm divorced I have no right to become possessive or jealous. *But I am.*

My good—no, fantastic—mood from a few moments ago sours fast, but Seb hasn't noticed. He squeezes my hand a little tighter and continues to walk towards my room. He leads me in, but doesn't cross inside. I think it may be some unspoken rule that he has about my space after we've been together. But I want to stay with Seb and delight in his loveliness, not sit alone in my beautiful room.

"What's wrong, Isabel?" Seb hasn't missed my mood change after all.

"Nothing." Not looking at him, I walk over to find the robe hanging in the wardrobe. My nakedness is suddenly very uncomfortable.

"Isabel, you need to talk to me and tell me how you feel. This won't work if you aren't honest with me. I understand that you find it hard to express your feelings, but you need to work harder at it."

Won't work. I spin around and look at him standing in the doorway. "No, really, I'm fine. I'm just tired. You kinda wore me out." I try to sound a little sassy in my response.

"If you're simply telling me what you think I want to hear then we will have to rethink things pretty damn quick."

"No, no. I go into my head quite often. I'm alright. I just checked out a little."

"Okay, but you know I like to check on you. This is new to you, and you need to tell me if I go too far. Look at me, Isabel. Do you understand?"

"Yes, Sebastian." I'm being honest in my response. I wanted and enjoyed everything he did to my body and can't wait until we are together again. It's my selfish insecurities that are putting my mood off.

Seb leaves me in my room, but I don't have the energy to get changed yet. I cuddle up on the bed for a moment. The changing directions of my emotions are taking their toll on me. On so many levels, I'm not dealing with them. My actions, however, are clear. I am sitting in Seb's apartment after he fucked me senseless and fulfilled my innermost desires. I am taking something that I want for a change, rather than being the invisible wife to a man who clearly doesn't love me. That thought resonates around my head for a few moments before I get up from the bed.

Seb is sitting in his chair again as I enter the lounge. I move to join him, kneeling down by his feet like the other night.

He seemed to like this last time, and I liked it when he was stroking my hair.

"There you are. All okay?"

"Sure, just tired. Thank you." Seb hands me a glass of what I think is sparkling water as I get comfy, and sure enough, he starts to stroke my hair.

"Did you have any specific expectations before we started this? About what 'more' meant for you?" His question catches me off guard and I have to muddle my way through the fog of feelings to find what they were before Seb.

"Well, I knew I wanted to give up control, to be bound and not have to initiate or direct the sex. I didn't want to be responsible for giving myself an orgasm. But I wanted the fantasy as well. The passion and desire, the intimacy."

"Nothing more than that?"

"No, not really. Is that wrong?"

"Oh no, sweetheart. I wanted to check in with you. I've been testing how much of the BDSM element you crave. Introducing them and giving you first-hand experience. I'm going to continue to do that." The fact that he wants to keep seeing me eases my mind and I relax a little more. It's easy expressing myself like this, at his feet. I'm very happy to sit by him. A tiny nagging thought is burrowing into my mind, though. *What are Seb's expectations?*

"Can I ask you a question?"

"You may."

"Do you have any expectations of this? Of me?" With my heart in my mouth, I wait for his answer, clinging to his words from a moment ago.

"In truth, that really depends on you."

"I don't understand." *Why can't he ever answer me straight?*

"No, I don't suppose you do. I've told you that I saw something special in you, Izzy. Well, you've proved my initial assumption of you right. You are wonderfully submissive and probably haven't realised that until very recently. Having said that, I've put myself in a compromising position by engaging in these activities with a married woman. I'm not proud of that, yet I'm not prepared to give you up. After talking to you and getting to know you, I simply couldn't turn my back on you knowing how easily I could help you find the sort of sexual experience you were seeking."

This is the first time I've gotten a good sense of how Seb is feeling about our situation. I'm both moved by and fearful of his words. The consequences of my actions are never far away.

"How did you know?"

"Know what?"

"That this is what I wanted? That I was... submissive?" I blush, acknowledging Seb's description of me.

"Lots of things, really. Initially our mutual online interests, what you told me about your relationship. Plus a few things you're probably not aware of."

I hear the smile in his voice at the last point, and I am pleased I can lighten his mood. I can only guess at the wealth of knowledge he has to be so adept at deciphering and reading people. I think of the photographs in the hall and again wonder whether they are of women he's been with.

"Izzy, I'm going to be in Manchester on Thursday and Friday this week, so I don't think I'll be able to see you again until next Saturday." His tone and manner have returned to business, the warmth in his voice from a moment ago now in shadow. He speaks to me with no sign of disappointment. I try to think about my week ahead and realise I'm in Liverpool Thursday night for an early-morning training session on Friday. "That's okay. I'll be in Liverpool on Thursday evening anyway."

Seb's hand stills in my hair for a moment before he continues.

"Well, that's fortunate. Maybe we can make the best of our situations. Would you meet me in Manchester?"

Really?

"Yes," I respond before I realise I've opened my mouth. I turn around and grin at him before I climb into his lap to kiss his soft lips. I'm giddy with excitement. He wants to see me even though we're both away. My unsettled nerves are forgotten in his embrace. My mouth closes over his lips, and he circles his hands around my waist to pull me in deeper until I'm as close as I can be. "Thank you," I whisper to him. He pulls back slightly so he can look down at my face.

"What for?"

"More." My answer is as simple as it can be.

His brow furrows, as if he doesn't quite follow my answer. "More?"

"Yes. All of this, all of you. I don't think I've thanked you. It's... I'm... I—"

"Shhh, Izzy. It's my complete pleasure. Believe me." He gives me his wickedly sexy smile. I think I do.

Fourteen

Since I started seeing Seb on Friday evenings, we haven't been out casually for coffee or a drink at the bar. Although I love the time we spend together, I also miss the easy friendship we had built. I wanted the friendship as much as the intensity we shared when we were together as lovers. I feel consumed by Seb, but in a very good way. I hope that Seb feels something towards me, too. Even if he doesn't say it, he often alludes to strong feelings for me. *Or am I just seeing things again?*

We haven't discussed the details of meeting at his hotel, just that we will. And surprisingly, I haven't heard from him since I left on Friday night, apart from the customary text to check I was home safely and feeling okay.

My week is going to be fairly quiet with sessions, but I do need to ensure I'm prepared for Friday. The presentation I am delivering is new content on social media benefiting SEO and managing return on investment. I've incorporated some basic SEO slides from a colleague.

Despite my attempts to keep focused on work, I want to see whether Seb and I still have that spark outside of the bedroom.

I miss him as a friend almost as much as I miss his touch. A part of me is scared I will lose both.

I pull out my phone and text Seb.

> How would you like to brighten my Tuesday and meet me for coffee at lunchtime? Izzy x

I set it back on my desk, sit back in my chair and stare at it. *God, what is happening to me?* I'm nervous and panicky about his response. *Will he respond?* Or does Seb only want to see me for sex? No, Seb is kind and considerate, and above all else, he is my friend.

But, as they do so often, my insecurities win. I convince myself that it's just part of Seb's nature, to explore domination and submission. He said that he saw something in me and wanted to see if he could help me. When he becomes bored, he'll simply stop. He'll be gone from my life as easily as he came into it and I'll be left with only the knowledge of what could be.

I stare at the clock on my computer and check to see whether it's still functioning. *How long does it take to answer a text?* He always answers my texts. I see the phone light up and buzz, and I nearly jump out of my chair to reach it.

> I could meet you briefly. I have a meeting at 2:30. The usual place at 1. S

My heart hammers in my chest at the prospect of meeting him, but the tone of his text has made me nervous. It sounds brisk. I shake my head and decide that I'm reading too much into everything and I need to trust Seb. I put my phone away after a quick confirmation and busy myself with preparation for work.

Seb waits for me with two lattes in front of him on a small table. I pause. He turns around and gives me his sexy smile and I find my feet again. Seeing him immediately stirs feelings deep in my stomach, and I subtly clench my thighs as I sit down. I thought I was doing well with my homework this week, but realise that meeting Seb might spark my arousal.

"Hi," I whisper.

"Hi, it was nice to hear from you. I was meaning to contact you about the plans for Thursday night."

"Oh, okay. Well, that's sort of why I thought we could meet."

"Sort of? Come on, Izzy. That was a rubbish lie."

Oh, shit. He gives me a reassuring smile, but it doesn't touch his eyes.

"Sorry." I look down and fiddle with my hands in my lap. "Can we sort the plans first, though?" I steer the conversation in a safe direction and try to relax. I'm feeling self-conscious. I fidget in my chair and try to focus on talking with him, but the ache between my legs distracts me.

Seb hands me a piece of paper and I reach to take it. As I do, he glides his other hand to the pulse point on my wrist. My breathing hitches with that one touch.

"These are the instructions for Thursday. It tells you where I'm staying, what train to get, and I've given you a few options for your return journey."

"Thank you." I smile at him and wait, not really sure of what else to say.

"What else did you want to talk about, Izzy?" He cocks his head to the side with his sexy smile still on his face. His stubble is maybe a little longer than usual and his eyes are a darker blue. He is always observant and seems to be able to read everything I'm thinking, while I struggle to read anything from him. I take a breath and lean forward to pick up my coffee. I hold it in front of me as a makeshift shield.

Why am I so nervous? Come on, Izzy. He's seen you naked.

"I just wanted to check that things between us were okay. I mean, we haven't seen a lot of each other... I mean, we haven't spent... Um... we haven't gone out socially together for a little while." I give my tongue a rest.

"You mean since 'more'?"

"Well, yes." I don't say anything else, waiting to see whether he'll take the lead.

"And you were worried because?"

"I'm not worried. I wanted to check that we could still be friends, you know, do this." I gesture to the coffee in my hand and take a sip. He doesn't answer straightaway, and I immediately feel a wave of dread replace my lust.

"Do you still want this, Izzy? Being friends outside of what I'm showing you? Because that may not be as easy as it seems."

I don't know how to respond for a moment. It seems for once my internal paranoia was warranted.

"Oh, of course. Okay." I blush and realise that perhaps this was all too good to be true.

"I offered to show you, Izzy, because you needed someone who would take this path with you safely. To support and guide you. I still want to do that. I will show you what you clearly want and need, but please think about everything else. You are married, and if I'm honest, I thought when you discovered how submitting to a man turned you on, it would help your marriage. I thought you would take the experiences you and I have had home, to Phil, and pursue a new relationship with your husband."

I'm floored. I don't say anything, but stare at his face. His beautiful face. Am I really asking more of him still? To not only meet my sexual fantasies, but keep the easy companionship we had as well? I think back, and there was always an underlying current between us. A hidden temptation and desire that provided the energy between us. That is definitely still there. Would I be able to cope with the very real physical temptation of Seb if we were to return to friends? I don't say anything.

"Izzy, I will have coffee with you, have drinks with you and be a friend to you. But think about what that means, okay? Think about why you told me about your desires, your marriage, what Phil did to you." Taking a sip of his coffee breaks the damning words from his lips.

"Don't you want to be friends?" My desperation rings clear in my ears, even through the quiver in my voice.

"Izzy, this is about you. I've shown you the rules I play by and you've followed. But how far that goes is your choice. This relationship between us started in order to give you the experience of BDSM—the submission you've craved. You're married and that doesn't look to be changing. Don't do something that you can't undo."

"What's that supposed to mean? I've already let you fuck me."

Cold, blue spheres lock on to me and hold my stare. Usually his eyes are sexy and dangerous. Or frustratingly clear. These eyes are laced with a disapproval I don't want to see again. I shrink under his gaze, and the slow shake of his head confirms that he is disappointed in me.

"Think about what I said, Izzy, and I'll see you Thursday. Unless you change your mind." With that, he stands and walks away, leaving me alone and confused.

I sit and mull over his words, trying to understand what he was saying to me, without actually telling me. He wants me to come to my own conclusion. *But about what?* My eyes burn as tears threaten, the emotions bubbling away. I don't understand what Seb's problem is with being friends. That's what we were before. Silent tears escape my eyes and stream down my face. *Why are you pushing me away, Seb?* No. He wouldn't do that. Not after everything. He said he would be there for me.

I dash the teary streaks from my face and leave the bar. I set out to ensure I could keep Seb's friendship and I'm pretty sure I've ruined it. The conversation plays in my mind, but I keep coming back to his question about my marriage. Has being with Seb helped my marriage? The honest answer is no. In reality, being with Seb has shown me everything that is missing from it. And that goes much further than the simple lack of sex. I want a connection—a companion—and I don't have it with Phil. *Shit!* As I stop in the middle of the pavement, realisation dawns.

I pull out my phone and search the contacts for Seb's number and press call. It rings but goes to voicemail. At the sound of the beep, I squeeze my eyes shut and open my mouth.

"I'm so sorry, Seb. Truly, I am. I asked you for a relationship. Not just sex, not just guiding me into what could have been a scary world of submission and dominance. I understand wanting friendship as well blurs the lines that we've already crossed, even further. I've shattered my marriage vows." I pause, not wanting to speak with Seb's voicemail. "I still want to see you on Thursday. I still want... you. Thank you."

I end the call in a rush and stuff my phone back into my bag. Seb is, in a strange way, trying to protect me. He's revealing the real me, the one who is hidden behind years of disappointment, neglect, and uncertainty. Buried under a marriage I don't want to be in any longer. He is helping to give me the perspective to make my decision—the one I should have made a long time ago—to leave Phil.

My heart swells as I try to take it all in. I'm on dangerous ground, in over my head. I've bitten off more than I can chew. It doesn't matter which cliché I use. It all boils down to the same. I want Sebastian—not Phil. *So much for keeping emotions at bay!*

* * *

Jess looks at me impatiently. "Please spit it out, Izzy. I know when you want to tell me something. Is it Phil?"

I hug a pillow to my chest and glance at Jess curled on the opposite end of my sofa. "Yes and no. Okay, well..." I take a deep breath and mentally cross my fingers. "You know the guy I met at the bar, well, I'm afraid I have feelings for him." I pause. "I didn't plan this, not to actually have proper feelings anyway. I wanted to feel again. I wanted an emotional connection with a man. I wanted to be adored and cared for." Jess is smiling at me as if I've just told her some big happy news. "Why are you smiling at me?"

"Because you deserve to be happy and you finally sound like you've realised that means moving on from Phil. So, you're sleeping with this guy?"

"Yes. Yes, I am. I'm sorry, I know how you feel about cheating, but..." I let the admission hang in the air, hoping that Jess can somehow understand or at least try to see where I am in all of this. "He's helping me to... um, he's helping me explore... you know, sexually."

Jess raises her eyebrows. "What? You mean like that *50 Shades* book?"

I can feel my cheeks turn scarlet. "Um... yeah... kinda like that. But I'm scared now it's become something more than simply physical. I have feelings for him, beyond being a friend or caring about him. I don't know what to do for the best. I'm scared." My head drops to my hands in defeat. Jess scoots closer to me on the sofa and wraps me up in a motherly hug.

"I don't know what to say, Izzy. I think you need to work out who you want in your life. You don't seem to accept the idea of divorcing Phil, yet you're having an affair. What does that tell you?"

"It's not an affair. It's just..." *God, I don't even know how to finish that. It is an affair.* My feelings are involved now.

"It's what, Iz? You know, I've seen you almost 'check out' on life over the last year. You are a shell of who you were, and it's because of Phil. But that doesn't mean I agree with you on this. You are having an affair and you need to admit that. An affair won't magically fix your marriage, and you know what, I hope it doesn't. You need to do what's right for you, and I doubt that includes remaining with Phil."

I'm having an affair. An affair. The word rings about my head and I feel the full weight of its meaning right through to my heart.

"Look, Iz. I know you're hurting. I can see it and I'm here for you, but sort your marriage out first and then see where your relationship with this other guy goes, okay?"

I'm glad that Jess can't see my face at the moment. The floodgates have opened. She scoots along the sofa to me and holds me as I weep. I'm ever grateful for her, my rock. After a long time, Jess releases me and gathers up her things. "Think about what I've said, Izzy. You're hurting and I want to help, but I don't want you to get hurt more than you already have." Jess's words sound like a warning. She's only doing this for my own good, but after everything else, I need to feel some support. Her tough love approach is too tough at the moment.

She leaves, and I feel worse for telling her. I needed her to understand. I can't leave things between us unresolved like this.

> I'm sorry I sprang all of this on you but I feel lost. Seb seems to be the only one who makes sense at the moment. Please try to see it from my point of view. Izzy

> OK, Izzy, but regardless you need to sort this mess out. I'm sure Seb's not happy with playing around. If he's the kind of guy you say he is, he deserves better and so do you.

> I know. I just don't know how to start things with Phil. Izzy

> You need to tell him, Izzy. From what you've said, I think the sex stuff was just the final straw.
>
> I'm scared. Izzy
>
> I know, hun. Be brave. I'm right here.

A few hours later, I'm in a familiar position, curled up in bed, running everything from the past few days through my head and waiting for Phil to come home. My mind is a jumble of conflicting emotions, guilt and excitement, sorrow and pleasure. Finally, I slip into a restless sleep, alone, fighting with my emotions and my heartache.

I wake with the ringing of my alarm. I reach across to silence the blaring noise and slowly draw myself out of the covers. I'm alone in bed. Phil didn't come home. We really do need to try to sort things out for once and all. A text message is waiting for me, sent sometime in the middle of the night.

> Sorry, Iz, crashing at Jackson's. See you tomorrow night.

I try to call his phone but I'm sent straight to voicemail, so I look for Jackson's number instead.

"Hello." A groggy male voice answers and I'm not sure I even recognise it as Jackson.

"Hi, Jackson. Sorry it's early. Can you grab Phil for me? I can't get him on his phone." There is a pause for a few moments and as I'm about to check he hasn't fallen asleep on me, he pipes up.

"Phil? Why... oh... yeah, hey, Izzy. I think he left already. Sorry."

"Okay, um, thanks. If you see him, will you tell him I'm looking for him?"

I take a deep breath and hang up. Jackson lied. *How stupid can I be?* I know that Phil's having an affair, and has been for far longer than I have. A daunting feeling surfaces within me every time I think about confronting Phil. It's taken root in my stomach and makes me restless and anxious. My concentration is shot.

I need to confront Phil. It's what I should have done a long time ago.

* * *

Phil is home when I return from work. I'm not going into the office tomorrow, so I have an extra bag full of resources needed for the training session on Friday.

"Hey, you." Phil greets me in the hall, all pleasantness and smiles. That isn't going to work.

"Hey, I think we need to talk, okay?" He looks a little anxious, and suddenly I'm scared. He pulls me into the front room almost before I can dump my bags down, and sits me on the sofa.

"Look, Iz, I know I've been a little distant recently. I think maybe all this stuff has been building up and I've not been dealing with it well. I'm sorry."

I don't reply straightaway, confused as to why Phil is acting like this. I sit there, looking at my hands and biting my lip.

"Say something, Iz. I'm sorry for a lot of stuff, and we've got a lot to sort out between us, but I love you."

"You love me?" I am shocked at how surprised my voice sounds.

"Of course I love you. I'm your husband." The temper he's holding in rings loud and clear in his response. Perhaps I've dented his ego.

"Where were you last night?" I murmur and hold my breath. This has been coming for a while and I need to brave it now, before I lose my nerve. I want us to be honest with each other for once.

"I was with Jackson. I crashed last minute, okay? I'm sorry. It's just I've not been good dealing with you recently. You know, since…" We both know he's referring to the night I asked him to tie me up.

"You can say it, Phil. I won't bite." My voice betrays my words as I snap them out, immediately defensive at where I can see this leading.

"Iz, you're the one who's changed everything with the whole kink thing—"

I cut him off before he can continue.

"No, Phil. You were missing from this relationship long before I even suggested the sex. Were you even at Jackson's last night?" The thought of him trying to put the blame on me about where we are in our relationship suddenly brings my anger to the forefront. *No. We are in this together.*

"Of course I was! Why would you question that?" His overreaction screams of a guilty conscience. "You're the one who wanted me to hit you, Izzy. Not me. Things were fine before."

"I don't believe you. I called, you weren't there, and if you think this all started with me, we've got even more problems, Phil." I will myself on. I will not back down on this now. *Stay strong. Don't break. Don't break.*

"So we're fighting again. Shit, Iz… I don't know what to do, how to fix whatever has happened. Will you try to help out or what?"

"Help out, after how you've treated me? Give me one reason why. You won't even tell me the truth." I look up at him and shake, trying to hold myself together, but I'm well past that and if I have to bottle it up any longer, I fear I may explode. Phil is pressing all my buttons tonight, and not in a good way.

"So you're still angry I wouldn't hit you. Great."

"Ask yourself if you really think everything was okay with us before I asked you to tie me up and spank me. If you can look me in the eye and tell me yes, then we can talk about what happened in the bedroom, okay?"

I hold my nerve, keeping my eyes locked onto his, and watch. Frustration and anger cross his face and I can tell this wasn't the reaction he was hoping he'd get. *I will not be ignored any longer.*

"You know what, forget it. I can't talk to you when you're not going to listen."

"No, you're not going to walk over me this time. We aren't working, Phil!" He turns around and storms out of the living room. I wait for the door to slam. But it doesn't.

"You can't just run away and hope I won't fight anymore, Phil."

The silent response suggests he hopes just that.

I can't sleep. It's been a pretty rough couple of days. It's been an intense few weeks—the most intense of my life. Seb has been the driving force behind it. He's brought into perspective exactly what's missing from my marriage, both on a physical level and an emotional one. He's shown me that men can be supportive and comforting as well as strong, domineering, and sexy as hell. I've grown as a result of his influence, even if it's just enough to stand up for myself. And I care for him. I feel we share an emotional bond.

My mind is clouded with doubt and worry. *Guilt.* I can't escape it. My phone buzzes and I look for it in the gloom of the bedroom.

> Sorry it's late but I wanted to check that you're okay. I'm looking forward to seeing you tomorrow night. S

> I've had better days. I'll see you tomorrow. Izzy

> Do you want to talk about it? S

There he goes again!

> Maybe not over text. Phil and I had a fight, but he's left now. I need to sleep. I'm sure tomorrow is going to be a busy day. Izzy

> Are you sure you're OK? S

> Yes, thank you. Izzy

> I'll leave you to your bed. You'll need to be well rested. Goodnight. Sweet dreams. S

My skin prickles at reading his words and the restlessness that I've been feeling suddenly switches into the more familiar feeling of frustration. God, I must be a horrible person. Cheating on my husband, fighting with him, and then being turned on after a simple text exchange from the man I'm sleeping with.

> Goodnight. Izzy

I take Seb's advice and will my eyes to close. I'm tired and I should be asleep already, but my subconscious decides to weigh in on my warring thoughts. I toss and turn all night.

I wake tired, as if I didn't even bother to go to bed, but that restless frustration hasn't dissipated. I pull my body out of bed, noting that Phil still isn't present, and head for the shower.

The warmth reignites my body and helps bring me to life as I go about my usual routine. But as the soap washes away, my right hand follows the flow of bubbles and comes to rest at the apex of my legs. Seb has told me not to touch myself or make myself come, but I feel that a release is what my body has been craving.

Seb put these delicious images of what he can do to me into my mind, and I want to act on them. Before Seb, it had been months since I played with myself. Now, with my homework and the memories of being with Seb, I can't quiet the simmer of arousal through my body. Giving myself the attention and pleasure of these orgasms is something I need. With all of the emotional turmoil, I need to find a moment of relief. I'm torn between what my body wants and obeying Seb. *Obeying—where did that come from?* I want to please him, to be obedient, give back in a small way for all he's giving to me.

Even as I think those thoughts, my hand seeks out and explores. My fingers take on a life of their own and search for my clit. I touch the tight, fleshy bud and circle it, teasing it. I close my eyes to think of Seb and picture his fingers touching me, his hand restraining me, pushing me down against the kitchen bar again. His voice is in my head, his breath in my ear, and I shudder as my body tenses at the imminent release I'm seeking. Tighter and harder I rub until I crash against that sweet spot.

I'm warm from the blood racing in my veins and the water washing away the juices from my fingers. As I calm my body, my thoughts turn to Seb and how disappointed he will be in me. Once more, I've failed.

Fifteen

Seb asked me to text him as the train was leaving Macclesfield.

> Train on time, due in at 6:39. I really can't wait to see you again. Let me know where to find you. Izzy x

My body and mind urge the train to speed along the tracks and I want to know where to meet him. *Why on earth is he being so secretive about his hotel?* The envelope he gave me has only limited details, and my own curiosity is getting the better of me. At 6:30, he finally texts back.

> Looking forward to seeing you again, too. Turn left when you exit the platform, go down the escalators and take a taxi to the Hilton Hotel. I'll be waiting in the lobby bar for you. Drop your case with the concierge and join me at the bar. I'll have a G&T waiting for you. S

Never one to disappoint with the exact details of what I have to do, Seb is controlling me even now. Even down to what I'll be drinking. *I love it!* Now that my curiosity has been satisfied, I relax. In preparation for this evening, I selected thigh highs instead of tights. A just above the knee pencil skirt and my favourite confidence-boosting heels—that I can still walk in—complete what I'm wearing. They are dark grey court shoes but have a good four-inch heel. The sexy, professional Izzy is going to meet Seb at the bar and try to avoid telling him about her failure with his homework.

The taxi darts through the streets of Manchester, and after a short while I ask how far away this hotel is.

"Oh, about another ten minutes, love. It's that glass tower building there."

I crouch down in the back of the cab to peer out of the window. A tall glass tower juts up in the near distance with a somewhat precarious looking overhang halfway up. Sleek, modern, and different. Very Seb. I can feel the excitement in my stomach as we draw closer to my destination.

I cannot wait to see Seb again and wonder what he has in store for our brief evening liaison. I have checked trains to Liverpool and need to be on the 10:07 train to be in bed in time to be effective in my training session tomorrow. *I really shouldn't be doing this. I don't really have the time.* The taxi pulls up underneath the canopy by the entrance. I slide out as gracefully as possible before I muster all of my confidence and stride in. *As though being in the wrong city to meet a man who has agreed to unleash my naughtiest desires is the most natural thing in the world.*

As instructed, I leave my coat and bag in the cloakroom and make my way to the lobby bar. Seb is perched on one of the bar stools with two tall glasses with ice and clear liquid inside them. My insides turn to jelly, all my confidence evaporating as I see him. He turns and catches my eye. A wry smile spreads across his face and I walk across the bar to meet him.

"Good evening, Isabel. Did you have a pleasant journey?"

"Very pleasant, thank you, Sebastian. Have you been here long?"

"Long enough to do all I needed to prepare for your arrival."

I look into eyes clouded with desire. My heart rate picks up and the last shreds of control I thought I had dissipate. I lock away all the delicious thoughts of what could be in store, and focus on where we are, trying not to get too carried away with myself.

"How come your company puts you up in classy hotels like this? I get shoved into the basic range places."

"We don't, but I have come to an agreement with my boss. I don't want the inconvenience of being away from home worsened by staying in some crummy backstreet hotel. He isn't allowed to authorise more than the budget so I book my own places, charge the company the budget and make up any difference myself. Sometimes I prefer quirky country places, sometimes an excellent bistro with rooms, and sometimes sleek and modern. I think this is appropriate for tonight."

"I was thinking in the taxi that this hotel is very you."

"Oh? How so?"

"Well, it commands over the city. It's modern and sharp but holds a precarious edge of danger."

"Very nice. I tended to think of it being suitable for you—beautiful, slender, looks fragile on the outside but has hidden inner strength to remain standing even in the most challenging moments." He looks right into my eyes as he speaks and it resonates down to my soul. Heat rises in my cheeks and I'm suddenly queasy. His clear, aqua-flecked eyes stare at me, watching for each of my reactions before he breaks the connection and I'm free to take a breath. "So, how have you found your homework this week?"

My eyes instantly drop to the floor, my reaction speaking much louder than any words.

"Do you have something you need to tell me, Isabel?"

I have to admit it. There is no way I could ever lie to this man. So I peer up and nod my head slowly.

"You failed to do as you were asked?" I nod again. He leans in to me and whispers, "Don't take another sip of your drink until you go to the ladies, which is in the corner behind you. Remove your knickers, take a few moments to get yourself 'interested', and come and hand your knickers to me."

I gasp at his words, mentally saying I can't possibly do something like that, especially in such a public place. My body responds to his command the way it always does and I slip off the bar stool and walk to the ladies.

I enter the ladies and find an empty cubicle. Almost frantically, I hitch up my skirt and pull my knickers down over my shoes. It is mad, insane. If I stopped to think about it for more than a second, I would be too scared to even contemplate that I am here. A married woman, keenly removing her underwear in a public bar for some man who is not her husband. *Don't think about it, Izzy. Do it and enjoy it.* And that's the problem. I am not surprised that after five minutes of simply being in his presence and assigned my punishment, I am already nicely wet. A few tentative strokes with my finger through the lips of my pussy are plenty to confirm that I am more than 'interested'. Time to go back. I screw up my black lacy knickers into a tight ball in my hand, flatten out my skirt and unlock the cubicle door. Then it hits me.

Shit, shit, shit. What the hell am I doing? This is too dangerous, walking across a bar with no knickers to a sexy, dangerous man who wants to punish me.

Drawing several lungfuls of air, I hold my head up high and regain my composure. I don't want doubt to creep into my time with Seb. This is no different than every other line he's helped me cross. *I can do this!* Plastering on a smile, I exit and stroll out of the ladies, slightly surprised at how… how… 'okay' it is to be naked beneath my skirt in public. Seb knows, but no one else has a clue, and being honest with myself, it hardly feels any different. Just sexy.

I arrive back at the stool and before I sit I hold out my hand with the tight ball of material scrunched up inside it for him. He puts his hand underneath and I carefully loosen the grip of my fingers so my knickers discreetly fall into his palm. He smiles and quickly slips them into the outside pocket of his suit jacket. I hop back onto the stool with a spring in my step, feeling a small sense of achievement that I've been able to follow his instruction.

"How are you feeling?"

"Good, surprisingly. Really good, actually." As I admit it, I realise I mean it.

"Isabel, do not be surprised at how you feel. Enjoy it and realise that you are getting what you want and need."

I take a deep sip of my G&T, leaving one mouthful left in the glass.

He places one hand on my leg, above my exposed knee at the hem of my skirt. He slips his hand up my leg until the tips of his fingers are gently probing at the point where my legs have been stuck together with superglue in order to retain some dignity.

"Relax," he instructs in a soft but commanding whisper.

Ha! Easy for you to say. You're not the one sitting here with no knickers on. I force myself to do as he asks, again unable to do anything but obey his commands. My tensed legs relax and Seb draws his stool closer to me. His fingers trace up my leg and venture under the hem of my skirt, his position obscuring his movements. Anticipation fizzes through me at his next move as I silently beg that he doesn't continue on his current track.

I reach toward the bar, trying not to think about how close his hand is to my wanton flesh, and finish off my drink. Perhaps if I drain the glass now, we can finish the evening somewhere more private. His glass is already empty and I set mine down to meet it. He slowly withdraws his hand and gives my knee a gentle squeeze.

"Would you like another drink, Isabel?"

No. No, I 'would like' you to take me somewhere nearby and fuck me senseless! Make me come so hard it shatters my body into a thousand tiny pieces, and if you would like to spank me again, like you did over your breakfast bar, then that's fine by me. My cheeks pink and my pussy throbs at the heat of my thoughts.

"Isabel?"

His tone shakes me from my daydreaming.

"Yes, that would be lovely."

He smiles and gives me a little wink, suggesting that he knows exactly what I was thinking. I don't really want another drink, but he is in charge. Seb catches the barman's eye and he comes over straightaway.

"Same again, please."

It's the little things Seb does that send a shiver down my spine. He's so confident and in control that he doesn't even bother to ask me whether I want the same drink. There is no debate. Few questions. A complete lack of the annoying 'are you sure?' conversations that are so draining.

The drinks arrive and as soon as the barman has turned to walk away, Seb strokes the inside of my leg again, briefly, but a little higher than last time before he takes his hand away. Fuck, he's teasing me again. *Like with the pasta.*

We sit in silence for the first few sips. With Seb, even silence is powerful. He is still and although we are quiet, he looks thoughtful. I sit and sip my drink. The cold liquid soothes my rising temperature. Seb looks like he's playing something over in his head. I wonder what he is thinking and hope he's pleased with how well I am receiving my punishment by sitting here as requested and letting him tease me. I catch the insane grin on my face and have to admit that I am enjoying this.

He breaks the silence and leans in towards me to whisper in my ear. "Come on and drink up. We need to go upstairs for your punishment."

Oh no! I thought sitting here having a drink with no knickers on was my punishment. His words wipe the smile from my face. I drop my head and stare at my shoes, gathering my courage. I take a few more sips of my G&T, trying not to rush, before I place it back on the bar. All of the pleasure I was experiencing from doing as I was told weighs heavily in my stomach, replacing all of the lust that was building. *I am in a hotel with another man and about to be punished.* That thought trumps all of the Dutch courage I have consumed. But it also ignites my blood and sparks the adrenaline in my veins. Fear and trepidation mix a cocktail much more potent than alcohol.

Seb swallows his last mouthful, leaving his glass half full, before he steps down from his seat. He holds out his hand to steady me as I step down. With his hand at the small of my back, he guides me to the lifts at one side of the lobby and presses the call button. The lift doors slide open and he glances around before we step into an empty car. He promptly presses the number 21 and the doors slide closed.

Before we start to move upwards, he turns around and faces me. He consumes me with a passionate and forceful kiss, exploring my mouth and lips with his tongue. I can sense his hunger for me. We have never kissed quite like this before. It's raw and has a ferocity that hasn't been there before. It knocks me off kilter.

His hands are on me a second later, pressing through the material of my skirt against my pussy. The embers of desire rooted in the centre of my body leap to a full burning fire of want. My legs tingle and my head goes light, dizzy with excitement. The feeling of being totally wanted adds to the elixir of anticipation already flooding my veins. He cups his hand against me—a silent promise of what will come later on.

The lift slows and comes to a stop, and he is off me in a second. The doors open and I obediently follow him down the short corridor to a second door. He slides his card key out of his pocket and opens the door.

He holds his hand out to me in front of the open door and we walk into his rather grand executive room with study area, small lounge and a king-sized bed. Floor-to-ceiling windows line the far wall and provide a dazzling view across the night-time cityscape.

"Did you enjoy the ride up?"

"Um, yes." I grin up at him.

He takes me to stand in front of the window, still holding my hand as we admire the view together. I get it, the similarities to the building and me—fragile but slowly finding the inner strength to stand up on my own. I have grown so fond of Seb guiding me, of him holding my hand. My body is still sizzling after the brief frisson in the lift and I desperately want him. He seems to be light and shadow tonight, intense and dangerous one moment, calm and nonchalant the next. The scene is set for something important, and I sense that the hand-holding is because he is about to take me somewhere dangerous.

He turns to me and looks me straight in the eye. His icy eyes validate my fears. The look confirms that he won't be holding my hand through this. His body seems bigger, more intimidating, and I bow my head slightly, feeling shy. I chance a look up at him through my eyelashes.

"Isabel, you have been a naughty girl. You made yourself come when I expressly forbade you from doing so."

Oh, shit.

He lets go of my hand and walks around behind me, leaving me to stand on my own.

"Don't look around at me. Keep looking out of the window at all those people in the city below. I am going to turn off the lights. At this height, you will be able to see them. As you are in the darkness, they won't be able to see you."

I'm plunged into darkness with only the soft gleam of the window offering any light. My pulse races at the uncertainty around the impending punishment.

"Isabel, strip naked for them."

"What?" I can't help my shocked voice and automatically start to turn around, but catch myself at the last moment.

"You heard. Stand there at the window and strip off all your clothes for all those people in the light below. Show them what a naughty, sexy, beautiful woman you are. Not for me, Isabel. I'll sit behind and watch you strip, but you are not to look at me at all."

I want to turn my head around to see his gaze, try to understand his tone, but know that I shouldn't.

"Isabel, if you turn and look at me, I promise you I'll put you over my knee and spank you so hard that you will be reminded of it every time you sit down tomorrow."

He answers my thoughts again. *Put me over your knee and spank me? Yes, please.* Although as I think about it, I'm not sure how hard he would go. Above everything, the swarm of thoughts and images in my mind makes me wet. This situation, although scary, makes me feel wanton and provocative. I can almost feel my desire dribble down my thighs at his words and am instantly reminded that he has my knickers from earlier. *Breathe, Izzy. They can't see you, and you can do this.*

My hands move to my top, cautiously picking it up and pulling it over my head. *Shit, shit, shit. I'm really going to be standing here in my bra in front of an open window!*

Thank goodness for my recent lingerie shopping trip. Okay, what next? I weigh my options and start to panic. *Expose my breasts or expose… Shit! Expose my naked pussy.* I'm not sure I can do this. He is really testing my boundaries. But I want to. I want to be daring. I want punishment. I want danger. I want excitement. I can do this. *Do what he says. Strip for them. Show them what a good girl I can be.*

After my mini pep talk, I reach behind me and unfasten the clasp on my bra. Refusing to give in to my insecurities, I toss it to the side. I run my hands to the small of my back, reach for the zip at the back of my skirt and slide it down. As my hands slide around my waistband to pull it down, I become acutely aware of my nakedness underneath. It makes me feel sexy, feeling my skin with the tips of my fingers. It sparks a warm comfort through my blood. *Here goes.*

I pull my skirt down and step out of it, revealing myself to the window.

"Completely naked, Isabel."

Oh no... The shoes. My reluctance is clear as I slowly step out of my shoes and roll down the thigh highs. The ability to do this with any finesse or seductive quality has been stripped from me with the rest of my clothes. I'm now utterly naked. It is strange that the lack of shoes is the biggest blow to me. Standing in bare feet makes me feel small and vulnerable, and I realise that I have closed my eyes.

"Admire the view, Isabel."

I guess he may be able to see a small reflection of me in the glass and know that my eyes are closed. I force them open to gaze out at the view below. The lights of cars move like a model train set on the streets below. Lights are on in buildings and the city gives off a glow.

"Seeing as you are so good at it, make yourself come for them, Isabel."

Fuck, no. Please, that's too much.

"Isabel, take your finger and slide it onto your clit."

His words both dismay and soothe me. I follow his instruction, focused on his commands. I'm unable to do anything other than obey.

So I slide my finger down between my legs. I am soaking. My whole sex is wet. My mind has been struggling with the position I am in, but my body? My body betrays me, and it is clearly showing how much I want this. Or how much this is what my body needs.

The touch—my touch—on my clit feels amazing, and as I stroke, everything else fades away and I submerge myself in the desire of my body.

"Good girl. Now open your eyes and enjoy the view, the sheer naughtiness of what you're doing."

I gaze out at the city below and stroke longer, amazed that even with this vulnerability the sensation is amazing. My finger glides over my clit and my hand moves faster. I pant and my mind focuses on the frustrations that have consumed my body over the last few days.

Faint noises distract me for a moment and draw me from my observation of the people below. I can't look around but low, reverberating breaths tell me Seb is as excited by this as I am and that he's enjoying the show.

I know that this is my punishment—to test my comfort zone, and see if I can truly follow instructions. But having Seb enjoy my submission gives me the inner courage to do as I'm told. I can listen to my body and the desires that I have and respond to them in a way that I'd never previously considered. It's exhilarating and I'm spurred on even more by my impending orgasm. The danger is an aphrodisiac and knowing that Seb watches my arousal, is himself turned on by my actions, holds the key to why I'm now racing to come.

"Come for them, Isabel."

His words are the final encouragement I need. I open my eyes wide and my orgasm rips through my body. I press tightly on my clit as my body pulsates around my hand. My finger is the only thing keeping me standing and stopping me from collapsing under the weight of the pleasure coursing through me. I'm so caught up with my body's feelings that I don't hear Seb until he's pressing at me from behind. His deep dominant voice growls in my ear.

"Lean forward, place the palms of your hands on the glass and spread your legs wide apart." I do as I am told, and he helps to bend my torso. My hands above my head press against the cool glass, but my bum is on clear display for him and with my legs this wide he can probably see my throbbing pussy.

He's naked and I hear the tear of the foil condom packet before his hot skin covers mine. His hard cock nuzzles the entrance to my pussy, and the next second he slides inside me.

"You naughty girl. You're about to get fucked for everyone to see. They will see me fucking you from behind, filling your dripping pussy with my cock. God, you're wet. You are a naughty girl, Isabel. What are you?"

"I'm naughty," I moan, lost in his words.

"And you feel so damn good."

I try to process what is happening, but the feelings and emotions swamp any rational thought. I simply surrender. I watch in the reflection as Seb fucks me and it only adds to the fire that has ravaged me. All I can do is feel the assault on my body, my mind, and my soul.

The glass offers no form of concealment—there's nowhere to hide. I'm as open and vulnerable as I have ever been. Seb's punishment, his choice of task, has left me raw. I gaze away from this pornographic sight and look directly out of the window to the lights of the city.

Condensation builds on the window directly in front of me and my hands slip down the glass a few inches, emitting a squeak and leaving an erotic trail of finger marks down the pane. *How can something so obscene feel so damn good?*

My first orgasm isn't even going to register against the one that Seb will force from my body. Long, hard strokes send sparks of pleasure from my clit. They radiate out in a wave that reaches my fingertips. He increases his rhythm and I have to focus to keep my hands against the glass. My arms burn. My pussy aches. My throat is arid from my ceaseless moans of pleasure. Then he starts to tense, to plunge into me harder. His fingers grip my hips like a vice and he comes. With his last thrust, I, too, burst into another climax from deep inside. He slowly circles his hips into me, making sure I've completely come apart, and pulls me against him tighter so I can feel the sweat against our skin.

He sweeps his arms around my waist and lifts me up off the floor. He picks me up and carries me the short distance to the bed. I collapse in an orgasmic mess in his arms. Sated and exhausted, he positions me on the bed and presses a wall switch. Floor-to-ceiling curtains glide closed on the stage of my punishment.

Snuggling up, he spoons behind me and pulls the sheets over us. I float in the ecstasy of all the sensations I have experienced. I have no idea how long we lie there. Time could have stood still for all I care. He slowly pulls away and lifts himself off the bed.

"How are you feeling?"

"Wonderful," I mutter, still in something of a dream state.

"Izzy, I fucked you really hard in what was, in effect, a stress position. Your muscles will ache badly in the morning unless I deal with them now. Roll over onto your front, baby." His words are soft and filled with comfort. Although I register the tone, I'm not sure what he's talking about so I flop over on the bed as he asks. Warm, smooth hands glide over my back as he rubs my skin with oil. Fingers and hands gently knead my shoulders, lifting the tension away with his magic. He certainly is a man of many talents.

I must have drifted off into slumber, as Seb wakes me with soft kisses on my cheek and down my neck.

"It's time to wake and re-join reality, Izzy."

No, no, no, no! I want to stay in this room forever. I pull myself to sitting on the side of the bed. I notice my clothes, neatly folded and arranged on the chair to the side. My knickers are on top. It's obviously time to get dressed and catch my train. On the table to the side is a light snack of a Caesar salad and a long glass of freshly squeezed juice, which I devour. Good, dirty sex seems to give me an appetite.

When I'm dressed and finished with the supper, Seb comes over to me and offers his hand to help me stand. He presses the button to open the curtains and we look out at the view once more. His body presses against my back, the stubble on his jaw tickling my cheek.

"Nice memories, Isabel?"

"Oh yes. Very, very nice."

He brings his right hand around and gives me one sharp slap on the side of my bottom. And in one simple movement, he sets my sated body on fire again. *Will I ever get enough?*

"You're a brilliantly naughty submissive, and I love it."

"I love it, too. Thank you." *Thank you for everything.* For pushing my boundaries, for encouraging me to do those things an hour or so ago, for lifting the lid on the box in which I had put all these desires and then rummaging around the bottom of it to find even more hidden beneath. *Yes. Thank you, Sebastian!* I battle with myself, wanting to share all of my emotions and feelings with him. Will he understand how much he means to me after such a short time? Will he believe me considering I'm still married?

He takes my hand and steers me toward the door of the room. I still feel unsteady on my feet. Despite the good massage, I understand what he meant about achy muscles. We step silently into the lift and exchange inane grins all the way back down to the ground floor. Practically laughing, we step out into the lobby of the hotel.

I can't remember the last time I laughed this effortlessly or had this much fun during sex. It's so refreshing to be able to share it with him and see his lighter side as well. We collect my coat and bags, and he escorts me to a taxi waiting outside in the cold air.

"Goodnight, Izzy, and good luck tomorrow." He kisses me formally on the cheek as I depart.

I turn and look up at the building, to the glass windows of the rooms high above, and smile. I'm now disappearing back into the city—the city which I stripped for, came for, and was fucked in front of. I dash into the back of the cab before my blush becomes too obvious.

Thinking of myself as a high-class escort had never featured in my fantasies before tonight. But as I am driven through the streets back to the station, that is what I feel like. Seb's escort, visiting him in hotel rooms and swanky apartments. Although that makes me feel ridiculously sexy—a fantasy I didn't realise I had—it also sours my stomach. Maybe to him I am just his latest plaything, a challenge, and a free one at that. Am I using him or is he using me? This started by simply wanting to explore some what-ifs and to see whether what was in my head was the missing piece to my happiness. The sex and the submission are great. But the relationship between us—the connection that has been built on trust—has grown in my heart. I want more from our relationship. I want it to continue. I need it to. But does he?

Sixteen

I enjoyed Manchester, Izzy. But I haven't finished with your punishment. S

Punishment? For what? I thought we already did that. Izzy

Yes, but for some reason you seem incapable of following my instructions. I've got a specific task I'd like you to follow through for me. Will you do it, Isabel? S

My heart is in my mouth because I know instinctively that I will. At least, I'll try. Self-doubt lingers when it comes to carrying out some of Seb's instructions, no matter how much I want to fulfil them.

Yes. Izzy

Good. I'm sending you an email that sets out my requirements. I hope you will find it an enjoyable challenge. S

I'm as impatient as ever and excitement whirls in my stomach. I immediately check my emails. Nothing. I return to my previous browsing on Tumblr and try to put Thursday night's encounter and Seb's recent challenge from my mind. I have a report I probably should be finalising for tomorrow, but my mind has been less than focused of late. *Well, focused on anything other than Sebastian York.*

After spending the rest of Sunday evening and most of Monday checking my emails every few minutes, I give up and decide that this is another part of Seb's game. He's purposefully teasing me and making me wait. And that stirs all sorts of wanton emotions. Sexual frustration and lust haven't featured in this way before. My sexual appetite has been kick started, and now I mentally picture myself and Seb in all of the images I find online.

By Tuesday morning, I'm fighting the urge to call or text Seb and see whether he's forgotten to email me. I manage to make it to work without giving in. Just.

As I open my email to remind him, there it is. I click it open and then close it just as quickly, realising where I am. Instead, I grab my phone and scroll to load my most recent emails.

> Isabel,
> It seems you struggle to follow my instructions, even when consequences are involved. I have yet to decide if your actions are deliberate and you misbehave in order to be punished. Regardless, I'd like you to follow these instructions—hopefully an enjoyable challenge. You will be making some purchases. You have a budget of £300. My credit card details are at the bottom of the email. The items you buy must either intrigue or excite you and will be:
> Something to spank you with.
> Something to tie you with.
> Something to put inside you when I'm not able.
> And something that scares you a little.
> Happy shopping!

S
5555-1103-1479-2709
11/16
476

Holy shit!
I re-read the email a few times before I finally close it and bury my phone in my drawer. My heart soars at the thought of pleasing Seb by actually completing his request. To know he is happy with me will be a greater reward than any awkwardness or embarrassment I may feel buying these things. *You already have a vibrator. Purchasing items that fit his request will be no more difficult.* I mentally prepare myself and think about the task he's set. *I can do this.* I can. All I have to do is buy a few items online. I'm eager to start my task, wanting to please Seb and bring a smile of approval to his face. My mind is made up—I'll get this done as soon as I'm home from work tonight.

* * *

I sit on my sofa with the laptop perched on top of my knees. Seb's instructions flit across my mind as I start my search to purchase some items more intimate than I perhaps would have imagined a few weeks ago.

With trepidation, I start with the CELLO website where I found my pretty pink vibrator. I feel as if I'm doing something illicit, like watching porn. I scold myself for being so silly. While it's not a pastime I'd share with my mother, I'm an adult. There is nothing forbidden about buying sex toys. I'm comfortable with watching images of BDSM, this should be easy. But the anonymity that the BDSM websites or Tumblr provide makes it safe. This is real. I'm going to give them my name and my address.

I relax into the sofa cushions and click through the different sections of the site. I'm turned on by considering all the possible items that would satisfy Seb's instructions. *Something to spank you with.* I add a small black flogger with suede to the basket. The kiss of the tassels is something that I long to feel. Will they tickle, sting or hurt me? *Something to tie you with.* The blindfold and satin ties ooze luxury, and I can imagine the cool material binding me. *Something to put inside you when I'm not able.* My heart skips as I imagine what the larger vibrator will feel like, pushed into my core. The sleek vibrator is in the basket and I'm eager to explore the next requirement. *Something that scares you a little.* His instruction gives me the courage to add items that I've thought of, but shied away from.

My nipples are sensitive, so I add a delicate silver pair of tweezer clamps that are connected by a silver chain. Next, a small leather paddle with intricate stitching catches my eye. It's a contradiction to me. It looks sensual and pretty, yet dangerous at the same time. How would my body react to being bent over Seb's breakfast bar and paddled? I press my thighs together, seeking relief from the arousal spurred by the thought of Seb applying the contents of my shopping basket on my willing body.

In less than an hour, I have everything. At the last moment I add love beads and a sensual hot oil candle. I couldn't resist the idea of the beads, the ability of them to keep me on the edge of arousal, wet for Seb, is too much after mentally playing over my fantasies. I put my laptop to the side and stretch out my legs. It's suddenly very hot.

I grab my phone, keen to share my small accomplishment.

> I've completed my homework. I hope you'll enjoy what I've bought. Izzy x

> Did you have fun with this, Izzy? S

> After I realised the computer wouldn't explode if I looked at sex toys, yes, I did enjoy it. Can I keep the items at your apartment when they arrive?
>
> Of course. I look forward to them arriving. And seeing you soon. S

Everything I ordered is due for delivery before Friday. I feel awash with an inner strength and sense of calm, as though I am carrying a really good secret that no one else knows about. I fight the need to email or contact Seb. Not speaking to him until everything has arrived will be more difficult than I had thought. The easy friendship we first shared is tempting me. I want to be free to have the friendship and the affair, to grab hold of it and take it. But I can't yet, not until I've resolved my marriage.

I have barely seen Phil the past week. I want everything out in the open with him, but it's difficult to confront him if he's never home. Neither of us wants to initiate the argument that will be the final blow to our marriage. We are stuck in limbo and I'm desperate to move forward, yet terrified at what that will mean.

* * *

On Friday, I leave the office early with my new items in the boot of my car. They arrived on Thursday, wrapped in beautiful shiny boxes and neatly packed. Everything looked so pretty and exciting. I got all of the items out and spread them on the bed. The vibrator, the flogger, the paddle, the nipple clamps, blindfold and ties. Plus the 'extras' that caught my eye: the love beads and the massage candle. It was like a birthday where you got everything you asked for. As I leave the office, I send a quick text to Seb.

> I have a delivery I'd like to drop off if that's okay? I'm looking forward to playing with them together. Izzy x

> Of course. Although I'm not home tonight. You have your key. S

A pang of hurt and disappointment snakes through me. It was wrong to expect Seb to be home, although I'd hoped he'd make an invitation. It has been over a week since we saw each other in Manchester, and I don't know when I will see him again.

> Yes, I do. Thank you. Maybe I could wait for you? Izzy x

I hit send and point the car toward Seb's apartment. I keep trying to reconcile my feelings towards Seb. How can my feelings for Phil be replaced so thoroughly by what I feel for Seb? Yet Seb is everything that I want, he's caring and considerate as well as dominant and assertive. This is what I need in a lifetime partner. This is what is so lacking in Phil.

The one dark spot in my euphoria is that Seb sees our relationship with clearly defined limits. Seb is guiding me in an exploration of my sexual needs—full stop. There has been no further talk of combining that with the friendship we first started. As much as I might long for my relationship with Seb to provide everything I dream of in a lifetime partner, to turn into a fairy tale, it won't. He won't let it.

I park the car and head up to Seb's apartment, still not looking at my phone. I take my boxes and head straight for my room, avoiding looking at the photographs on the wall. I set about carefully placing all the individual items in one of the drawers of the dresser. As I handle each one, I fight the growing sense of arousal as the anticipation stirs. My stomach is in knots and I know that I'd be wet if I slid my finger down into my knickers. It couldn't hurt just to try one of two, could it?

The love beads were my curious buy, so I unpack the box. Two silicon spheres sit innocently in the packaging. My cheeks pink at what I'm about to do with them. I push them between my swollen lips and inside me, enjoying the feeling of being filled. After a moment of adjustment I'm used to them and a dull ache is the only reminder to my private pleasure.

I pull the silk ties out of their box and run the red material through my fingers. The cool silk heats my arousal further. I resist the urge to play with everything in the drawer and halt my exploration, suddenly feeling foolish for indulging when I'm at Seb's house alone.

After all the toys are safely away, I steal a glance at my phone. Sure enough, there is a message from Seb.

> Not tonight, Izzy. I already have plans. I'd like to see you tomorrow at 7 p.m. sharp. S

Okay, so another night to wait.

> I'd like that. See you tomorrow. Izzy x

I try not to think about what his plans are for tonight. I have no right. Perhaps a little distance for an extra night will be good. But I don't want an extra night. I want to be here with Seb. Tonight, as well as tomorrow night and perhaps every night. I want him to feel like I do, eager to see me, excited at what could happen. I'm sure men don't get the same stomach-churning nervousness, but whatever their equivalent is, I want him to feel that.

Seventeen

I wake feeling slightly groggy, having tossed and turned all night. I even got up at one point to try and tire myself into sleep. Questions about Seb and what I want from our relationship ran through my brain, and they only quietened with his texts.

> Izzy, tell me straight, how much of this stuff did you get solely because you want to try it and how much is because you think this is what I wanted you to buy? S

> I bought these items for me. Well, us. It's what I wanted. Did you want something different? Izzy

> No, Izzy, it's perfect.

> Have you tried out any of it yet? S

> One or two things. The ties and blindfold are comfortable. And the balls... okay, weird but for the few moments I had them in they were nice.

> See you tomorrow. S

He was thinking about our future time together, and that was enough to calm my turbulent emotions and send me to sleep.

* * *

My morning alarm vibrates on the bed table and I stretch and turn over. Phil is in bed with me. I'm stunned. It seems like weeks since we last shared a bed.

"Good morning, Iz."

"Morning, Phil. I've not seen you for a while."

"Sorry, Iz. I've been trying to sort some stuff out. I needed space."

"Okay." I move to get out of bed, not liking the idea that he joined me in the middle of the night and I wasn't aware of it. He reaches for my arm.

"Come on, Iz. We need to talk."

I sigh and sink back down, scooting to the edge of the bed. I need to get this conversation sorted. Phil is keen to talk for a change, perhaps I should hear him out.

"I know that we've not been close lately. You've been distant, off doing your own things all the time. But I want to sort this out." Phil's sudden change in tack and direction throw me. He hasn't said more than two words to me in a week. He didn't like me challenging him before and now he's playing nice.

"Well, you're never here, Phil. What do you expect? For me to wait around and mope until you notice me again?" Phil visibly stiffens at my words and I ready myself for my defence against him.

"This isn't my fault, Iz. You're the one who wanted to get all 'kinky' in the bedroom and expected me to hit you."

"We've had this argument before. I'm sick of this. This is so typical of you. I didn't want you to hit me. I wanted you to take care of me. To fulfil a desire I have and listen to me. As usual, you couldn't do it."

"What do you mean, as usual?"

"This didn't start a few weeks ago, Phil. I've taken your constant neglect and selfish behaviour for a long time. It seems like a lifetime ago that we were happy. I thought that if I stood up to you, pushed harder for my wants, we could still try and work things out. Obviously I got that wrong and you've been running ever since." I stand and my voice grows even stronger as all the hurt and desperation courses through me. "I'm tired, Phil. I've supported you and us for years. We were young when we got married and I thought the distance between us was normal. I am as much to blame for that as you, as I let that happen. But these last few years have been worse." Countless nights spent climbing into bed alone and the continued rejection of anything that I wanted swamp my memories.

"Izzy, you make this sound like a huge deal. So I didn't want to do anything kinky to you."

"But it's not just that, Phil. I've tried to tell you this, but you never listen." His attitude is making me angry. "You've never once acknowledged any of my needs. All of the times I'd ask you to make me come, to actually show me some attention, were ignored. I thought that our marriage was more important than having a good sex life. But you really don't understand me, or even show a basic interest in me. You never ask about my day, want to socialise with my friends. Hell, by now you'd have thought we'd have our friends. Not yours and mine still. If it's not all about you, then you don't want to know."

Phil is quiet for a moment and the pause is primed, ready for me to say what I need to.

"Look, Phil, you should know that things aren't right and I think you and I both know why."

He stands abruptly. "Shut up, Izzy. I don't want to hear this."

"No, you need to hear this. We can't go on like this."

"I said shut up."

"No! I won't take it anymore."

"What's gotten into you? You're gone just as much as I am."

"Only recently, and only because I've finally woken up to you."

"You don't know what you're talking about." Phil seems flustered. I'm so close now. I need to hold my nerve.

"I know you've been having an affair, Phil, and I think it's been going on for a long time." I leave the accusation hanging in the air, thick with anger and frustration. We face off against each other, the bed separating us, and I wait for him to answer.

"Maybe I should be asking you the same question? Perhaps you've even had some help in the kink department, because you certainly seem different. Sure as hell you haven't been sleeping with me."

All of my anger and conviction to finally clear things up with Phil crumble down as guilt takes their place. You're so close. *Come on, Izzy! Courage.*

"So that's your answer? To throw it back at me?"

"Well?"

"Well what? You're the one all over another woman in front of me, who doesn't come home, who says he's working when he's not. Are you going to answer that?" My final challenge shakes him to the point of action.

"No, I am not!"

He stalks around the bed, ratcheting up the tension. I'm caught in his grasp before I can escape. I shake like a rag doll as he snarls into my face and throws me to the bed. F*ear*. Genuine fear slices through me at where this argument might end. I wait for it—the slap of his hand against my cheek—hoping that I didn't see the anger there in his eyes.

"Iz, I'm sorry." His soft apology is more shocking to me than throwing me to the bed.

"What for? For accusing me or for throwing me on the bed?"

"I said I'm sorry. Just lay off if you know what's good for you, Izzy."

"Why won't you just admit the affair? Tell me the truth for once? Then we can move on."

He stands there at the edge of the room with no words, and I can't take it. I need him to admit that he's part of the problem. But he won't. He's always taken the easy way out and ignored me. I won't be the quiet wife anymore. I know what it feels like to be listened to, cared for, and it's finally opened my eyes.

"You know what?" I shout. "Sod it. I'm not going to stay here. I can't stay here with you like this. I want the truth from you. When you're willing to have a conversation with me without you getting angry we can put everything on the table. I'll be at Jess's until then." I walk to the bathroom and slam the door. *Calm. Breathe. Don't cry yet. Hold on.*

"So it's alright for you to run, then?" he shouts.

"I'm not running. I'm leaving!" I scream back at him through the door. "Unless you're ready to tell me the truth?" I listen, but his confession doesn't come. I pull things together in the bathroom, grabbing everything I need for a few days before I open the door. Phil sits on the bed with his shoulders slouched. His whole demeanour has changed in the space of a minute.

The resentment and pain that was so potent a few moments ago now leaves a sick feeling in my stomach. We are both destroying anything left of our marriage. I have no right to feel the way I do and place blame on Phil while I'm off being unfaithful. But I'm not sure that the marriage vows alone can be enough to keep us together. There hasn't been 'for better'. There has only been 'for worse'. Marriage is a partnership, something that needs love and understanding as well as hard work. I haven't got anything left to give. We are married in fact alone and that gives me the courage I need to carry through with my actions.

"I'm not going to stay here, Phil. This isn't something that has happened overnight, and it won't fix itself that way either. You need to admit to me that you are having an affair. And I think we have some other conversations ahead of us." I dump the items beside him on the bed as he slowly looks towards me. He doesn't say anything. The rage I witnessed earlier is gone, replaced by despair. Regret sours his face and tests my courage to follow through with my actions to leave. I've never stood up to him like this before and it's left him shaken. I grab my clothes and stuff them into a bag before adding toiletries on top. He watches my movements around our bedroom as he continues to sit. I desperately try to hold onto my anger, but the guilt and sorrow are unstoppable.

This is it. This is a pivotal moment in our relationship. One of those moments when no matter what you try, you can't prevent it from happening. I feel part of myself pull away, growing distant to the scene playing out before me. I can't ignore my actions. I'm physically running from Phil—walking out. I'm not even sure I'll be back. The emotions of everything that has happened over the past few weeks and years have built to this point. Now I'm balanced on a precipice. The potential ruin of our marriage waits below.

I can't stay. Staying would concede some imaginary defeat and give Phil the signal that he can get away with ignoring me. It might have been alright in the past, but not now. That is not what I want. I'm stronger than that. *Thanks to Seb.*

"Don't leave like this, Iz."

"What, like the last few times you walked out on me? You need to take a look at our marriage and decide what you want to say to me. Clearing the air isn't enough, and neither is trying to blame everything on me. If you won't talk to me, then I'm leaving. I'll be at Jess's." I reach for my bag, bolt out of the door and down the stairs. I grab my keys and I'm in my car before I know it. I'm not heading for Jess's house. I'm going to the one place I can be myself and hopefully feel some comfort in this whirlwind of feelings.

It's still early on Saturday morning and I don't even think to check that Seb is home. I fire off a text to let him know that I'm on my way over.

> Why do you need to come over, Izzy? I'm not home at the moment. S

I read the message once I'm parked in one of his spaces. I fled here without thinking because I needed to feel safe. Seb has been the one to offer me comfort and reassurance, and I desperately need that now. The thought, though, that Seb might not be home at this time twists something in my chest and I can barely keep the hurt inside.

> Phil and I had a fight and I wasn't sure where else to go. Is it OK? Izzy

> You can wait for me. I won't be home just yet though. S

> Thank you. See you soon. Izzy

I can't sit any longer. I need to go inside and lick my wounds. I rush up to the sixth floor and open his door. Bursting into my room, I fling myself to the bed. As I nestle into the pillows, my body relaxes and the emotional turmoil raging within my heart and my head lets loose. The first wave of tears dampens my eyes and then the pillow. I let my body take over, pulling great sobs from my chest. I let it all out—the guilt, the pain and more guilt.

This was supposed to be simple. Seb shows me what I craved, the bliss from placing my sexual gratification in the hands of someone else and having it met. Submitting to someone else's dominant nature. My curiosity satisfied. Simple. Now I know what I'll be missing if I stay with Phil, but ending our marriage still hurts when I think about it. I thought it would be forever. I've given so much to our marriage. Can it really be over?

Seb has given me vastly more than I expected. Yet I don't know him. He's doing all of this for me, and he's asked nothing in return. Will he send me back when he's had enough? Is he doing this for other women as well?

More sobs tear at my chest and I can't contain them. It's no use. I'm a mess and can't think properly at the moment. Everything is in gloom-tinted glasses. As my tears dry, I try to focus on this morning. Things have been building towards this for a while. Meeting Seb just sped it up. But I came to Seb. I wanted to be with him. I'm not going to be able to walk away from Seb. I'm falling in love with him. *Oh no, no, no...*

I halt my thoughts, trying to reverse my realisation. I can't feel like this—not now, not ever. Seb will never settle for someone like me. He must have been with dozens of women, could have any of the women in the photographs. My eyes sting and burn as more tears fall. My face is raw and puffy. I keep my head buried into the plush, now wet, cushions and pull my knees up to my chest.

* * *

I wake as the light shines through the bedroom window and drifts across my face. I must have fallen asleep. Crying out my emotions has helped to focus my situation. I need to acknowledge my marriage is over and deal with what that will mean. That I've failed at something that I thought would last a lifetime. I'll have to leave Phil and start a new life. Easier said than done.

I need a shower, so I uncurl and head to the bathroom. The pulse of the water washes over me and I will the jets to wash away the ache in my heart. Instead, it merely numbs my senses as I turn the heat as hot as I can stand. It doesn't erase all of my thoughts from the morning or the emotional break I had on arriving, but it certainly helps.

I feel Seb before I see or hear him—a gentle caress down my spine, a warm hand snaking around my hip to pull me towards him. It's suddenly so clear, like turning on a light in a room that was filled with shadows.

I've fallen for him. It was the last thing that I thought would happen, and the realisation hasn't the best timing. Perhaps all the tears that flowed this morning washed away the final barriers I had built between what my head and my heart were feeling towards Seb. As these thoughts cascade through my mind, he brings me back to the present by sinking his teeth into my bottom lip. I feel it in the pit of my stomach. My thighs tense as need for him washes over me like the water running down my body.

His lips devour me and bring every nerve in my body to attention. The kiss is wild and holds a hunger—a desire—that has me whimpering. He pauses for breath. I take the moment to adjust to his onslaught. He's usually so controlled, so planned, but with my emotions so raw, I want to feel his emotions, too. I want to hear him tell me how desperate he is to have me, that he can't stand the time we are apart. My kisses beseech him to tell me how he feels. His body answers with consuming lips and scorching hands.

I wrap my hands around his neck and into his hair, trying to get closer to him. I want him all over my body, touching every part of my skin. His tongue plays with my lip and dominates my mouth, and I moan at the sensations he evokes. I'm constantly ambushed by the response of my body to Seb. He brings me to life every time he touches me, as if he has a magical switch. I weaken in his arms. I want him to control and guide me as he always does.

His hands run through my wet hair, and he gently pulls so I am forced to tilt my head to him. The water runs over my face and down my neck. He dips his head to lick up my throat, and electric shivers shudder through me. *Oh my God, I want to come.* The water runs into my mouth as he opens it with his lips and thrusts his tongue inside again. His hands are wandering, impatient and demanding.

He runs both hands down my back, into the dimples at the base of my spine and over my bottom, pulling me closer. His cock sears my stomach, a clear sign of how aroused he is. My hands move to his chest, spreading out, and grasp around his neck. I love feeling his body in my hands. He's warm and strong and I want to feel all of him.

Seb's kisses grow harder, more urgent. He explores my body with his lips. He kisses my cheeks, my throat, my collarbone, and back up to my lips. I slowly move my hands down his chest to caress him, but he grabs my wrist before I reach him. With a show of strength, he forces me against the wall of the shower. I gasp as the cold tiles press against my back. *Yes!* I'm suddenly desperate for Seb to take the lead, to rule over my body and be inside me. A gentle moan escapes my lips.

"Shhh, Izzy," he whispers and lifts my leg around his hip. I tighten my leg and cling to him as his hand runs up my thigh to squeeze my bottom.

His hand continues to explore over my hip and down my stomach. Dipping between our bodies, he slips his fingers into me, feeling how wet I am. My response shows what Seb does to me. I grind down onto his finger, thirsty for more.

"Izzy, I want you. Let me have you," he moans into my mouth.

Izzy? You called me Izzy? He never calls me Izzy when he's intimate with me. He always calls me Isabel. A formal reflection of where our relationship lies. Before I can listen to my head, my body gives in to his assault. His lips and teeth are at my throat again, at my ear, and I'm panting hard.

"Yes," I keen, unable to stop. My body already trembles. He pauses to cover himself in latex before returning to me. He lifts me above his hips, pinning me to the wall as I wrap my legs around him. He removes his hand, takes his cock, thrusting up into me while he grabs my hips, and pulls me down onto him.

"Umm," I purr as he penetrates me. A wave of heat radiates from my core. There is a carnal power in how Seb is taking me, as though he can't quite get deep enough inside me. I can't get enough of him. Each thrust is harder, deeper, and I can't escape him. I don't want to escape.

Wet tendrils of hair stick to my face as we get lost in this primal need. My body is coiling already, unable to resist Seb in this most demanding state. Trying to escape the elation that is building with my orgasm, I tilt my head back and close my eyes to keep myself together. I relish the feeling of him filling me, taking me. My respite is only momentary, though, as Seb cups my face and pulls it back to him.

"Look at me, Izzy."

I blink open my eyes through the water to stare into his. Beautiful glinting eyes lock onto mine while he continues to push inside me. It's so intense, staring right at him with our bodies joined in such an intimate way. My whole body tenses with anticipation. I can't keep quiet anymore. I gasp and moan louder and louder the closer he gets to winning my climax. The ache in my pussy is ever-present and I long for Seb to take my body to the wondrous high where I lose all senses.

"Please!" I beg him. It's all too much.

His chocolate voice rumbles with raw emotion. "Come for me, Izzy."

My eyes drop, closing off my vulnerability to him as my body starts to fly. I feel the words right through my body. I take a deep breath and let go.

"Oh... my... yes, yes... yes!" My thighs tighten around him as I ride out the shudders raking through my body. My back slides up and down the wall with each breath.

"Look at me." His command forces me to obey him. My pussy clenches around him from the force of my orgasm and I hope he feels it, too. He stares deep into my eyes, making sure we're as connected as physically possible as he thrusts and pulls down on my hips before he lets go.

"Oh God, Izzy!" With the last thrust, he comes deep inside me. I close my eyes and lean my forehead to rest on his, taking a moment to calm my breathing. We stay in that position, the water still flowing down between us, for what seems like forever. He slips out of me and holds me up so I can unwrap my legs, lowering me down into the shower. He pulls me to the centre of the shower and lets the water soak my hair, warming my body in a completely different way than he did a moment ago. I'm pulled into his bare chest as he holds me in his arms and I feel like I've come home, secure and blissful in the hazy afterglow of the amazing sex.

I hope he echoes my feelings. I don't have the courage to speak of it. I let him wash me, enjoying being soaped from head to foot in vanilla cocoa butter. Silently I pray that he never stops doing this to me—touching me, holding me, cherishing me.

He washes every part of me before he turns the shower off and grabs a towel to envelop me. The way he took me felt... different, as if he were staking a claim on me, and now? Now he's treating me as if I may break. My head is dizzy with thoughts as I let him wrap and dry me. But the one thought that predominates is why did he call me Izzy?

He's done it a hundred times before, but not once while I was submitting to him. *Why now?* He places a kiss to my forehead before he dries himself off and leaves me in my bathroom.

This was the most intense, body-shattering orgasm he's given me, and we were not Isabel, submissive, and Sebastian, Dominant, but Izzy and Seb, friends and lovers. I'm not sure how to straighten this out in my mind. I hope that Seb will talk to me later. I walk into the bedroom and curl up in bed, exhausted. It doesn't take me long to drift, but before sleep finally claims me, I'm conscious of one resounding thought.

I love him.

Eighteen

"Wake up, Isabel."

I hear Seb's low, velvet voice and I slowly roll over. A smile creeps across my face as I look up into his eyes.

"Come on, Isabel. Wake up. You've been here for hours, and I don't want to spend the time I have with you watching you sleep."

Hearing Seb talk about the time we have together brings me out of my sleepy haze. I glance at my watch and I'm pleased that it's only two in the afternoon.

"I've had your recent purchases in my house for over a day with the knowledge that you've already been playing with some of them without me."

I blush as I remember gently slipping the love beads inside me to see what they felt like. Somehow, thinking about that act with Seb being in charge makes it a lot more sexy.

"You've made excellent choices with what you've chosen. Now that you're here, would you like to find out what I'm going to do with everything?"

His words heat my building desire, and I want him to know that I want this, here, with him. I sit up in bed and lean forward to kiss him. I crush my lips against his and slide my tongue between them, staking claim to his mouth. My actions speak for me and tell him how much I want him, how much I want what he does to me. He pulls me close towards him, wraps his arm around me and lifts me from the bed as he stands. I wrap my legs around his waist as he carries me into his room, locked together in a passionate embrace that I hope is a prelude to much more.

Seb quietens the kiss, nipping my bottom lip between his teeth before he lets go completely. His eyes sparkle and glint in the light like cut crystal. He sits me down on the bed and all I see is the dominant standing before me. "The thought of using these toys on you makes me a very happy man, Isabel. Would you like to see what happy feels like?"

I nod. My stomach drops and my sex throbs. I've been imagining what Seb could do to me with the items I bought, but the reality will be far superior. Being with him is the best experience of my life. He takes me to places I didn't think possible.

"Come with me." He leads a few feet from the foot of the bed. "I think you've 'seen' enough for the moment. From now on, you will only feel. If you want me to stop at any point, say 'black'. Understand?"

Black if I want to stop? Why not just say stop?
"Okay."

I suddenly feel nervous and very exposed, but in a turned-on and excited beyond belief kind of way. A red silk blindfold is in his hand. He raises it and covers my eyes. The material is cool and light against my skin and my eyes relax. I take a few deep breaths to calm myself, and I feel settled. *I trust Seb.*

"Very nice, Isabel." Seb's lips brush against my ear as he whispers to me. Butterflies swarm in my stomach. His hands run down my arms and wrap around my wrists. He gently pulls me forward and I go with him. He turns my back to the bed. He pulls my left hand upwards and I feel more silk being tied around my wrist. He removes his hands but my arm remains aloft. There is some movement, telling me that the silk stretches to the tall wooden bed post, but I'm not bound directly to it. He repeats the action with my right arm so I'm standing, tethered to the bed, arms upraised. Seb's restrained and blindfolded me before, but my chest heaves, sucking in oxygen in anticipation of what he might do this time.

He brushes my neck with kisses and tiny electric currents spark at each contact point. His hands snake down my stomach and follow the contours of my body until he cups my pussy.

"If I slip my finger between your lips, will you be wet for me?"

Yes. God yes.

I can't speak, but as I try to articulate something, I open my mouth and a tiny gasp escapes, betraying how turned on he's made me.

"I think you like this, don't you, Isabel?" He thrusts his finger inside me without any resistance, demonstrating how slick I am. As quickly as he entered me, he pulls away, leaving me with no physical contact. I can't hear anything except for my heartbeat. The anticipation builds again and it's a heady mix of lust, nerves and excitement.

Seb's tongue lightly flicks my right nipple before he sucks its tightening bud into his mouth. It sends more lightning strikes through me, this time directly to my clit, and my soft panting replaces my heartbeat in my ears. He moves his head and pulls my right nipple into his mouth, continuing to use the left as a plaything between his finger and thumb. *Oh yes, please, keep doing that.* He twists both nipples now and I feel needy and desperate. "I think if I keep doing this, I may be able to make you come. What do you think?" As if to make his point, he pinches my right nipple hard and I squeal. "Oh yes, Isabel. But not today. Let's see how you respond to this." He replaces his fingers with something cold. A burning sensation replaces coolness in a single moment as he clamps my delicate tip. The hot rush gives way to a tingling sensation as he clamps my other nipple. My attempt to quiet my whimpers is lacklustre. My mouth drops open and I pant loudly. "Not so scary now, are they? You look fucking delicious with this chain across your chest. If I want to get a reaction from you, all I need to do is—"

He gently tugs the chain. "Umm" My nipples strain and throb.

"Oh yes. Perfect."

I try to focus on something other than my aching breasts, but Seb isn't touching any other part of me. My body is drunk on a whirlwind of intense pleasure.

A low buzzing reaches my ears. It's the vibrator. Its cool, firm head presses against my inner thigh and tickles my skin with its dull vibrations. Seb slowly draws the vibrator upward toward my pussy. He lightly skims my swollen lips and back down my other leg. He leisurely draws patterns with the top of the vibrator over every inch of my legs. Up and down, up and down. Each time he passes the apex of my thighs, I tilt my hips to achieve greater pressure where I want it.

Finally, Seb places the tip directly on my clit and it sends me into a breathless panic. I pull against the ties on my wrists and widen my legs. I can feel all the tiny sparks building around my clit, my sex weeping at Seb's assault on my body. But as I feel my muscles tighten deliciously, the vibrations stop.

"Nooo." I pull deep breaths into my lungs, the tension in my limbs waning, and the rush of my orgasm dissipates. Seb thrusts his finger inside me. His fingers explore me, inside and out, coating my pussy in my wetness. He hits harder, finger fucking me and building a deeper wave in the pit of my stomach.

I hear them again—the vibrations—and they signal another onslaught of pleasure. But I'm starting to feel overwhelmed. Seb's quietly going about my sexual torture and I'm desperately on the edge.

Seb focuses his attention—and the toy—on my exposed and very wet pussy. He draws the tip back and forth through my wet lips. I wait eagerly for the head to breach my entrance and finish what Seb started with his fingers. He plunges the vibrator inside me, filling me up. My release dominates my thoughts.

"Don't come, Isabel." His warning has me fighting against my body. Seb turns up the vibrations and I moan and mewl in response. I am so close to that beautiful edge, but he pulls on my nipple chain and I cry out, not expecting the pain to intensify my feelings of pleasure. He removes the vibrator.

"No, please!" I'm desperate to come. Seb has worked my body to a crescendo, playing each erogenous zone in time. My clit throbs and my arms ache. I can barely feel my nipples. They are just a numb tingle. But Seb doesn't let me finish. He continues his mix of stimulation, bringing me to that gloriously divine crest, but stopping a heartbeat away from where I want to go. The pleasure is growing darker, ebbing closer to pain, and my head is muddled.

Seb continues to play with me, touch me and tease me. My whimpers grow louder, my pleas falling from my lips in a continuous stream.

"Please, Sebastian. I can't... No more. I need to come. Please." But he doesn't respond. He continues his torturous actions. "Seb, please. No more." And to my utter relief, he stops. The knots loosen around my wrists. My arms drop to my sides and I nearly slump to the floor. Seb catches me and turns me around.

"You need to learn to enjoy what I'm doing to you, Isabel, to trust in the pleasure that I give you." His voice is harsh. "Place your hands on the bed and keep your beautiful arse in the air. Don't drop your chest or your nipples will be in trouble."

He moves my body into the bent position, and I feel each movement through my breasts as the chain dangles between my clamped nipples. My head is fuzzy and I can hardly catch my breath. My body is raging with my mind. I don't want to be treated like this. He's not listening to me. Seb is normally so gentle and considerate of my wants. But this is different. *Is this what being a submissive would really be like?*

"I'm going to fulfil the last request from my list. Something that scares you. You're making me so fucking pleased." I know he's talking to me, but I don't hear the words. Seb's warm hands massage my bottom, pinching and squeezing. My pussy aches in response. Fear, desire, pain and pleasure flow through me in a confused mix.

I hear a soft whoosh of the paddle. A dull thud sounds as leather smacks my bum.

"Ow."

He follows with two more strikes. The sting isn't too painful, but every nerve ending in my body is calling out for release. I'm hyper sensitive to everything. I want to come so badly, and the spanking makes me feel vulnerable and desperate. *Thwack, thwack, thwack.* Three more hits, harder than the first. My skin registers pain over anything else. Seb's hitting closer together and harder, with little rest. I lock my arms, stopping myself from collapsing onto the bed. At each spank, my nipples throb, my pussy aches, and my clit sends tiny little pulses throughout my body. I'm scared I'll come. I'm scared how my body is reacting and I'm scared that I don't want this. *Thwack, thwack, thwack, thwack.*

"God, your arse is a glorious pink." The paddle lands on the bed next to my hand. Seb shoves two fingers inside me. He finger fucks me again and I'm building. The muscles in my stomach pull tighter and my skin hums, radiating from my core. Seb stops again and I cry out.

"Oh God, no. Seb, please. I can't take it anymore, please." It's too much for me. Tears fall from my eyes, instantly absorbed by the blindfold. Every fibre of my body is screaming for release but I hold it in. *I don't want this.* My climax is bearing down on me, the pressure mingling with the pain and adding to my impending release. I want to give in to my body's demands, but Seb won't award me that pleasure. His fingers retreat. His hand strokes my fiery bottom, and he slaps me several times with an open palm. I jerk with every hand fall. The pain swamps my mind. I don't want to be with Seb like this. The brush of his legs tells me where he is. He stands behind me and runs his hard cock through my wet folds, covering himself in my juices. He surges forward, penetrating me hard and deep.

"Argh!" My cry rips from my throat as I'm assaulted again by the sensations he compels from me. He stills for a moment and moves his hands around to my front. His voice is a harsh whisper in my ear.

"This might hurt, baby. Take a deep breath."

I don't understand his words. He cups my breast and then I understand. A searing pain rushes to my breasts as he releases the first and then the second clamp before he pumps into me.

I'm sobbing now. He's massaging feeling back into my breasts. They feel heavy and sensitive, and it adds yet more fuel to the fire that burns wild inside my body. I'm hurting and I haven't climaxed. My body is screaming at me and I want to retreat from Seb. He releases my breasts and grips my hips to anchor himself as he powers into me.

My arms give out and I collapse to the bed.

My abused nipples scream at the contact while Seb's cock splits me in two. It's too much. I'm overwhelmed. I feel abused rather than cherished.

"Stop, please, Seb. Stop," I sob out, my throat raw with emotion. Seb has never once been like this—this intense, this painful. He's given me too much stimulation at once. The paddle was the item I was scared of. I knew it could hurt, but I trusted that Seb would know how to use it to extract pleasure. With all the new sensations bombarding me, I can't find the connection to Seb, the one that we were so quick to establish. I'm lost inside my head with just the heated pain and my fears. Seb doesn't stop, and I fear he's lost the control that he's always kept in check.

I grit my teeth, clench my fists and try to block it all out, but I can't. He seeks out my clit with the tip of his finger and I nearly convulse off the bed. Despite my mind telling me that I don't like how Seb is acting, my body is still burning to climax.

"Yes, Isabel. Yes. Come with me," Seb growls. His finger suddenly rubs my clit in quick circles and I know that I will. He thrusts a few more times. The frustration and feelings that have been growing inside me finally edge closer to release. Fire rages through me. I don't want to come. Not like this. I don't want a climax ripped from my body rather than willingly given. Painful thrusts penetrate me and my orgasm explodes around his cock, pulsing and drawing him in deeper. I'm left broken as it washes through my body, unable to cope with the feelings that come from it. I don't want the pleasure that he has forced from me. Finally, he stops and he slowly pulls out of me.

As soon as I'm free, I crawl up the bed and sag into the pillows. I wrap my arms around myself and sob, giving in to the wave of emotions. Resting on my side, I pull my knees up tight. Protectively.

"Izzy, god, Izzy. That was... Let me get your blindfold, Izzy." Seb's voice is close, but I don't want him near me.

"No!" I grab for the blindfold, tear it off and throw it to the floor.

"Shhh, baby," he croons at me, but I don't want to hear it.

"No. Please, just... don't touch me. Don't... Don't touch me."

"Izzy, please." Now it's Seb who's pleading. I pull myself up and try to get off the bed. My legs are weak and I feel as if I may fall, but I make it to the door.

"Stop, Izzy. What's wrong?"

I turn to him so he can see my tear-stained face. I must look a state.

"Oh, Izzy. Why are you crying? Come here. I need to take care of you."

"Take care of me? You hurt me, Seb. I... I didn't know how to stop you. You wouldn't stop. You wouldn't listen to me." I must look confused and lost as my words hang in the air between us.

"No," he shakes his head, but his brows knit together before his focus returns to me. Scrutinising me. "You were fine. You didn't say..." His hands fist at his sides as anger and regret register across his face. "Black. Izzy, you didn't say black. I thought you were okay. God, Izzy." His fists continue to flex and he drops his head. "We were good. It was so powerful, you letting me... I'm sorry. You didn't say black." He steps towards me and I let him, his arms inch out, careful not to startle me. His embrace is rigid with tension and the contact puts my nerves back up. I move away and can see the pain darken his eyes. My heart wants to stay with him, to reassure him, but my body isn't quite ready yet. I need to be on my own, to process my own thoughts. I turn from him, walk as fast as I can to my room, and close the door behind me.

* * *

I must have been asleep for a while. The light has faded in the sky and the room is cast in shadows. As I let my eyes adjust, I remember why I'm in my room alone. *The blindfold, being tied, the vibrator, the nipple clamps, the paddle.* I turn over onto my back and wince as the cotton sheets rub against my sore behind. I ache from head to foot. My head is pounding, probably because I've barely eaten or drunk anything all day. *And the crying.*

Where is Seb? The pain etched on his face once he realised I wasn't okay is what I remember most. Now that I'm calm, I want to check he's okay. But what do I say? Something happened to Seb earlier. He wouldn't normally act that way towards me. Up to a point, I wanted everything Seb was giving to me. Even with all he put me through, he still made me come—my body wanting what he gave to me. He brought me to the edge so many times. My head and my emotions couldn't keep up. I didn't know what to do with it all.

I need to speak to Seb and talk all of this through. It wasn't the same as the other times we've been together. He'd always been careful. He was introducing me to this lifestyle gently. There was nothing that felt gentle about earlier. I normally feel more connected to him after we've been intimate. This is uncharted water. It's as if he reached a new point with me today. His focus was on what he was doing to me, not on me. It gave me a glimpse of what might be hidden beneath his muscled body—a need that went beyond what he's already shown me. Perhaps all the previous times had been a warm up for him. Warming me up to show me the joy of submission before sampling the pain that can also come from it? *No.* Seb would never intentionally hurt me. I know he cares for me. This was as much my fault as his. I didn't realise that saying stop wouldn't make him stop. He told me, but I didn't understand the true meaning of his words. I was too eager, too excited. I need to apologise.

I pull on my robe and crack the door open to peep out. The rest of the apartment is quiet and shrouded in darkness. I walk to his room and push the door open but he's not inside. As I continue down the hall to the living room, I see him sitting on the floor against the wall. His head is slumped forward, his arms propped on his knees. Hanging from his hand is what looks like a champagne bottle. I take a closer look around the room and notice several things out of place. The table by the sofa is knocked over. There is another bottle of champagne lying on the floor, empty. Glass shards litter the floor by the door. *How did I not hear all of this?* As I survey the wreck, I notice Seb lifting the bottle and taking a drink. I'm suddenly nervous.

"Seb, are you alright?" My voice is weak even to my own ears, and I'm not even sure he's heard me. "Seb, are you alright? Come on. Talk to me?" This is partly my fault. If I wanted to stop, I could have, but my safeword hadn't crossed my mind since we first talked about it. "Seb, can you hear me?" I step closer to him and kneel down by his side. He lifts his head and locks eyes with me. They are glassy and unfocused against his pale face.

"Izzy... Hey, baby." His words are slurred and his usual chocolate smooth voice is hoarse and gravelly.

"Have you been out here all evening?" I wait to see whether Seb can string a sentence together, concerned that he's downed several bottles of champagne in a few hours.

"Yes, I've been out here." He starts to stand up but stumbles as he rights himself and braces against the wall. "Seems I can't even get drunk enough to pass out."

"I'm sorry. I am. Perhaps we can talk about it when you've slept this off. Come on, Seb. Let me help you get to bed."

"No. You should be running by now Isabel. That's what you do—run. Why aren't you out the door?"

"Seb, please. I don't want to run, but you're drunk and I can't talk to you like this."

"Come on now, Isabel. Aren't you ready to run back to your safe, boring marriage now?"

Tears trickle down my face once more. My eyes sting as I try to blink them away. My heart beats faster and my aching body is suddenly numb. All I can hear is my heart beating in my ears. I don't understand. Why he is saying he wants me to leave? I want to talk to him about why I reacted the way I did.

"No, please. I'm sorry I came apart earlier. I don't want to go." I talk to the floor. I can't bear to look at him for fear of seeing the rejection and disapproval I hear in his voice.

At this moment, I realise it doesn't matter what happened in his bedroom. I was as much to blame as he was. I need to learn to communicate and not be so frightened to speak my mind. If I'd done that before retreating to my room, Seb wouldn't be here drunk. We can get past this, though, I know we can.

"Seb, please. You're drunk—"

"Yes, well done, Isabel. How perceptive of you. I'm very drunk. Why are you still here? I'm damn sure I've shown you 'more' by now. Or have I not fulfilled my part of the deal yet? You get a walk on the wild side and what do I get? What's in this for me, Isabel?" His voice is raised, his words slurred. All I hear is a bitter anger. He walks towards the armchair—his armchair—and I try to follow him.

"Go, Isabel. There's the door."

"Please, Seb, don't push me away. I'm not running. I won't run. I'm sorry." I plead with him. I don't want to lose him. I love him.

"Yes. You. Will. You wanted to play out your fantasy but you got scared. Well, the tour is over. Go back to your marriage."

"I don't want to!" I scream the words at him. He looks at me and then towards the door before he launches the champagne bottle at it. It crashes against the wood, smashing into a thousand pieces. As the glass falls to the floor, my heart echoes its action, breaking into a hundred pieces.

"I said there's the door." With that, he stumbles his way past me and down the hall towards his room. The door slams behind him.

* * *

I need to leave.

I go back to change into my clothes from earlier and grab my bag from the wardrobe. The velvet box is sitting in its usual place, the anklet nestled safely inside. It wasn't around my ankle. Did it matter? I want to submit to Seb. I have since the first time we were together. That hasn't changed. I grab the box and open it. The overwhelming urge to take it with me has me closing the box in my hand. But it's not mine to take. It was a gift and a sign of my submission—our secret language. I pause and close my eyes. Tears have escaped the corners of my eyes, but I don't care. I let them fall and put the box back down and leave it in my room.

Moving silently through the apartment, I dig his key fob out of my bag and leave it on the kitchen counter. Part of me wants to write a note to say that I was sorry. I wanted to ask him why he went so far. Why he didn't listen to me? Would it be like that again? Would it be so intense and overwhelming? A thousand thoughts stream through my head and I can't focus on just one. I leave. *He made his feelings pretty clear.*

I walk to the front door. The glass crushes beneath my feet and as it splinters under my weight my heart aches for the man who I have barely begun to love. I came here to escape my marriage and found someone who I could be my true self with. Who I could give all of myself to. He opened a door that I always assumed would be closed to me, the one that took me to a place where I felt wanted, desired and free to experience my internal desires.

Now, with my heart in pieces, I open the door of Seb's apartment and creep over the threshold that only a few weeks ago held so much promise.

Nineteen

The door echoes in the hall as it closes behind me. Unsurprisingly, the house is empty, with no sign of Phil. I drag my body up the stairs, fall into bed and curl myself into a tight ball. I feel drained of everything. My eyes are sore and puffy and I desperately want to let my emotions win and have a good cry, but I can't. If I start, I may never stop.

I watch the numbers tick over on the clock on the bedside table and try to make sense of the last few days. I think back to when Seb and I met, when we were friends. Would I have preferred not to take the step that led to us being lovers? Would I have been happy to settle at always wondering, always hoping that Phil would work harder at our marriage? Would I stop the affair and work at getting back to where we used to be?

Lying in bed feeling as numb and broken as I do, I can't answer those questions. I'm not ready to analyse anything. I try to close my eyes, but when I do, I see the drunken glazed look in Seb's eyes before he told me to leave.

More

    I will my body into getting up and looking after some basic needs—eat, drink, and take a shower—there isn't anything else I want to do.
    It's nearly five in the morning. I must have slept because I don't know where the time has gone. I've lost a day. I'm supposed to be up and going to work in a few hours, but the idea of that makes my stomach turn. I pull the duvet over my head and wrap up tight, trying to cocoon myself from the outside, from everything and everyone. Even Seb.
    The alarm wakes me but I immediately turn it off.
    I've been over Saturday so many times in my head I'm not sure what really happened and what is my own thoughts playing tricks on me. I've not moved since coming home in the early hours of Sunday morning and although I still don't want to do anything, my bladder is in desperate need and I should check my phone, if only to call work. Hobbling to the bathroom, my body is stiff from the bed rest. My phone is dead so I plug it in and check for messages. There is one text from Seb.

    Sorry. S

    Reading that one word sets me off. My eyes sting as they fill and overflow with tears. My legs crumble. I slump on the floor and bury my face in the bed, crying about everything that those few letters convey: my pain and my hurt heart, the worry about my feelings being reciprocated, my marriage. It's all been below the surface. I'm scared as well. I'm in love with another man and I don't know whether I'll ever see him again. The thought hits me in the stomach, and I rush to the toilet and heave into the bowl. I've not eaten for a while so nothing comes up, but that doesn't stop the nausea. At least now I can legitimately say I'm too ill to work.
    The day comes and goes, and I spend most of it wallowing in bed. After getting over the initial shock of possibly never seeing

Seb again, I calm down enough to make some sense out of all of this mess. There isn't anything to say that I'll never see him again. No matter how I look at the situation, I have no regret over meeting or being with Seb. He made me feel more alive, more connected to someone than I ever have before. What we shared was more than just a physical connection. Our relationship was real, even if it wasn't conventional. If there is ever to be the smallest chance of having anything with Seb, I must first settle things with Phil.

We've been skirting around the issue of our marriage for weeks and it's time to be grown-up about it. Phil wouldn't answer my confrontation the last time we argued. I won't have that again.

Seb once told me to have courage, and now I feel that I need it more than ever. I grab my phone and call Phil but it goes to voicemail. I don't leave a message but send a text.

> Phil, I'm home. It's time to talk.

I press send and wait. And wait. It strikes me that I've been at home since early Sunday morning and haven't seen Phil. *Surprise, surprise!* I crawl back into bed and try to get some rest. Before I fall asleep, I send a text to Jess to fill her in. I need someone on my side at the moment.

When the alarm goes off the next morning, I decide to ignore it again. I doze before making myself call into work.

"Hi, Mark," I mumble, my voice weak and tight with emotion.

"Hey, Izzy. Are you feeling better?"

"Um, no. I'm not doing very well and doubt I'll be in for the next few days."

"Okay, well, thanks for letting me know. I hope you feel better soon, and make sure you let me know when you'll be back to work."

"Thanks, I will."

I seem to be able to sleep much more easily now, and I drift in and out for most of the day. I make it downstairs to cook some pasta. I take a few mouthfuls, but that's all I can stomach.

The house is still quiet, and it makes me sad to see where I could end up at the end of all of this. Completely alone. Suddenly this is all so serious. I'm looking at leaving my husband with no guarantee of anything after it. But should that stop me? Seb and I never talked about being together. He said he would show me what submission and dominance can be like. That he'd give me what I've been pining after through my Tumblr blog and BDSM sites, not jump into a relationship with a married woman, or a married woman seeking a divorce.

Divorce. It doesn't seem so distant now. Perhaps this is what I should have done weeks ago. Before Seb, I would never have thought this was a way out or even a possibility. Now... I should be proud that I'm making progress of some kind, but I'm not. It numbs me further.

It's not only the house that is quiet, so is my phone. No calls or texts from Phil and nothing further from Seb. Not even Jess has gotten in touch. I'm desperate to speak to someone, to have someone reassure me about my life, but I'm on my own. I shouldn't need anyone else. This is my life, and I have to take charge of it.

In the shower, I realise that I'm wallowing in self-pity and need to get over it. Quickly.

I always think better in the shower. The water clarifies my mind and calms me. I can think clearly for the first time in days. People get divorced all of the time. It doesn't mean the end of the world or that I've failed. *It shouldn't.* I climb back into bed, feeling a lot brighter. I am only thirty-two years old and I have a good job. My marriage or relationship should not define me as a person. It shouldn't.

As I try to fall asleep, I can't help but think of Seb and wonder what he's been doing. Because of the text he sent, I know he hasn't drunk himself into a coma. Seeing so many different sides to him hasn't dulled my feelings for him. He's shown me what having a real relationship can be like. I want to grab hold of it and work at giving Seb as much as he's given me. I want our relationship to hold trust and understanding, give and take. Plus the freedom from submitting. It's so much more than I thought it could be from sitting behind the computer screen and imagining. Even though the time I had with Seb was brief, not being with him, not having him as part of my life, makes my heart ache.

* * *

A bell rings in my ears, and it's not my alarm. As I come round, the ringing turns to banging. I'm suddenly wide-awake and panicking. *Could it be Seb at the door?* I fly out of bed and into my dressing gown before I head downstairs. I don't even care that I've not put a comb through my hair or brushed my teeth.

I pull the door open with my heart in my mouth, but it's not Seb. Jess is standing on my doorstep with a huge bouquet of flowers in her arms. I look at her and I see her concern for me. I feel the lump in my throat and I step back to let her in.

Before I can say or do anything else, she thrusts a heavy cream envelope into my hand, followed by the flowers, and walks past me into the kitchen.

"I found these on your doorstep. I'm putting the kettle on for a cup of tea."

The envelope has my name handwritten in black ink. It has to be a note from Seb. It is far too classy to be from Phil. My heart seizes in my throat. Is this a formal good-bye? Or is it an "I'm sorry. Let's try again?" I don't have the courage to look. The flowers, though, are beautiful. Purple hyacinths are surrounded by white roses, tuberoses, and tulips. It's such an unusual arrangement.

"Thanks, Jess," I venture tentatively.

"Are you going to stay in the hall all day, Iz?"

I bring the envelope and the flowers with me and place them gingerly on the table, not wanting to damage them. My heart races at the prospect of what the flowers mean or what words he's written, but I will need to be alone to confront them. In my heart, I know it won't be good news. How can it after the way I've treated him? I pick up the cup of tea waiting for me.

"So, are you going to tell me what is going on?" Jess sounds sad and a little bit resigned to the fact that this isn't going to be a happy meeting.

"Oh Jess, things are a mess. But I need to talk to Phil. I can't stay with him, Jess." I say the words as confidently as I can, but my voice breaks and the words taste bitter in my mouth.

"Well, that's a very positive start to the conversation. I'm proud of you, Iz. I thought I was going to have to talk you into it." Jess is nearly smiling now, and for the first time in days, I manage a lacklustre smile in return. I sit down at the table and Jess joins me. "You know, you've made the right decision and I'm really pleased you made it on your own."

"It doesn't feel particularly positive. But I know what I should have done before getting involved with Seb. Phil and I... I've been in denial. I didn't want to admit to failing."

"You are not failing just because you have an asshole of a husband. Iz, you know he's been staying at Jackson's, but he's been spending a lot of time with a blonde."

Hearing that from Jess is little consolation.

"That's not a surprise, Jess."

"Well, I know you had your suspicions. I'm merely confirming them."

"He won't admit it to me."

"I know. And he's turning everything around to be your fault."

"My fault? It's not my fault!"

"Calm down, Iz. I'm just saying. Phil's playing the confused, doting husband who doesn't understand his wife anymore."

"Well, he doesn't understand me. That's part of the problem. We hardly talk, and we don't even know each other anymore. We haven't done anything as a couple that we both wanted to do for years. Plus, he's been having an affair." My self-pity suddenly boils up as anger. How can I be having such a hard time trying to resolve my feelings over our marriage, yet he seems content with going to another woman rather than working things out with me? Hypocrite.

"I'm sorry, Iz."

"I need to talk to Phil but he won't call me. I want to do this right, for us to talk like adults." Frustration builds at my lack of control over the situation.

"Oh, sweetie. I know, but if he won't, what will you do?"

"I want to do this right, Jess. I need Phil to talk to me and admit that a divorce is the best option for us, that our marriage is over, and we've both moved on. He's moved on with Sophie, it seems. I wasn't even looking for a friend when I first met Seb. I was starved for any form of interest or affection and when Seb gave that to me…"

"And what about Seb? Have you seen him recently?"

"Not since the weekend."

"What happened?"

I can't tell her everything. "We had a fight. I started crying and he got drunk. He asked me to go back to my marriage."

"Oh, Iz."

She moves towards me to offer a hug.

"Don't. Please. I'll start crying, and I've spent too much time crying. I need to make sure things are sorted with Phil before I can start to sort things with Seb. It's not fair to Seb, otherwise." I look down at my now-cold tea and take a moment.

"Look, I'm here for you, Iz, but I need to get to work and so do you."

"No, I'm not going to work this week. I can't. I'm a mess and need some time."

"Okay, okay, I'm not your boss."

"I'm sorry. It's just… I can't. I can't." I break down. I was doing so well. I sob onto Jess's shoulder and cry it all out.

* * *

Jess leaves once I get my crying under control. Now, I'm left with the flowers and the envelope.

I arrange the flowers into a vase and I take the time to do it right. They are so fragrant. The perfume from the hyacinths is overpowering. I try to make it as pretty as possible but I can't do them justice. I've not received flowers for such a long time and certainly never like these, an unexpectedly beautiful and unique gift.

I stare at the envelope in my hand. I want to hear from Seb. I would give anything to hear from him and be told that everything is okay. Now, knowing that he has committed his feelings to paper has me scared. It's selfish. I'm a selfish, horrible woman, but I can't help my feelings. I should be ashamed.

Jess has helped to brighten my dreary mood. She always has a positive influence over me, even with her giving me the tough love I deserve. Although I didn't tell her too much, I know she's there for me and is supporting me. It still hurts to think that Phil would rather be off with another woman than talking to me about our marriage. But how can I force it? I also need to hear Phil admit that we were broken before I can admit to my own actions. Our broken marriage was the catalyst for me. If he can't admit we were in trouble… Two wrongs certainly don't make a right, and I don't think we'll ever be right again.

The envelope is thick and feels heavy as I turn it over and over between my fingers. It reminds me of his business card when he first gave it to me. I peel open the letter and pull out the paper.

> Dearest Isabel,
> I'm deeply sorry about how things ended on Saturday. It was never my plan, nor my intention for the evening to be so challenging for you. You wanted to experience more and I'm confident that's what I've given you, but I don't think I can offer you that in the future.
> I hope, in time, we can still be friends. Our friendship was precious to me.
> Take care,
> Sebastian

My blood runs cold as I read his words. He doesn't want anything else from me but friendship. He certainly doesn't love me, like I do him. My hands shake as I hold the letter and I can no longer see the words. My eyes blur and the letters swim in front of my eyes.

I can't take this. I don't want to go back to what my life was like before Seb. My heart feels as if it's going to burst from my chest it's beating so fast. No, this can't happen. We had something that can't be forgotten. Seb has taught me to feel more in the last few weeks than I ever have in my life. There was something between us. I felt it.

The tears flow down my face. I thought I'd cried myself dry already. Obviously I was wrong. I sob, howl, and cry until my body has nothing left.

I have nothing left.

Twenty

Two weeks later

"I'm going out, Iz. I'll be late so don't wait up," Phil shouts up the stairs to me before he slams the door behind him. I'm where I've spent most of the last few weeks—holed up in my bedroom.

After getting Seb's card, I've completely shut down. I took the flowers up to my room and pretty much stopped living. Day by day, I watched the flowers fade and wither away, and with them, my hopes and dreams and all of my feelings.

I haven't seen anyone or gone to work. I told Mark that I've had a family emergency and agreed to take some unpaid leave. I've sat, slept, and thought about all that I've done and how much my entire world has changed. *Changed without actually changing.*

Phil came home the day after the flowers arrived. I listened as he talked at me. Sure, he apologised for not listening to me, for arguing. He told me it was all because of stress. He wouldn't admit to his affair. I told him that we couldn't be together. That too much has happened and we can't just pretend everything is alright. Resorting to form, Phil ignored me.

That's how it was left. Phil talked at me, and I didn't say the magic words, "I want a divorce." I didn't have the energy to fight it out with him. I too, have resorted to form, but with a few exceptions. I have insisted he sleep in the spare room and I have as little interaction as possible with him.

I have well and truly hit rock bottom and can't think how to pull myself out of my misery. Not even a rather stern pep talk from Jess has helped.

The flowers are dead in the vase. I can't even throw them away. It feels like if I do, I'll be throwing away my last connection to Seb. Gone from my life. He hasn't contacted me since sending the flowers, and I've resisted getting in touch with him. My marriage is over and I wonder what it will take for Phil to realise that for himself. Every time I see Phil, I mentally picture him with that girl, Sophie, and hate myself for not saying anything. Then I feel even worse for not coming clean about Seb. All Phil is doing is trying to placate me. Nothing has changed for him. Yet everything has for me.

There was a time, years ago, that I would have been outraged and heartbroken at the thought of Phil with someone else. Not now, though. I promised myself that I wouldn't continue to see Seb without telling Phil. Perhaps if I tell him about Seb, Phil will see the futility of continuing as we are.

* * *

"Get up!" I'm woken by Jess screaming at me.

"How? What? How did you get in?" I'm half asleep, shocked and a little scared at the look on Jess's face.

"It doesn't matter. I'm sick of this shit from you. I'm not going to let you wallow any longer, so drag your sorry arse out of bed." There is little room for argument in her tone and it's not as if I've grown a spine overnight, so I sit myself up in bed. I stare at her, waiting for her to make the first move.

"I've let you sit and fall apart for long enough. No more. Up, shower, and you're coming with me. No arguments."

I don't say anything. I just stare at her. She's flipped. She's never been this angry with me before.

"Move it!"

The scary look on her face encourages me to hurry along and climb out of bed and into the bathroom. I turn the shower on, avoiding the mirror, and ready myself to tackle the bird's nest that is my hair.

Half an hour later, I creep out of the bathroom and see Jess drinking a cup of tea in my chair.

"Get dressed. We're going out." She stands expectantly as I wander to the wardrobe and look through my options.

"Where are we going?" I venture a simple question to test how angry she is.

"You'll see. Now hurry up and get dressed."

Focussing on the task, I'm stiff and awkward. I've barely moved in two weeks and my limbs are protesting.

When I'm finally ready, Jess marches downstairs and I dutifully follow. She stops only to put her mug in the kitchen before she heads to the door. Her intent is crystal-clear. She really does want me to leave the house. Grabbing my bag, I check for the essentials and shove my phone in as well. I peek at her, the pleading clear in my eyes. She doesn't sympathise, and humphs as she heads out the door.

Twenty minutes later, we're parked and she's marching me towards the entrance of a swanky salon. She marches me through the door and goes to speak to the receptionist. As I loiter in the waiting area, it becomes apparent that she has organised this and has booked me in for who knows what. She walks back to me with a staff member in tow.

"Hello, Isabel. If you'd like to follow me?" The pretty member of the salon staff beckons me towards the back of the shop. I look towards Jess, who nods her head towards the back, so I follow. Reluctantly.

I'm seated at the basin and she washes my hair, which feels wonderful. Then she escorts me once more to a station in front of floor-to-ceiling mirrors.

"Andy will be with you shortly."

"Thank you." Jess has arranged for me to have my hair cut. *As if this would shock me out of my funk.*

"Hi, Isabel. I'm Andy," says a very tall brunette, who appears to be the one doing the cutting. I try not to imagine what Jess has given them permission to do. I guess I don't really have an incentive to keep it long anymore. Seb was the only one who ever said anything about my hair. Visions of him stroking my hair and tying it up flash before my eyes, and I try to suppress the lump forming in my throat. His hands were sure and comforting, and although every fibre of my body wants to feel that again, my rational head tries to tell me that it won't happen. I close my eyes and squeeze to stop the tears. I would give anything to feel him wrap my hair around his wrist, to feel his skin on mine.

"Isabel, are you alright?"

"Yes, sure. Um, sorry. Just… whatever my friend said."

"Okay, well, if you're sure?"

"Yes." I'm definitive and settle back into the chair. I try to force my melancholy thoughts away and let this very nice lady do whatever Jess wants with my hair.

An hour and a half later, I walk out of the salon with Jess, and she seems happy with her work. "Coffee?" she asks.

"Sure. Where?"

"Do you like it?"

"Like what?"

"Don't be stupid, Isabel. Your hair? You haven't said anything since we left the salon."

"It's fine. Thanks. I know what you wanted to do and I love you for it. Thank you."

"Stop, stop, stop!"

I sigh and stop my feet from carrying me forward. I know what she's going to say, but I want to get past this.

"Iz, of course I did this for you. You needed something to snap you out of your depression, to try to make you feel special again. I know it's just your hair but hopefully it's a start. I won't let you give up on everything you wanted. You were so sure of things a few weeks ago. And now you've given up. You're not even you at the moment. I want to help get you back. I'm here for you."

"I know, Jess, and I'm really thankful. Really I am. And I do like my hair."

"Really?"

"Yes. Now come on. I just need some time. I'm not quite ready yet. But this has helped."

"Okay, so coffee now?"

"Yes, please."

"Okay. Here's a bar that looks good."

I look up and my stomach rolls. *Oh, God no. Not this bar... Please.*

"There's better places for coffee. Come on."

"But you said you wanted coffee. It doesn't really matter." With that, she grabs my arm and drags me inside.

I know this bar, well. It's where Seb and I always met. Where we first met. It hasn't changed. Why would it? It's only been a few weeks.

"I'll grab a table if you get the coffees. I'll have a latte." She heads off towards a quiet group of tables off to one side. I walk to the bar to place our order. It's fairly quiet for a... I realise I don't even know what day of the week it is. I turn around and look out at all of the tables. I can remember feeling good about being here. It was always where we would meet, before we complicated it all with more. *When Seb and I were friends.*

Waiting for the coffees, I can feel my lips struggling to put on a smile. Jess'll hound me for the reason why I can't try to be happy, and I so don't want to upset her after everything she's done for me today. My mind begins to drift.

"Stop it! Stop it now."

"I'm fine. Leave it, Jess." I try to gather myself, but there's no fooling her. My voice even cracks a little as I try to convince her that I'm alright.

"No, you're not. I can see it all over your face. You're sad—beyond sad. It's like you've given up. I want the real Izzy back. Forget about Seb and Phil, and start again. Why can't you see that it's them who are making you miserable?"

"I… It's not that simple. You won't understand."

"Only because you won't tell me. Talk to me. You've completely closed up and I've only had the edited highlights of what happened between you Seb."

"If I try to explain, will you leave it?"

"Maybe. You needed an intervention. Now talk."

She'll never leave this. She'll back me into a corner. Maybe talking this through, getting it all out in the open, can give me some peace and I can move on?

"This is the bar Seb and I met in."

"This bar—this bar we're in now?"

"Jess!"

"Okay, okay. I'm sorry."

"Yes, this bar. It's where we would meet."

"And…"

"And, we slept together, you know this. We weren't just friends anymore. He showed me what being with someone who cared for me could be like. He gave me what I'd always been missing from a relationship… from sex. He gave me more. But I ruined it and he told me to go back to my marriage. It's over. End of story." I turn my head away from Jess and try not to have a meltdown at the words I've just spoken.

"You love him, don't you?" Her words hit me in the chest. I can't lie to her. Not about this.

"Yes." I can't look her in the eye.

"Then why is it all over? I don't understand."

"The last time we were together I did something stupid. We both hurt each other and didn't talk it through. He asked me to leave. He sent me the flowers and a note and told me he wanted to be friends. I haven't heard from him since. Now can we leave it? Please?" I drink my coffee far too quickly, turning my tongue numb with pain. I play with the napkin, folding it up and trying to occupy my hands. The loss I've felt since walking out on Seb is bubbling up and threatening to choke me from inside, and I feel trapped.

"I'm sorry, Jess. I can't be here just now. I need to go. Thanks, though... for today. Despite everything, I know you're there for me, and it means a lot. I'll make it up to you, I promise." I almost trip over myself as I hurry out towards the door. I'm nearly running as I crash through the door and straight into someone entering.

"Oh, I'm sorry." I sniffle my apology, not looking up.

"That's quite alright... Isabel?"

His voice. Smooth and rich and everything I've longed to hear. I would recognise it anywhere but I still can't look up. I'm on the very edge tears as it is. I can't break down in front of him. *I can't.*

"Izzy, are you okay?" Seb holds my shoulders now, keeping me standing, but I still haven't raised my eyes.

"Izzy, look at me."

Such a big part of me wants to follow his simple instruction. I can't. I can't let him see me like this. *I can't.*

"Look at me." The rumble in his voice shifts the air around him. I'm falling apart in his arms, and he leaves me powerless to do anything but obey when he uses that voice. He helps by lifting my chin so I'm looking directly up into his eyes. That's when all of my resolve falters and the first tear slips from my eye. Seb's thumb eases it from my cheek and at that simple touch, that kind and gentle action, he melts me to my core. I can't stop the tears now and I cling onto Seb for the support I need.

"It's okay. Let it all out." Seb's words seep through me, soothing my tortured mind. Strong arms close around me, cradling me to him, and I simply give up. I give in to the churning mass of emotions inside me.

"What's going on?" Jess's no-nonsense voice breaks through my Seb armour.

"It's fine. I've got her." Seb replies without missing a beat, before I get a chance to say anything.

"And who are you?"

"A friend. Who are you?"

"You're him, aren't you? Seb."

"Yes. I told you, I've got her. She's fine."

"I don't think you're anyone to judge that. Now leave her alone. Come on, Iz."

"Jess, " I step back from Seb to look at her. "It is okay. Really." I say it softly, without putting any conviction behind the words. It's all I can manage, but I doubt that Jess will buy it.

"No, it's not okay. You're crying and you're in no fit state to know what you want. Now come on." She begins to pull me away, but I don't want to leave Seb.

"Jess, please…"

"Yes, I think you should listen to Isabel."

"Oh, wow! You're the one who needs to leave. Have you any idea what you've put her through? You've no right to have anything to do with her."

"Isabel is perfectly safe with me, I assure you."

"Safe with you is a relative term. She's emotionally broken."

"Enough!" I can't stand here and let them bicker about me as though I'm not even here. I have to muster all of my courage to get this one sentence out. I turn to Jess and hope that she'll understand.

"Jess, I love you, but I'd like to talk with Seb. I'll follow you home shortly." It feels like I'm taking sides. Looking at Jess, I can tell she thinks I picked the wrong one.

"Fine." She doesn't say anything more and turns to walk away. She's done nothing but support me, and I've thrown that all back in her face. As much as I want to go after her and say sorry some more, Seb is standing in front of me, still holding onto me and providing the support to keep me standing. The irony that it's his words he wrote on the card that have caused me to fall apart is not lost on me.

I lower my eyes and stare at his chest.

"Izzy, please look at me."

"Seb, I—"

"Isabel, look at me." He doesn't force me this time, but he doesn't need to. My eyes drift up to his. They are still the beautiful aquamarine I love gazing into, the same mix of blues and greens that sparkle and reassure me. My vision blurs as the tears fall.

"Oh, Izzy. What's wrong? " He pulls me into him and places his arms around me in a soft embrace. He strokes my head as I weep onto his chest in the middle of the bar. He lets me cry, lets me have this moment. His hands run down my newly cut hair and it feels lovely.

"You've cut your hair."

I nod against his chest.

"Okay, we can talk about that later."

"What do you mean?" I look up at him and push back a little.

"I'm sorry. I didn't mean to sound like that. I would like to talk, Izzy. Please?" I continue to stare up at him. Could I really cope with just being friends? Is this what he wanted to discuss? I hear the words from his card ring loud in my head. *Only friends.* Suddenly I don't want to hear him say it to my face. In my chest throbs a deep pain that no amount of fake smiles can disguise. Will I feel like this every time I see him?

"Seb, I'm not sure I can be just friends. There's too much… I feel too much for you to forget and move on." I start to back away. My thoughts make my stomach churn. I'm the one who is suddenly talking about cutting all ties. From the devastation I felt after reading his letter, I was sure that friendship would be better than not having him in my life. Now that I see him, I'm not sure.

I love him. How can I pretend that I don't feel that way about him and go about being friends? Coffee, the occasional dinner, text chats—I can't do it. I continue my retreat.

"Wait, Izzy, please. Forget about my note for a minute. Just talk to me." He's getting agitated. I can see it and I don't want to fight again.

His hands mess his hair, as if he's fighting with himself, but I can't stay to find out. Turning on my heel, I quicken my pace to the door. I make it a few steps down the street before my shoulder is pulled backwards and I'm stopped abruptly.

"Isabel, no!" he shouts. "No. No running. If you won't talk, then listen."

"Seb, please. I can't…"

"Shhh. Yes you can. I'm not letting you go. You can listen here on the street or back inside."

As much as it will hurt, listening to what he has to say might offer me some closure. I nod my acquiescence and he grabs my hand to pull me back inside.

He plonks me down at a table—the table we usually sat at—and takes the seat opposite me. I don't say anything; I'm afraid I'll tell him I love him and he'll kindly dismiss it.

"Izzy, I'm sorry."

"You've said that already. The flowers were lovely, thank you."

"Stop. I'm trying to tell you something, so be quiet," he snaps back at me, and I recoil like a scolded child.

"I… I can't get you out of my mind. I've been visiting here for the last week just on the off chance I'd see you. I don't want to lose you."

"I can't fall back into just a friendship with you. I'm hurting. I know you're sorry. I'm sorry too." I start to stand but Seb grabs my shoulders to keep me sitting. He leans his forehead against mine and his hands cradle my face.

"Spend the weekend with me?" *The weekend?* I try to stop my heart from soaring. This isn't something that a friend would ask of another. I shake my head. I won't survive being kicked out again. The last few weeks are proof of that.

"Izzy, I'm ashamed at how I left things between us. I should never have gotten drunk and said such hateful things to you. Truthfully, I want a lot more than the occasional night with you. I want to explore what has already grown between us. The possibility of an us. There's so much more." He pulls away to look at me and a tiny smile creeps across my lips. As it does, his thumb brushes over it, closely followed by his lips.

He kisses me hard and forces my compliance. *I've lost.* Almost as quickly as he started, he stops. He pulls me up and walks around the table to squeeze me tightly in an all-encompassing hold.

"Come on. Before you change your mind."

"What? Wait. I can't go now. What day is it, anyway?"

"It's Friday, and I'm taking you home."

Friday? Oh God, I've been such a mess I've even lost track of the days. He can't take me home, though.

"Can't I meet you later?"

"No. And I don't mean your home. I mean mine."

"Oh. But I don't have anything. I need to grab some things."

"No you don't. I'll take care of you. Come with me."

I'll take care of you. How I've longed to hear those words, feel their meaning. After everything that has happened, he still wants me in his life. I love him. That hasn't changed. Do I want to be asking myself 'what if' for the rest of my life? I already thought that would be my fate. Is it too much to hope that I can find happiness with this man? "Okay." I say it before I talk myself out of it. I don't want to think anymore. I want to feel. Seb smiles back at me and squeezes my hand. I want this—my heart wants this—I know that. But I won't deny the part of me that's scared of exactly where this may lead. I'm still a wreck, and one who hasn't been to work in three weeks. I'm being trampled by my husband and I'm in love with another man.

Twenty One

The journey back is quiet and tense. Seb constantly adjusts his position in his seat. When I think he's finally comfy, his fingers start to drum on the steering wheel.

We walk in to the lift. The silence is heavy.

"How's work?" Seb asks.

"I've not been at work a lot. I've... had some time off."

The conversation dies before we reach his door. We've never been awkward around each other, and it feels alien.

"Would you like a drink?"

"Umm, tea, please."

He escorts me into the kitchen and I sit on a bar stool while Seb goes about making a pot of tea. I zone out. My head rings loudly with the alarms of what being here may bring. As I'm about to voice my troubles, Seb shocks me back into the present.

"Izzy, I'm sorry for many things. I did mean what I said in the note. I never meant to take it further than you wished to go. You just..." he pauses, as if he's searching for the right words to say. "With you... you completely give yourself to me. You trust me to bring you pleasure and pain, but safely and for our mutual benefit. And you want that for more than a quick scene or hook up." His words aren't anything new, but I feel how each one means something to him. He's sharing a part of himself with me. "I've been able to take you further than I ever imagined you'd want to go. I got lost in you—in us. I shouldn't have lost sight of your reactions to me. To what I was doing to your body. You didn't use your safeword, but you are very new to this. I misjudged the situation. I'm not proud of my behaviour afterwards. I pride myself on being a caring and considerate Dom, and I was everything but. Will you forgive me?"

I can see this is hard for him. His face is etched with the pain and worry of all the words he's spoken. I know that he is utterly sincere. But I'm as much to blame as he is, and I can't let him take the responsibility for this alone. I have to explain my feelings to him.

"Yes, of course I forgive you." I turn so I'm facing him. "It was all... all too much. I'm sorry. I forgot about my safeword. I didn't mean to. It was all so... intense. It felt different from the other times we were together. I'm sorry I reacted so hysterically. When I came to my senses, I wanted to talk to you about what had happened. I wanted to understand. I found you drunk in the living room. You threw me out after smashing a bottle against the wall. I didn't know what to think. All I got was one text that said, 'I'm sorry'." I don't hold back. "I wouldn't have run, but you pushed me out. You crushed me." My words hit us both. Even though I've felt everything I've said, saying it out loud slices through my heart again.

"I was furious with myself. I'd fucked up. I'd lost control in the moment. That has never happened to me before, and it shook me. I was angry and I shouldn't have taken it out on you when you came to find me." Seb pauses to pour the tea and he joins me at the breakfast bar. We aren't looking at each other, just facing forward in silence.

We've both said our piece but where does it leave us? Regret is heavy in the air between us. Although we're talking, the earlier tension hasn't abated.

"I'd like it if we can relax over the weekend. A bath might help you with that?"

"A bath? On my own?"

"Yes. Let me take care of you. I'd like to do something to make you feel good."

"Okay." I turn to smile warmly at him. This I can do. I can cope with a bath.

Ten minutes later, Seb has run a deep bubble bath. Citrus and floral scents fill the steam in the bathroom. I'm suddenly feeling shy. I look at him and raise my eyebrow, trying to indicate my hesitancy.

He shuts the door behind him and I smile to myself. I undress and lower myself into the bubbles. The heat instantly relaxes my body. Two weeks of sleepless nights and tension gang up on me and I doze off.

"Izzy, are you alright in there?" Seb's voice drifts into my consciousness and I wake with a small splash.

"Um... yes. Give me a few minutes. " I quickly wash my hair, having already ruined the salon effect, and pull myself from the bath and smother myself in a robe. I crack the door to find Seb waiting patiently for me.

"I must have dozed off. Sorry."

"Please don't be sorry. It's been a hard day." He offers me his hand and I gingerly place mine in his. He pulls me forward and into the lounge, where we sit on the sofa.

"You used to like me playing with your hair. Let me brush it for you." He twists in his seat and I position myself so my back is to him. He slowly and methodically pulls the comb through my tresses, gently tugging at the few knots at the end. Sure and confident fingers replace the comb and begin to massage my scalp, and my head lolls from side to side with pleasure. A cat-like purring escapes my throat.

"You like?"

"I love. Thank you."

"You are very welcome. Why did you get your hair cut?"

Oh no—he doesn't like it! I remember my thoughts as I sat in the chair at the salon. I never even considered that I would be back in Seb's company so soon. *If at all.*

"Well, it wasn't really my idea, and I didn't think it mattered anymore." I shrug a little, hoping he'll sense that I don't want to go into the details.

"I don't understand."

I let out a sigh. "Jess dragged me out of bed to get it cut. It was her 'intervention', as she put it. New hair, new me, I suppose. I let her do it. And I didn't really think I needed to keep it long. You said things were over. Friends don't get to decide on the length of the other's hair. Well, apart from Jess… You know what I mean."

"Relax. I like your hair and it's still long enough to tie up." He doesn't ask the question but leaves the meaning clear. The unspoken words fill the air with tension. I want him to reassure me. To be clear that after all our apologies there is still an us.

"We'll take things slowly, but I'd like to continue our relationship. I think you'd like that too." He knows what I'm going to say, what my answer is. I wouldn't be here with him if I was unsure. My current feelings for Seb dwarf what I felt the first time I came here. Excitement and exhilaration have been replaced with love and affection. The nerves are still there, though.

It is nice to feel something other than numb—all I've been managing recently.

After ensuring my hair is tangle-free, Seb pulls me around and into an embrace. I relax into it—into Seb—and let him comfort me and hold me. I instantly feel cared for. We sit, wrapped in each other's arms, for what feels like hours. Then I look up and notice one of the beautiful women artfully posed in black and white on his wall.

"Can I ask you a question?"

"Of course you may. Anything."

"The photographs. Why all of the photographs of women?" I try to make my question sound more 'interested' than 'jealous/paranoid'.

"I admire the female form, Izzy. I think it's a beautiful thing."

Are all of these photos girlfriends he's tied up and spanked—women he's helped to explore their sexual desires? I know it's my insecurities getting to me, but I'm always insecure. I can't help it, especially now.

"I thought, perhaps you had taken them, that they were photos of your previous partners." I hold my breath for his response.

"No, not mine. I've simply bought from a few photographers whose work I particularly like."

"So not the others... others you've been with?" It's out of my mouth before I can stop it, and I inwardly cringe at my own words.

"Definitely not. Is that what you've thought? All this time?" He sounds shocked.

"I wasn't sure. They've always, well, made me wonder. That's all."

"Wonder if these are women I've slept with?"

"Well... Um, yes... sort of." I try to sit up and free myself from his embrace. My pride is slightly wounded by how stupid this all sounds. Now I think it was a mistake to bring it up at all.

"What do you mean yes, sort of?" He hasn't let me free myself and he won't forget I started this conversation.

"Well, if these pictures are what you like, I'm not like them." My voice is small and I almost squeak out my greatest insecurities.

"Stand up." He helps me up and then sits me back in the chair. "This is a lot to ask, but close your eyes for a moment, and keep them closed."

I look at him and my hesitation shocks me.

"I promise I won't touch you."

I nod, unsure of what he is planning. I close my eyes and try to relax. I hear him walk about the room before it all goes quiet and I can't tell where he is.

"Do you know what I'm looking at, Izzy?"

"No," I reply, even more lost as to where he's going with this. I start to feel uncomfortable.

"I'm looking at the most delightful, enticing, and attractive female form in this apartment."

My heart sinks at his words and I pull my knees up to my chest. I keep my eyes shut and squeeze them tightly to stop more tears.

"Would you like to see which one is my favourite, Izzy?"

There is only so much I can take and right there—that was it. "I've had enough. That was cruel—" I jump up from the chair and smash right into Seb. He is standing, looking down at me.

"Silly girl," he mutters before he pulls me in for a breathtakingly soft kiss.

It doesn't stay soft. His next kiss is hard and possessive, pushing and pulling against my lips, his tongue teasing my mouth open. His hands are in my hair, pinning me to him, and all thought of taking our physical relationship slowly vanishes from my mind. My hands explore his body now, roaming under his shirt to find firm, hot skin. I want more of him. He follows my lead and runs his hands over my dressing gown, but it's not enough for me.

"Seb," I murmur between kisses.

"I'm sorry."

"No, don't stop."

"No, we do this slowly."

"Please…" I kiss him harder, pulling myself closer to him still. My hands scrape down his back, digging in to his flesh and signifying my growing need for him. I don't want to walk on eggshells with him. I want to take the second chance we have.

He lifts me off the ground and carries me back down the corridor towards his bedroom. He places me on the bed but keeps constant contact with my lips. We're working each other up, frantically clawing at the fabric that separates our bodies. I want him. I want all of him. My hands move to his belt buckle but he stops me.

"Izzy, slowly."

"I can't. I want this. I need this. Please."

His hands hold my head and he rests his forehead against mine. "This isn't what I had intended."

"It's okay. Don't make me beg."

"Oh, God." He pushes me back and unties the robe, baring all of me to him. "Izzy…" he whispers as he trails kisses up my stomach and between my breasts, up my neck. I tingle everywhere, as if he's awoken all of my nerve endings. A constant current thrums through me. He pulls me forward so he can take off the dressing gown. He runs his hands down my arms to hold my hands before he lays me back down.

"May I ask you something?"

"Yes." My breathing is heavy and I don't want him to stop. He fingers my wedding rings and looks back up at me.

"Would you take these off while you're here this weekend?"

I stare up at his face and look into his beautiful eyes. If I do this—take my rings off—what will that mean? A gesture that goes some way towards what I should have done months ago? A symbol that my marriage shouldn't stand between us anymore?

I nod my head and see Seb's answering smile. He gently wraps his fingers around the rings and slowly and carefully pulls them off. He sets them to the side before he lifts my hand and kisses my ring finger. His lips are soft and caress my naked skin, licking up my finger before sucking it into his mouth. His eyes seek mine and the heat I see in them scorches me. If I didn't need him before, I do now.

He eases me back to the bed and resumes covering me with kisses. Despite the look in his eyes a moment ago, he takes his time and runs his hands over every inch of my body. He moves my arms up and above my head and weaves our fingers together, keeping them there while he works his way down my neck with his lips and tongue. I kiss him back when he reaches my lips and pour all of the hurt and pain, all of the sadness and regret that I've felt over the last few weeks in to my kisses. He takes each of my emotions and returns passion and beauty through our kiss.

Seb's clothes rub against me and it makes me crave his touch. He forces my legs apart with his knee and my hips cradle him. He still has my hands clasped in his so I can't move to undress him.

"Seb, clothes," I pant.

"Patience, Isabel," he says between kisses. "Keep your arms above your head."

"Mmm," is all I manage.

He lets go of my hands and moves his slowly down my body. He trails them over my breasts, around my waist and over my hips. I try not to squirm under his touch but I can't help it. My eyes plead with him.

He doesn't take my silent hint and continues at his own pace. Finally, he stands up and strips his clothes off. He grabs a condom and crawls back up my body. He pushes my legs apart, making room for me to cradle his hips. His cock eagerly presses against me and I relax my legs further. He grasps my hands over my head again before he grinds his hips into me. His very hard cock rubs me and slips over my clit. I know I'm wet because he glides through my folds, sparking small pulses of pleasure. I'm aching for him to grant me the final relief, to drive inside me. I try to lift my hips to meet him, but he leans his body weight down onto me.

"Isabel, I wanted to wait, to look after you. You wanted to take it slow. I'm tryi—"

I cut him off. "Please, I want you inside me, Seb."

With my words, he lets out a frustrated moan from deep in his chest. "We'll go slow. At my pace."

I nod in agreement, heeding his warning. But I'm secretly hoping he doesn't stay true to his word on this.

He lifts up to push inside me and slowly enters, stretching me, and I moan in pleasure. He pauses when he's seated deep and kisses my lips, softer this time. He doesn't move. I wiggle my hips to encourage him, but he doesn't take the hint.

"I won't break. I promise," I whisper in his ear.

"Shhh! Stop it. My pace. Now let me take care of you."

I look up at him and nod. I'm rewarded with a hard and deep thrust that has me crying out. He slowly—torturously slowly—pulls out and pushes back in. Each time he grazes my clit to keep me humming. He holds my hands tight, our fingers interwoven, and he stares into my eyes. The connection he builds between us is more potent than just having sex. Our bodies and hearts are joining invisible fibres between our very beings.

He speeds up slightly and hits harder, right when he's buried the deepest. My climax builds and I want it. I need it to let everything out. At each slow assault, I moan as the pleasure builds. He strains more and more, attempting to keep to his word. He watches my face and I try to stay focused on him, but my eyes keep threatening to roll back in my head. He controls every movement, every action. I try to meet his thrusts this time and he lets me. Slow and gentle doesn't last long. The passion between us spills over into fast and needy.

I'm so close. I want Seb to tip me over, to release the pent-up need that has been dormant since he came into my life. I focus on Seb's weight on top of me, how he is treating me now. He's making up for the last time we were together by showing me how controlled he can be. He's driving me crazy with need. That's what my focus is now on.

"Yes. Please, Seb. Yes."

"Yes, Isabel. Tell me."

"More... There... Yes... oh, oh, oh."

"Come for me, Isabel."

I do. I fall apart under him, and convulse and spasm around his cock. My body tenses and my climax radiates throughout my body.

"Yes. Oh God, Isabel. Hmm." Seb follows after me and we are both spent. All I can hear is the sound of our mingled breathing and my heart pounding in my chest.

After a long while, Seb rolls over me, lying beside me. He pulls me into him and wraps his arm around me. For the first time in weeks, I feel content and sated. This was important to both of us. After what happened before, building our trust in one another is crucial. I'm going to have to show Seb that he can trust me, like he's just shown me. I fight it, but within a few moments my eyes close and I fall asleep.

Sebastian

The light shines through the curtains and it wakes me earlier then I'd like. I stir, but then freeze. Izzy is still sleeping beside me. Her hair is a mess of brown strands falling over the pillow and the light gently shines on her shoulder. She has nestled into my side as if she is seeking heat from me. She's so close that I can feel her breath on my skin. In and out. In and out.

Warm. I feel warm from the inside out.

I showed her control last night. It was hard. God, the trust she put in me. She pushed me to go faster, causing my brain to struggle. I'm going to have to work with her on that. Trying to goad me. I won't let her top from the bottom. My problem is that I want her so badly. I want everything from her. Our previous night together proved that. I completely lost myself to her, finally finding the partner that I can be myself with.

Last night went a long way to repairing that damage. I stayed in control and we both got off. More than got off on it. It was amazing sex. We connected beyond anything else we've done together. Hell, I've connected with her more than anyone else in my life. *Fuck!* I want to have her in all ways possible. I want to test her further, watch as her submission grows and her barriers crumble. I want to be more than her occasional lover and Dom.

Seeing her again after how things ended was a sign. Perhaps one that I helped to engineer, but I want her in my life and I can't ignore what we have. I've revealed her true nature, and she can't deny that any longer. We both fucked up. I couldn't stand the thought of her going back to her safe marriage and leaving me with only memories. That reasoning lasted as long as the hangover did.

She moves slightly beside me, and I fight the urge to pull her in closer to me, to comfort her. It feels right, to have her next to me, waking up with the feel of her soft skin pressed against me. I don't want to give this up.

Fuck! I want her. I don't want our arrangement anymore. I want to be her everything: her Dom, her partner, her friend. I want to fucking own her.

I won't make her choose. All she needs is time and courage. I know she doesn't love the fucker. She loves me. I can feel it. I won't push her, though. This is her decision to make and one boundary I can't lead her to cross. I have always said that. The line is there for her to choose. I've tried to show her the possibilities outside of her marriage. But that final question still stands. What will she do?

Twenty Two

I wake up feeling warm and snoozy. I'm comfortable and feel Seb's body next to me. I smile.

"You're awake?" His question sounds as if he's surprised.

"Mmmhmm," I mumble back to him. I may be awake, but only just.

"Would you like some breakfast? We didn't eat last night. You must be hungry."

Although I would love to eat something, I'd rather stay in bed with Seb.

"Can I stay here a little longer? I've not slept particularly well for the last couple of weeks." I didn't mean for that to sound how it did and I regret it as soon as it's said. I don't want to talk about blame with Seb. "I'm sorry, that didn't come out right."

"It's okay, sweetheart. I understand."

I pull myself up to sitting in bed and bring the covers with me. Seb and I have never spent the night together before and it's a little awkward, especially after the last few weeks. I pushed Seb faster than he wanted to go last night, but I hope he doesn't regret it. I loved every moment.

"So breakfast?" he asks me again, and I nod. He climbs out of the bed and I scoot back down under the covers and snuggle into the Seb-sized gap. He pulls on a t-shirt and pyjama bottoms before he leaves the bedroom. As I watch him leave, I see my rings on the bedside table. The sun hits them, throwing sparkles in the light, and I'm hit with a wave of guilt. I don't think I've taken them off in the ten years we've been married.

I reach for them and turn them over in my fingers a few times. They don't hold the same meaning as they once did. They are pretty pieces of metal now rather than the symbolic representations of our vows to each other, our continual commitment. I put them back on the table and lie on my back. I know that this won't go away, this dull ache that the collapse of my marriage has caused. But I can't do anything today.

It's Saturday. Seb said, "spend the weekend," but I've got nothing to wear, not even a toothbrush to clean my teeth with. I think about why Seb wants the weekend with me. Last night felt different than all the other times. Has something changed? Or am I seeing things that I hope will come to fruition?

"I hope scrambled eggs on toast sounds good? I've got coffee as well," Seb shouts to me.

"Yes, that sounds great. I just need to put something on." I start to climb out of bed as Seb walks in with a tray of breakfast things. I stop and look up at him.

"Breakfast in bed," he says in his deep, rich voice, and it certainly sounds appealing. "I'll get you a t-shirt if you'd like?"

"Yes, please." I stay on the bed, still not comfortable walking around naked. "If you were serious about the weekend, I will need to go and get some clothes and toiletries. I don't even have a toothbrush." Seb smiles at me as he throws a clean grey t-shirt at my head. I pull it on and I'm engulfed in the smell of Seb. I breathe in deeply. I sit up against the headboard and Seb sets the breakfast tray on my lap before he climbs in next to me.

We eat in silence. I haven't eaten properly in weeks. The eggs and toast go down very well. We finish and Seb clears the plates and takes them back to the kitchen. He returns to the bed and raises his arm to give me room to cuddle into his side. I willingly go to him. He wraps me close into him and I rest my head on his shoulder. He plays with my hair for a little while, pulling it through his fingers, but doesn't say anything. Finally, I break the silence.

"So, are you going to take me home now?" It comes out wrong and I tense.

"No. I asked you to spend the weekend."

"I didn't know if it was a spur-of-the-moment offer or not. But I still need to get some stuff."

"Izzy, stop worrying. I want to spend time with you, and I'd like you to relax. I said I'd take care of you." He holds me tighter. "I also want to show you the pleasure that all of the items you brought can bring. Slowly, of course, but I'd like to do it right. I understand if it's too soon."

My stomach drops and that thudding nervousness is back. I think about his meaning. The paddle, the vibrator and the nipple clamps. They all held so much appeal, so much anticipation when I first unpacked them at Seb's house. The thrill was still there. There was pleasure before the pain.

"Okay." I mumble my response and try to wiggle closer to him. Being here with Seb is what I want, what feels right. And how he makes me feel is better than anything. My memories drift to last night and I fidget in bed. My body heats up and Seb rests his hand on my shoulder to still me.

"I think you like the sound of that, Izzy, even if your head doesn't quite trust it yet."

And he's right. His free arm snakes down my body until it reaches the tops of my thighs. He teases and tickles before he trails his finger upwards. My legs have relaxed and they part to give him access. He slides his finger higher and gently skims my labia. That single touch sets my blood heating and my sex aching for more contact. He slides his finger between my wet folds, betraying how turned on he's made me already.

"I like that you're still wet for me, Isabel." He kisses my ear and bites my lobe as he pushes his finger inside me. I moan in pleasure. He slowly teases me with his finger, rubbing my clit and sliding inside me to hit my g-spot. I'm lost to his touch.

"I'm going to give you what I should have done before. I'm going to show you how good it can be. How you can lose yourself to the pleasure, forget everything else apart from the contact I give you, the freedom I give you." His words make me hotter and wetter. My body moves up against him with his actions, which quickens his pace in turn. "Do you want that, Isabel? Your head needs to want it like your body does." He pulls out and circles my clit, rubbing it and tapping it, and I'm right there. My legs straighten and I flush. "You need to answer me. Do you want it?" He bites my ear again as he rubs my clit hard and fast, and it sends me crashing over.

"Yes. Yes... Please, yes!" My hips buck against his hand as my sex pulses with my orgasm. He doesn't give me that last bit of satisfaction by filling me with his fingers.

"Good girl," he whispers.

My entire body floats back down and I'm sleepy again.

"Mmm."

"Now, did you mean what you said, Isabel?"

I think about it for a moment and turn to look at Seb. His eyes are the familiar aquamarine that I love and trust. I've been over the actions of the previous time we were together so many times that I'm not even sure what actually happened and what I made up, trying to analyse everything. Now I can see I could have stopped it. I was more hurt by his actions afterward. And after last night—the control that he showed me—I'm sure he would never put either of us in that position again.

"Yes." I smile and snuggle in beside him, wrapping my arms around his chest. I make my decision like many of the others with Seb. I go on gut instincts.

"Seb, I need a shower, and what am I supposed to wear?" I stand in nothing other than the bath towel, quickly getting over my shyness from yesterday.

"Do you need to get dressed? I quite like having you half-naked in my house." Seb smiles as he pulls me towards him using the ties that hold the bathrobe together. He's being playful with me, and it's a lovely side of Seb to see.

"I have to get dressed, Seb, and at least brush my teeth. Can you drop me home and I'll grab a few bits?"

"How about we go out and get what you need?"

"No, Seb." I try to take a firm stand, but know it won't last. His hands are inside my robe now and he massages my bottom and pulls me closer into him. My mind thinks about sinfully good things—not putting clothes on.

"No, you don't want me to do this…?" He pulls me closer still, forcing me to fall into him, and I can feel he's turned on. He's in jeans and they rub against my now-exposed flesh. His hands hold me tightly and work at my backside. "I've got something planned for your very lovely bottom later, Isabel." My stomach drops and my heart races at the thought. I'm not nervous or worried. After last night, Seb will be in complete control and he won't get carried away. I trust that he will be checking me. I also know that I must use my safeword if it gets too much. "Okay, but later, please. First, I need to get some of my things."

"Fine. I'll drive you and then we're coming right back."

Seb sat in the car, engine running, while I entered the house. I'm as quick as I can be. Making a dash around the room, I grab my toiletries, change of clothes, and some clean underwear. I stop and think about all the very nice lingerie that Seb has yet to see me in. The black lace-up corset is what I want to wear, remembering my thoughts when I first bought it. *I hope it's still at Seb's.*

"There—less than ten minutes." I slam the door as I jump into his car.

"Okay. Home now. I want to cook for us. Do you fancy anything in particular?"

"No, I don't think so. I've not had a huge appetite, so whatever you have in mind is fine." I settle myself down and send a quick text to Jess. *Should I tell Phil that I'm not at home?* I've been gone since Friday morning and nothing. I don't know what I was expecting. A call, a text to check I'm alright or wondering where I am? I rub my ring finger and remember they aren't there.

Seb tries to break the silence, but I'm not even sure what he's said.

"Sorry, what?"

"I was just asking if you were okay?" He's concerned for me, and, I think, a little anxious that I'm now very quiet. I don't really want to admit what is on my mind, so I play it off as nothing.

"I'm fine. Just thinking."

"Don't."

"Don't what?"

"Don't hide from me. Open and honest communication. That still stands."

"I'm sorry. I was just wondering if I should tell Phil that I'm not home."

"I see." His immediate scowl at my words makes me question telling him, but it clears just as quickly. "Thank you for telling me, Izzy." His gratitude reinforces that I shouldn't fear being honest with Seb. He won't judge me like Phil did.

The rest of the journey is quiet. We're trying to work out how to be friends as well as lovers, although neither of us has actually said that this is what we're playing at. When we were friends before, it came so easily, so naturally we didn't even have to try. Now, the lines are blurred and we need to work out how to be around each other if we are going to try to make anything work in the future.

The quiet follows us into the apartment and Seb gets to work in the kitchen. I take the time to wander about the apartment. I venture back into my old room and take a look at everything. It's all still like it was. The red cushions are still on the bed and my anklet is still on the box on top of the dresser. Unable to resist, I walk over and pick it up, playing it between my fingers.

"It's still yours if you want it." Seb leans against the doorframe. I look at him and feel the release and comfort from submitting to him already imprinted in my mind. It was so fulfilling, and it went far beyond simply having fun or trying something new in the bedroom.

"I still want to, Sebastian." I stand still and drop my head slightly in a gesture towards him. Light footfalls tell me he's entered the room. He takes the anklet. With very sure hands, he runs his fingers down my leg, my ankle his clear destination. He kneels beside me and lifts my foot. He secures the anklet and runs his hands back up my legs as he stands.

"The same rules as before apply. You need to be clear with me if you want anything to change. But thank you for trusting me again." He pulls my face towards him and kisses me, slowly, bestowing the trust he now holds. It morphs into a fierce and passionate embrace, signalling our mutual need for one another. His lips demand my submission, and I want to give it to him.

"As much as I'd like this to continue, I want to feed you first," he whispers in my ear.

"Yes, Sir," I say with a big smile on my face.

"Come on then, Isabel." Seb pulls me out into the kitchen. "Lay the table, please." His tone has changed, confident and sure of himself now. It's the side of him that makes me go completely weak at the knees. I set the table but can't keep from stealing glances at him. It's reminiscent of my first night here. Now sure of my part, I go to the fridge and pour him a glass of wine. I hand it to him and smile sweetly. This is how we work the best. We know our roles and are more than comfortable in them, even though we've only known they exist for a short while. Something clicks between us when we're together in this way. He takes my submission and with it the worries I've been carrying. The angst from earlier evaporates.

We talk only a little but still enjoy dinner. I clear away the plates and finish my wine. While we were eating, I had something to concentrate on other than what would be coming next. I'm beginning to feel that nervous anticipation building, those excited butterflies that have my breathing all over the place.

"Did you enjoy dinner, Isabel?"

"Yes, thank you. It was delicious."

"Good." He takes my hand in his and caresses the back of it with his fingers. "I'd like you to come and join me in my room after you've changed."

"Yes, Sebastian." I pause, though, wondering what I should wear and whether everything is still in the room.

"You may choose what to wear, Isabel, and I've not touched anything in your room since you left." Once again, he answers my questions before they're asked.

"Thank you." My mind struggles to slow my thoughts as I walk to my room. I close the door and run to find the corset I thought about earlier. It's in the drawer with the rest of the black and lace. I match it with some black thigh highs and a lace thong. Usually I am scrupulous about keeping hair-free. But the last couple of weeks, nothing in my life has been scrupulous. My beauty therapist will kill me, but I grab a razor and jump in the shower to de-fuzz.

A few hurried minutes later, I stand in front of the mirror, fresh and silky and wearing a very desirable get-up. My hair is glossy and tickles the top of my shoulders. The corset, although a bitch to get on, gives me a great silhouette. Nerves get the better of me at the door, and I put the silk robe on before going to Seb's room.

He sits in his armchair. The lights are turned down low and the bed has been made since we left it this morning. At the end of the bed are a few things that I can't quite see, but can guess at. "Come in, Isabel. I'd like for you to sit on the bed." I walk over and set myself down next to some of the toys that I bought. "I'd like to show you what should have happened between us those weeks ago. You bought these items under my instruction to show you how pain and pleasure can work together for a heightened experience. You purchased the items that met the following: something to tie you with, to spank you with, to put inside you, and something that scares you."

As Seb speaks, I'm assaulted by the memories of that night. "I'm not going to let you be overwhelmed, Isabel. I promise. I told you that I consider myself a sensual Dom, and that is exactly what I'm going to be for you tonight. I will be using this, though..." He holds up the flogger. I don't think he used that last time—he may have. I was probably too far out of it to distinguish one thing from another. "This flogger will be better for you than the paddle. Do you trust me?"

"Yes." It's an automatic response, but one my head agrees with.

"What do you say if you want this to stop?"

"Black." Again, I say it with no hesitation.

"Good girl. If you want me to slow down say yellow, but remember you need to communicate. Now stand up and strip out of that robe. I'd like to see you." My stomach does the drop thing and my sex clenches at his instruction. Untying the belt, I let the silk glide from my shoulders. I'm not in skyscraper heels, but a more modest pair. I stand still and wait for Seb to say something, but he doesn't. He lifts his hand and motions for me to turn around with his finger. The heat in my cheeks is accompanied by a small smile as I slowly turn around for him, showing him every part of my lace-clad body.

"Very nice, Isabel. Did you buy this for me?"

"Yes, Sir." I want him to be pleased with me. I want to feel pride in his approval of me. His deep breath is my reward, and warmth spreads through me at his reaction.

"Thank you. Now, as much as it looks incredible on, take off your thong and turn so you're facing the bed."

I pull off the lace and turn so I face the bed. I shut my mind to the resemblance from last time.

"I will blindfold you because I already know you like that." His voice is right at my ear and goose bumps crawl over my skin in reaction. He gently fastens the silk around my head before he runs his hands down my body. "You feel very good in this corset, Isabel." He continues his exploration and then runs a hand over my bottom to the top of my thigh highs. "I told you I have plans for you tonight. I want to make you squirm and beg for me, Isabel."

"Yes," I whimper.

He proceeds to cover my entire body with his hands, running them all over my exposed flesh as he kisses my neck and shoulders. In his search of my skin, he avoids my clit, yet it throbs and feels swollen already. He massages my bottom, gently squeezing, and his fingers creep closer and closer to my sex. But before he grants me my wish, he stops. "Bend over and put your arms down. Yes, now spread your legs a little. Perfect. Now try to relax."

As I follow Seb's instructions, it doesn't feel like me. I've been replaced by this sexy and confident woman who knows what to do to please her man and is rewarded with pleasure. I enjoy this feeling, basking in the glow of his words. My body has already taken over. My heart pounds and my boobs all but fall out of the corset.

I feel a light slap on my bottom, which almost tickles, and I realise it's the flogger. The next few strokes land a little harder and feel more comfortable. Each strand lands on my skin but I only feel them as one. My skin warms. Each hit makes me clench my sex, and my clit begs to be touched. He pauses regularly and returns to rubbing my warmed skin with his hands. Keeping our connection through touch. This is nothing like the spanking Seb gave me last time. Each stroke lands in a slightly different position and I find myself pushing back, wanting more.

The thud of the strands sends a flash of pain before dulling to a warm glow, the feeling radiating throughout my body. My pulse races and my body breaks out in a sheen of sweat. I want some friction on my clit, and my sex gets wetter with the need for Seb to touch me. I can't help the little moans of pleasure that start in my throat but soon echo around the room.

"You like this, Isabel? Me flogging your beautiful arse until it's pink and you're wet for me?"

I groan at his words as they simply add to my frustration. I can feel how wet I am, how damp my thighs are.

"Yes." I try to answer him. I don't know what I expected from the flogger, but not to be this turned on, this desperate. The flogger lands at the top of my thighs and I jump a little before Seb's finger glides over my drenched clit.

"God, Isabel, you're so wet, so ready. I bet just a little…"

"Yes, please." His finger is dancing across my clit and I'm ready to beg.

"Not yet, sweetheart."

"No, not like last time." My head spins.

"Don't worry, Isabel. I won't deny you this time." His finger dances over the very tip of my clit before he smacks me with the flogger again.

"Yesss, Arghh!"

He stops and something cold is between my swollen lips. He nudges the vibrator inside me, but it's not turned on. It slides in easily and he fucks me with it, slowly and steadily. I can't rule my body's response, and I move my hips in time with his thrusts. I can't help it. The vibrator slides smoothly in and out, but I want more. I want to feel Seb. I want him to take my orgasm, to feel the pleasure he brings to me. To have me how he wants.

"You," I pant out.

"Yes, Isabel?"

"I want you in me. Please, Sir."

"This is for you, Isabel. Feel and let your body take over."

"Please," I moan. He hasn't stopped with the vibrator and I'm so close to coming I sound forlorn. "I want you!" I scream, utterly overtaken by my body's need. He stops and pulls back. A heavy pause clears my hazy mind as I wait on Seb.

"I know you do. And I'll fuck you when I choose to. Don't forget that." He glides the vibrator through my juices. In and around again and again, and I'm lost to the sensations. My moans are loud in my ears, growing wild with my imminent climax. But before I let go, he pulls the vibrator out. "You need to be on top. You won't be able to sit back on your arse."

As the blindfold is still on, I straighten myself up, disorientated, and wait for him to guide me. He takes my hands and pulls me onto the bed. I crawl up his body. "Wait…" Seb stills me and fumbles about. "Right, we're good."

I continue my track and brush my corseted chest across his stomach before I straddle his hips.

I position myself over him and I sink down onto his rock-hard cock. We both cry out as I take him deep inside me. He's right. My bum is tender, so I stay up on my knees. The blaze of my orgasm is but a few strokes from me, and I ride him hard and fast, rocking and grinding into him so I get friction over my clit. *Just a little more.*

"God, Isabel, you look so fucking gorgeous on top of me, your beautiful tits spilling out of that corset, tempting me, making me lose myself in you. I feel you clenching my cock. Do you want to come?" His voice is thick with lust and tells me just how much he's enjoying this.

"Yes!" I scream at him.

"Make yourself come." With his command, I slam down, rotate my hips and push him as deep as I can get him. I cry out as the heat and nerves that have been sizzling under my skin are set free and I arch up against him. I come hard as wave after wave of tremors run through me.

"You feel so good when you come."

I'm exhausted and slump over his chest.

"Not yet, baby." Seb holds me back up and I wrap my arms around his neck. He sits up with me and kisses me hard. With him still deep inside me, he moves us so I'm straddling him still but he's sitting on the edge of the bed. He stands and flips us over so I'm on my back but my bottom is off the edge—no contact with the mattress. I wrap my legs around his hips and he moves inside me. He mixes the pace, hard and then soft, hard and then soft. I'm building again. I moan and hear little sighs of pleasure coming from him as well. He breathes heavily, panting with me, and he tenses. He suddenly yanks my corset down to free my breasts, then he leans over and bites my nipple. The pain sends shocks through my body and to my clit, and I come again.

"God... Yes! Yes!" We're both shouting and gasping for air as we come together. Seb collapses on top of me, but pulls me onto him. His lips seek mine to claim my mouth as he just claimed my body.

"Now that is what I wanted to show you, Isabel," he whispers in my ear.

* * *

It's dark and the apartment is quiet when I wake. Seb lies next to me, his chest gently rising. The bed is a mess from the evening before. I remember making love but nothing after, having fallen straight to sleep.

I sit up and look down at him. Being here with Seb this weekend has cemented the feelings I have for him. This is where I want to be. If I was in any doubt of my love for him before, there is none now. I want to have Seb in my life, and for the first time in a long while, I can feel a sense of hope and even happiness at my future.

Twenty Three

Sunday morning comes and before I know it the afternoon is drawing to a close. We've settled into each other's company, calm and contented. Reality looms. I have to go back to work, as I've pushed my boss to his limit with allowing me time off. As my departure gets closer, I feel anxious about what the next few days have in store. I have to go back to work and face Phil. I've enjoyed being in the safety of our bubble.

"Stop worrying, Isabel." Seb's voice is firm and controlled. It reminds me of what he can do to me.

"I'm not worrying. Not really, more like I'm anxious. This weekend has been wonderful and I don't want it to end."

He takes my head in his hands and makes me look him in the eye. "I'm not going to let you slip through my fingers. I want this to continue." His words touch me and lift my heart.

"Oh, shit!" I suddenly panic. "My rings. I need my rings."

"I'll get them for you." Seb leaves me to retrieve my wedding bands. He takes my hand on his return and slowly pushes them onto my finger. His action has me holding back tears, and guilt wells up in me. It was Phil who put those on my finger all those years ago, making me so very happy. Yet today, it's another man. He wipes the tears from my cheeks and kisses me gently. Reverently.

"I'll see you very soon, Izzy, okay? Here." He takes the key fob that used to be mine for his apartment out of his pocket. "You'll need this again."

I nod and smile at him. I walk out of the apartment towards the lobby and out to the waiting taxi. I reflect on the similarities between my leaving now and the first time I left. So much has changed, and yet I'm still adrift in a storm of emotions—emotions that have grown far more serious than I ever thought possible. I didn't consider that I'd fall in love or be reminded what it is to be cared for.

On Monday morning I wake with a determination that I am going to sort everything out. Phil wasn't home when I returned last night. It meant that I would have to put off the fight for another day.

As I try to form a plan of when and how to tell Phil things are really over, I can't escape the thought of Seb and three little words. Words that I am suddenly desperate to hear. Words that I've not yet told him. *Should I tell him?*

* * *

I have a mountain of work to get through when I finally reach my neglected desk. It focuses my mind and stops my recent bad habit of letting my mind wander away. At least I won't be dwelling on the sorry state of my personal life. Luckily, I have a good relationship with my boss. He accepted my 'family emergency' excuse.

It's gone six before I dig myself out from my desk and head home. I'm astounded when I'm welcomed home by Phil, cooking in the kitchen.

"Iz, is that you?" I walk into the kitchen and stop. Years have passed since Phil last ventured into the kitchen, and even then I think it was because I was sick. "Oh good, I thought I'd make you some food and we could talk?"

"Okay. Yes, we need to talk." I say the words and my stomach turns. I feel sick at the thought of telling him I want a divorce. I go upstairs to change and also to check my phone. Seb has texted me a few times over the course of the day.

> How are you today, Izzy? S

> I enjoyed the weekend with you, Izzy. The apartment isn't the same without you. S

> Isabel, don't make me wait much longer to hear from you. S

The last text makes me giggle and I quickly send a response back.

> Sorry, Seb, I've had a mountain of work to get through. I've missed you. Izzy

My thumb pauses over the send button before I hit it. It's true. I miss Seb and being with him. I hope that's what he wants to hear.

> You were about half an hour away from getting a spanking and not the kind I gave you at the weekend. S

Heat indicates the blush on my face at his words and desire builds in my stomach.

"Iz, dinner!"

I'm startled out of my thoughts of Seb with the announcement from Phil, and I'm suddenly right back in the room. I take a breath and head down the stairs.

"Listen, Iz, I know we've been going through a rough time, but I want to put that behind us. I need you to come with me to my company's Christmas party on Friday." His sudden launch into conversation startles me, and I'm not sure what to say.

My skin crawls at the prospect of having to do this. Each year, it's the same. Some big venue plays host to different companies, hundreds of Christmas revellers out on their work parties, drinking the free wine and eating the free food. Phil insists on going and makes an effort with his co-workers, sucking up to the big boss, while I stay quietly at our table and hope that I get to leave soon.

"Umm..." I take a few minutes to try to process this, the first real sentence he's said to me in weeks. "Look, Phil. We both know that a rough patch isn't all this is. I'm still waiting on that answer from you, and I think we're delaying the inevitable." I try to make my voice sound strong although I'm shaking inside.

"I'm sorry, Iz." He doesn't look at me as he says it, revealing how insincere his apology is. He continues to shovel his food into his mouth, not paying me a blind bit of notice.

"This isn't going to be solved with you just saying you're sorry. It's much bigger than that."

He slams his knife and fork down and looks at me.

"What are you saying?" With those words, I suddenly hear my heart pound and my blood turns to ice. This is my opportunity to tell him how I feel, how I want to end things and get a clean break. But I turn to stone. I can't say the words. "Iz?"

"We're... we don't work anymore."

"That's not true."

"Yes, it is. I've been a mess the last few weeks and you've not even noticed. Not cared enough to help me. Hell, you didn't even say anything about me not being here this weekend." I find my voice and the adrenalin kicks in.

"Well, what do you want me to say?"

"We can't go on like this. I meant what I said, we don't work."

"You're being ridiculous. And I need you to come out on Friday. The area manager will be there again. You know the emphasis he puts on 'happily married' employees. It's important to my job that you are there."

"No. I won't pretend anymore. And I want you to be honest with me. Tell me about the affair." The look he gives me makes me cringe. Ice travels up my spine and freezes my body in fear.

"Would you drop that already? You're my wife and you'll come with me." He stands and shouts at me, as if to crush my resistance with sheer volume.

"You can't force me."

"Oh really? One thing, Izzy. That's all I want. Then I will tell you whatever you want to know. I'm going to bed."

His temper has always been quick to break, and I'm certainly seeing more of it now. I feel grim at the prospect of standing up to him and holding my ground. Making him take me seriously will be a challenge. But I have to. I have to get through to him.

* * *

The next few days are only bearable because of the texts and distractions of Seb. I should have told him what happened with Phil, but I don't want him to think I still want to be in my marriage. The happy distractions of Seb's lust-filled texts have brought the only ray of hope to me this week. Leaving him on Sunday night was hard. Something changed when we woke up together. We stopped playing at a fantasy and found our own sense of happiness together. Being in his presence and being consumed by him for two days straight made my body ache but my heart sing.

> Isabel, I'm the only one who gets to touch your body. Do you understand me? No touching yourself in the shower. S

> When can I see you? Izzy

> I'm afraid not until Saturday. I have a busy week. S

> Saturday then. Izzy

> I want you frustrated, Isabel. You will be desperate for my touch and I'm going to have your entire body to play with. S

If Seb keeps the pressure up through text talk, by Saturday I'm going to come at his first touch.

The constant worry about how to get Phil to listen has stifled my future hopes with Seb. After our weekend, I was optimistic and excited about our future. I love Seb and I hope he feels the same way about me. When I lie in bed, trying to sleep, I replay our weekend, all the things he said to me, how he acted with me, and I see it, feel it, there in his actions. He might not have told me he loves me, but I'm hopeful. He said he wanted to explore the possibility of an us. Is it too much to hope that Seb feels the same way for me as I do for him?

First I need to get over the worry around Phil before I can consider the big 'I love you' with Seb.

* * *

The week has flown by in a blur of work, frustration and arguments. Speaking to Phil has become like a broken record. We go over and over the same few words before he disappears on me. He hasn't backed down about Friday. He offers it as his bargaining chip. If I go to his party, we'll sort out the end of our relationship. It's stupid to think he will live up to his agreement, but I have to believe he'll finally do this. Playing wife to Phil at this party is the last thing I want to be doing, but if it is what's needed to end to our bickering and allows us to end things once and for all, then I'll suffer through it.

"Will you wear the red dress, Iz? It is Christmas and I love that dress," I hear Phil shout up to me in the bedroom.

"Really? You're even going to tell me what to wear?" It's not what I want to say, but if I'm going to get through this evening in one piece then perhaps conceding the dress will help.

"Thanks and hurry up. The taxi will be here soon." His voice is clipped and stern. I swallow down my frustrations and pull the red dress out of the wardrobe. It is a lovely dress, and I haven't worn it for a long time. The dress is red lace, cut in a fitted, Japanese style with beautiful detailing. The shoes I have to match wrap my ankles in an extravagant red bow. I can even wear some of my new underwear with it, at least the more modest pieces I didn't take to Seb's.

As I start to get ready, I can't stop my mind wandering to Seb and what he would think of me dressed up, my hair and makeup done, sexy evening gown with even nicer underwear beneath. I feel a pang of disappointment in my chest that I won't be able to do this with Seb. I would enjoy being out in public with him, accompanying him to his Christmas party. I would eagerly look forward to what he would do to me when we arrive home. I mentally picture accompanying Seb and all of the delicious things he would do with me. He would tease me all night, get me wet before even arriving home, and then strip me out of my dress and have me on the floor with my hands tied. My smile breaks across my face as I pull my thigh highs into place. I chose the thigh highs over tights because even though I won't be seeing Seb tonight, I still want to please him.

"Izzy. Come. On."

"Stop shouting, Phil. I'm ready. I'm only going with you to get my confession. After this we're done."

"I don't care if you want to or not. You're coming. You're my wife and I expect you to act like one." Aggression surges through his voice and leaves me shrinking back. I fix my dress and tuck a loose lock of hair behind my ear in a nervous gesture.

We don't speak in the taxi, just sit and wait to arrive. I'm lost in thoughts of Seb.

"You coming, Iz?"

"Sorry, what?"

"We're here."

"Oh right, sorry." I climb out of the taxi and walk next to Phil into the hotel. *Come on, Izzy. A few hours of being pleasant, that's all it is. Just concentrate and everything will be fine.* I close my eyes for a second to focus on tonight and squeeze Seb from my mind. If I can get through this, then I can finally move on with Seb.

We walk to check in our coats and read the huge table plan propped up outside the main room. There are about four or five different companies sharing the party, but at least we're at the same table as Jackson and his wife. I know them. My moment of pleasure is instantly soured by Sophie's name on our table's seating chart. *I'm a fool!* Phil has manipulated me, again.

I should be with Seb. I should never have let Phil coerce me into this pretence. He'll never change and is unlikely to ever admit what I know is the truth.

Ironically, the guilt I felt due to my adultery vanishes. My heart is completely Seb's. I sigh as Phil walks me through the doorway and I'm surrounded by people milling around and gathering drinks at the bar. The band is already playing 'Jingle Bell Rock'.

A stiff drink will go a long way toward making this evening endurable. "I'm getting a drink from the bar, Phil. Do you want anything?" Phil doesn't answer. As I turn around, I see why. He's too busy staring across the room at Sophie draped over some other man. I wonder if after all Phil's bluster I'm only here to make another woman jealous.

My eyes burn with the threat of tears, but I hold them back, unwilling to waste them on Phil. I turn away in disgust at both Phil and myself. I snake my way through a few people but then stand frozen in place.

"Seb?" I whisper to myself. I see him only a few feet away from me. He's wearing a smart, dark suit with an immaculate white shirt and there is a stunning woman on his arm. My eyes start to blur in front of me as I see his sexy smile on his face, the one I thought was only for me, and as I do, his eyes fall on me. His expression changes, turns hard, and his eyes turn dark.

I don't... Why? Why is he here with another woman? After what we shared, after what he said to me? Was he lying? Was it about having some fun? Getting to fuck me? No, he didn't have to do everything he did. The weekend... He loves me, too. My feet have taken on a mind of their own and walked me the few feet that were separating us. I stop in front of him and say nothing. He looks at me but doesn't speak, although it's clear that he wants to say something.

"Izzy?" Phil's voice follows me to where I stand. "Iz, where did you go? Come on. I want us over to meet Jackson and our boss."

I don't answer him and stay motionless, focused on Seb, the man who holds my heart in his hands.

"Excuse me, do you two know each other?" Phil says with a cocky grin.

"Um, this is Seb. He was in one of my training classes a few months back. Nice to see you again." I can't say anything else without my voice cracking.

"Yes, nice to see you again, Isabel."

Isabel? You call me Isabel now? With another woman on your arm?

"Excuse me for a moment. I'm going to find the bathroom." I nearly run out of the room. I turn down a corridor, but before I reach the ladies a hand grabs my wrist and pulls me further down the hallway, around a corner into a dark and quiet room. Seb closes and locks the door. My hands are held tightly above my head and his lips are at my ear. I nearly relax into his hold.

"What are you doing here, Isabel?" He growls out the question and it makes my nerves come alive.

"It's Phil's Christmas party. Why are you here and why are you with another woman? Who is she?" I can't hide the anger and hurt in my voice. Seeing Seb with another woman has brought out a reaction in me I didn't think I was capable of. A surge of jealousy rushes through my body and tells me how bad this is. The feelings engulf me. Not for Phil, not seeing Sophie pawing all over him. Only for Seb.

"She's a friend. And it's Natasha's Christmas party also."

"A friend? I'm a friend. Do you tie Natasha up and fuck her, too? Do you do what you've done with me to others? Or do you just play with them?" The accusation sits between us, unanswered. His eyes turn sad, though. They darken and I know I should have never said that. "I didn't think... I thought that after this past weekend..." My words stick in my throat and I have to lower my eyes, unable to be confronted with more pain from this man. "I thought I meant something to you?"

"Isabel, you are here with your husband. I am here with a friend. And my feelings for you have not changed since the weekend." His voice has softened.

"I'm so—" But I don't finish before Seb forces me back into the wall. His hands press my shoulders before he moves to capture my face, keeping it in place while he looks me straight in the eye.

"You want to know if I've done this before? Shown an exquisitely beautiful woman more? Held her hand and taught her there is more to her than being used by her husband for a quick lay? Taught her to listen to her body, to respond?" He hoists my arms above my head before he slides my dress up my leg with the force of his one free hand. "To respond to my touch, my voice, my command?"

I can hear his frustration, the restraint in him slipping. But the raw power in his voice has my muscles clenching, anticipating his next move. Need overtakes my thoughts as he pins me in place. His hand creeps closer to the top of my thigh highs and edges closer to my knickers.

"Isabel, you're wearing thigh highs for another man, and you're asking me why I'm here with another woman? What did the weekend mean to you?"

The thought that he would think this is for Phil spears my heart.

"You're angry at me? Well, I should be furious at you, Isabel." With that, he drives two fingers into me, and I moan my response as my body bows to him. He's hard and aggressive, but his actions are filled with a passion that speaks volumes. "You are wet for me, Isabel. You give yourself to me again and again, yet you are still here with him." He shoves his fingers deeper, and with those words he finds that spot that makes my knees weak and my breath catch. "You've said time and time again that you can't go back to how your life was before. I thought the weekend meant something as well, but you're still here with *him.* You dressed like a temptress in red for *him.*" His thumb finds my clit and I fight for shallow pants of air.

"Why are you with him, Isabel? Why do you still return to him? Answer me. Why are you here with him?" His educated hand works my clit. His fingers inside push my arousal higher.

"Because..." I start, desperate to concentrate on the words and not the orgasm his busy fingers are about to rip from my body. "I'm scared. I don't want to be a failure. I'm scared of the future and telling Phil I want a divorce. I didn't think there was a way out. But with you, I feel there is. There's a future... Please? I need to come."

"Come. For. Me. Isabel. For *me*." His voice rings in my ear as his fingers thrust into me one last time. I clench around them as I come around his hand. My body shudders against him, but it's not enough. I need to show him how he alone holds my heart and commands my body. My hands tangle in his hair and I pull him down to my lips.

"Don't stop, Seb. I need you inside me. I need you to hold me. I need to know I matter to you. Please..." I pant between kisses.

"You can't ask that of me. Especially now. Your husband is with you, and my friend is waiting for me."

My emotions are beyond saving at this point. I'm a complete mess. "Please, Seb... don't walk away from me."

"Izzy, now is not the time."

"What was all of this about then, Sebastian? Proving that you can make me do whatever you want?" I bite out, regretting the words as soon as they pass my lips.

"Isabel, don't push me. I'm not going to fuck you here, even if you beg me. We'll talk later." He takes a step away from me and I miss him instantly. I pull my dress down and try to compose myself. Seb holds me in an icy stare, so different from his normal warmth. I'm hurt and confused. I feel as if I'm going to break into a thousand brittle pieces. I want to leave. I quickly turn and leave the room—and Seb—and head back to find Phil.

"There you are. Where have you been?"

"I'm going to get a taxi. I'm not well. I'm sorry."

"Fine. You've gotten out of it. I asked you to do one thing, Izzy. One thing!" he shouts at me, and it actually helps me fight the tears.

I pick up my coat and rush to a waiting taxi. I give the driver my home address. *Home?* Is it really home? I live there, but it's not where I want to be. Phil and I should have ended even before I met Seb. I need to make Phil see that we are truly over. Divorce. That's the one thing I've not thrown at him. Maybe he'll listen then. The icy look in Seb's eyes haunts me and I hate the way I left. I need to explain to him that I didn't want to be there with Phil. I have to tell him how I feel, that I love him even if he's had enough of my cowardly behaviour. I lean forward and address the driver. "I've changed my mind. I want to go to a different address."

I'm at Seb's door before I know it. I look around at his elegant furniture, the photographs on the wall, the table, the breakfast bar. Even with his explanation, I still hate those photographs and how they make me feel. Walking into his room, I crawl into his bed. My mind runs through the horrible accusations I threw at him. All I can do is hope that he doesn't hate me, that he won't send me away again and that he might love me.

I hear the door open and close. I scurry from his room, not wanting to be caught somewhere I shouldn't be. Stopping at the threshold to the lounge, I look up. He stands across the room, his eyes focused on me. I cannot read anything in his stern expression. His tie is loose around his neck, the top button of his shirt undone, and he looks as handsome as ever. His eyes are clear and hooded with lust. He takes four strides towards me. He crushes his lips to mine and I melt. The force of his kiss doesn't stop. His weight forces me back and I go with him, back into his room. As he closes the door behind us, he spins me and presses me against the wood. His cock presses hard into my bum, and he encases my wrists in his hands and holds them tightly above my head.

"Why am I not surprised you're here? Why do you push me, Isabel?" He doesn't let go of my hands as he growls the words. "You want this, don't you, Isabel? What you begged me for earlier?" I can only groan in response. He moves my wrists so they are held in one hand and he peels my dress from my upper body. He doesn't take it off, though. With his hand, he pulls the hem of my dress up so it leaves my bottom exposed. "This is what you want, Isabel. You want sex with me. You crave it, you need it, and you're already dripping with want for me. Your body is crying out for it." He runs a finger through my wet pussy before his fingers delve inside me.

"Ahh"

"Good girl." He unzips his trousers.

I mentally beg him to take me. I want him to show me that I'm his. I want him to dominate me. I forget everything else from this evening and relax under his hands. He pauses only to cover himself with a condom before taking me. He thrusts hard into me from behind with my hands still above my head, and I arch into it. He lets my arms go and holds my hips viciously as I steady myself against the door. His lips attack my neck, my shoulder, and my ear, biting and licking. There is no gentle. No cherishing. No holding my hand and guiding me. This is Seb taking me and showing me that I'm his, if not in every way, then in this way. He's taking me exactly how I need, how I want. I can feel that I'm not going to last long. The intensity is too much. I want him too much.

"Yes, please…"

"Come, Izzy." Hearing my name on his lips does it, again.

"Mmm." My eyes roll back in my head and my mouth opens as my body tenses and grips me in my climax. Heat floods through my veins. Seb pistons into me, hard and fast. He hilts himself once more before spilling into me as he reaches climax. The small movements of my hair blowing from his breath tickle my face as he remains close. He steps away quickly to sit on the bed. I'm left leaning against the door, slowly calming down.

Seb holds his head in his hands. I go to him and kneel down.

"What's wrong?" I whisper to him.

"Isabel… God, you make me question everything I promised myself. This shouldn't have happened." He stops for a moment, and I'm afraid of what he'll say next. "I can't… I can't do this, Isabel. Izzy. I can't. Not when you keep going back to him." He looks up at me, his face a study in pain. "I told you I wouldn't let you slip through my fingers again, but I also told you I don't share. In the beginning, I was prepared to accept that you would leave at the end of the night, because I wanted to help you grow, to realise what you need sexually. But I can't help you anymore. I can't deal with you still being with your husband. I don't want you if you keep going back to him. I deserve better. I deserve more."

My stomach sickens and my body shakes as the meaning of his words filters in.

"You acted out of jealousy tonight? Well, think how I must feel. How I do feel. Fuck! I want your complete submission. To me. All of you."

"And I want to give it all to you."

"Do you?"

"Yes, yes of course I do. But I don't know how you feel. About… us." I try bravely to ask the question, to find out whether he feels the way I think he does about me. He pulls me up to sit on the bed with him before he walks away.

"Yes, you do."

"No, I don't!" I shout back at him. "I don't know. You haven't told me."

"Well, you haven't either, Izzy. Hell, this started with you wanting to experience what your body has been craving, what you've always longed for. Someone to care for you and show you the way through your sexual submission. Well, I've shown you. I've shown you how good surrendering can be. I've shown you how submission can join two people beyond sex. That's what I want. Now I want more." I pause and hold my breath at the possibility of hearing what I'm longing to hear. But he doesn't say it.

"Seb...?"

"I'm sorry, Izzy, but I can't do this."

"No..." My mind panics. "I love you, Sebastian," I blurt. He turns to face me.

"I know you do, sweetheart. Thank you for telling me, but that doesn't help. You still return to Phil. I think you should take some time and think about what you want, Izzy. Really think." He looks at me, my dress half on, half off from his impatience to fuck me, to claim me. "I think you need to leave."

"No!" I scream, but it has little effect. The aquamarine of his gaze is tinged with pain and darkness rather than the bright blues and greens that normally shine back.

He doesn't say anything further, just leaves me and closes the door behind him.

I'm crushed. My tears stream down my face. The rejection and guilt and myriad of other emotions rage through me. This is so much worse than when I left him drunk a few weeks ago. I told him I loved him and it still isn't enough. All my fears about what could happen have come to fruition, and it's my fault.

I won't be going back to Phil. Seb's right. I'm a coward and I'm selfish. I've done all of this to myself. What makes everything worse is that I never considered what this has been doing to Seb.

I hoped that he would feel the same towards me, yet never considered how he felt about the situation. My feelings were all that mattered. I can't expect Seb to love me until I'm worth loving.

That starts with me being honest with myself and with Phil.

More

To be continued...

Rachel De Lune

To be notified when "Forever More", Izzy and Seb's story conclusion will be released join Rachel's infrequent email list and get a FREE Novella. See next page for excerpt.
http://eepurl.com/bckw0r

Forever More

Excerpt:

"Are you ready to see me, Izzy?"

"Yes, Please…" I beg, and I'm not ashamed.

"Izzy, I'll warn you. Right now I'm caught between wanting to spank you senseless and worshipping you. It's been a long week."

"I'll love both from you. Please, Seb." He sighs audibly. "I can come over, I still have your key."

"I'm away in Manchester at the moment. When will you need to be home?"

"Boxing Day evening. Are you staying at the same hotel?"

"Yes, I'll meet you in the bar. Drive safely, Isabel. That's an order."

* * *

Nearly four hours later I'm parked and have my bag in hand as I walk through the entrance. There is a huge Christmas tree in the lobby, decked with beautiful glass ornaments. I have been distracted from the regular goings-on of Christmas and this sight makes me smile.

Now, standing looking at the tree, meeting the man I love for a rendezvous of passion, I feel Christmassy. The misery of the last week has evaporated. The conversations ahead of us won't be easy, but I'm not afraid. Not anymore.

I'm nervous and the butterflies are back in residence. Walking through the lobby I notice it's nearly deserted. The combination of Christmas Eve and the late evening have emptied the hotel. Seb told me to meet him in the bar—the bar where we met the first time at the hotel—and it seemed fitting. I sit at one of the bar stools and start twiddling with my ring. My stomach is churning and I long to be wrapped in his arms. Please, please, please!

I texted him as soon as I parked the car, but so far nothing back—it's torture. There isn't even a barman I can order a drink from, so I'm stuck with only my own thoughts for company.

I feel him before I see him. All the hairs on the back of my neck stand up and I start tingling in anticipation. "Merry Christmas, Isabel," he purrs at my ear, sending shivers through my body. He doesn't touch me, just hovers his mouth by my cheek. I tilt my head back and up towards him. "I think we should go upstairs. Come on." He steps back and offers his hand out to help me, which I gratefully accept.

His handsome frame holds a tension I wish I could erase. In jeans and a white shirt he makes my mouth water. His stubble has grown out a little and I itch to feel its scrape across my skin. He collects my bag and leads me to wait for the lift. He doesn't look at me or say a word as we wait, and I can't help but shift from foot to foot. I'm eager to be with Seb, for him to lay my worries to rest, about us and our future. If we have a future. The separation from him that I felt in our conversation is still there, bubbling through my veins.

The 'ding' makes me jump. Why am I feeling like this? Seb steps us into the lift car, dropping the bag. As the doors close, he pulls me into his arms and engulfs me in a huge cuddle. He crushes me to his chest and just squeezes hard. I melt at his sign of affection, but it is just what I need. He shuffles me a few feet without breaking his hold and he presses the emergency stop button. "For the next day, our time together here is just for us, Izzy. I want us to enjoy our time together without thinking about anything else. Our bubble again. Can you give me that?" I stare up him and know that he holds all of my trust. I'll do what Seb wants. "And I won't be calling you Isabel from now on." My eyes close and the tears run freely at his words. Our bubble! I remember that we've only really spent the night together one other time. Now, I'll be getting to spend Christmas waking up next to him.

My tears are happy tears, and I struggle out of his hold to wrap my arms around him. I lift my mouth to his and kiss him. I kiss him and it's wonderful. His lips crush into mine, expressing the passion that is always between us. His lips tell me how much more he wants. We show each other our base need through this kiss—his tongue pushing and penetrating me. He takes control, holding my jaw, and slows my overzealous attack on him. He turns the kiss into a slow, sensuous act. I'm desperate to be under him.

"What do you say, Izzy?" he reminds me.

"Yes....please," I mumble out, agreeing to his conditions. I would have agreed to anything after that kiss.

He pulls back, cradling my head in his hands. His beautiful aqua eyes bore into mine, past the teary sheen. A promise. Unspoken between us that the next few days will be an indulgence for both of us.

We'd like to thank you for reading More by Rachel De Lune. Desire *more* from your romance novel? Get a FREE Novella! Sign up for Rachel's infrequent mailing list and be notified of GIVEAWAYS, Advanced reader opportunities and Pre-order notifications!
Join us at:
http://eepurl.com/bckw0r

Made in the USA
Charleston, SC
22 February 2017